FANTASIA

VOXIAN SERIES

BOOK ONE

WRITTEN BY

RUTH WATSON-MORRIS

ISBN: 9798374523850

ACKNOWLEDGEMENTS

Andrew Gibbins, Karen Dempsey, Steven Watson-Morris, Shannon McRoberts, Natalie Watson-Morris & Bob Atkinson, donated from Pixabay-Wishing to be mentioned:- Shannon McRoberts, jcooper12,Parker_West, pendleburyannette, JuliusH, Tabz, fbartondavis, Majabel_creaciones, Rachealmarie, AlfredGrupstra, Eynoxart, NelsonDaSilva, UIEI4I0, Mystic Art Design & sergeitokmakov.

*This book has been written in UK English.
** The name Fantasia is Italian for Fantasy. Pronounced FANTA-SEE-A **

With Thanks

FANTASIA
(FANTA-SEE-A)

Book published by Ruth Watson-Morris 2023
RETOLD
Bad language & violence occur throughout this novel.

BEGINNING...

Residing in a bell-shaped Universe is Galaxia, a world on the light side of the wonders. There, rules the Goddess with her Angel children, who are immortal warriors of virtue.

To the south there is a nebula, bright and true, in the shape of an eye watching over the Multiverse, and inside rules the Angel King, Kathos, with his warrior superheroes, powerful soldiers with swords, fighting against the dark dimensions, protecting all in the Multiverse from Evil.

PLANET GALAXIA: 200 B.C.

The Angel Kathos was brought down from the Heavens with a challenge from those on a higher spiritual plane. He was to bring back Belial the dark Angel, the liar, bringer of wars.

It is said that Kathos promised he would never rest until the fallen Angel had been returned once again to Hell.

Through legend, Kathos would do all in his powers so that Belial could no longer cast his spells of evil, sucking out the energy from planets to feed his own powers and rituals of destruction.

Kathos would continue to search for his Demonic brother until he had defeated him and his army, bringing peace once again to the Multiverse. To this day Kathos has searched on, to keep his promise.

PROLOGUE

<u>PLANET EARTH 1942 A.D.</u>

Phoenix stood six feet four inches tall with a slender build, dark blue eyes, dark skin, and white hair. In the moonlight his large pupils appeared dark, as dark as his soul.

Having joined the British Special Forces at the beginning of the Second World War, he now stood in a smartly pressed German officer's uniform, having infiltrated the ranks of the SS in 1941.

Phoenix knew of *'The Book of Demons'* legend. He had also heard of Kathos, the Angel searching for the Demon. So, he was amazed, while walking through the back streets of Berlin, when he caught sight of the evil book in a small shop.

The shopkeeper, who had killed to own it, amused himself by displaying the book in the window, knowing full well that people who passed by would never understand or know its content or its origins.

"It's not possible!" Phoenix whispered. He could hardly catch his breath.

His heart raced with excitement. He had become a member of the brotherhood and taken the satanic pact many years before. Splitting his palm open, Phoenix signed his name to the Devil's pact, swearing to be a son of darkness. For all his life he would bear the scar and never be allowed to forget his promise to the Devil.

Phoenix walked through the door of the shop. His massive frame meant that he had to stoop to get in through the door.

"Good evening, sir, how can I help you today?" The shopkeeper said, standing nervously by his counter.

Phoenix approached him.

"I am interested in the book," he said, turning and looking over at the glass display cabinet. The book sat on a high plinth. It had a strange cream leather bound cover with metal casing around the edges and a fancy metal lock that flipped over the cover that matched. The cover was decorated all over with gold engraving in a strange language. It said: *'The Book of Demons'*. Underneath that it read in bigger letter casing: *'The Book of Belial.'* The detail was quite exquisite.

The shopkeeper walked slowly around to his chair behind the desk. He dropped and sat down, taking a closer look at the huge man standing in his shop. He was amazed at his colossal size.

Fear struck his face as Phoenix's appearance began to change. His face became tinted with a metallic black colour. He had bulges across the top of his cheek bones, also across the line of his eyebrows and at the top of his nose. He then noticed a flash of white, a small glimmer that turned his attention to the customer's teeth. Horror struck him as two sets of long white fangs protruded from his snarling mouth. The first set about two inches long, next to Phoenix's front teeth. Then a second set right next to them, only these were looking at least double the size of the first.

Before the shopkeeper had time to give it another thought, Phoenix pulled a sword from the side of his overcoat. It gleamed as the lamp light from outside caught it, sharp and willing. With hardly a sound to be heard, except a soft swish as it directed its blow, hitting the shopkeeper in the middle of his head, going straight through like a knife slicing butter.

A small line of red appeared on the man's head and worked its way quickly through the middle of his face. One side slid, showing a perfect dissection as his body split in half where he was sitting. His intestines poured from his stomach, landing in a pile on the floor.

There was the sound of glass breaking as Phoenix picked the book up from its casing. He wrapped it in a blanket, and then without even looking back smiled, walking out into the night air.

He wiped the blood from his sword, replacing it back into its cover in his overcoat.

Looking around the night was silent. No one had noticed the commotion in the shop. Phoenix walked through the alley to his car. He carefully placed the covered book in the boot;

6

his devilish smile said it all. He had *'The Book of Demons.'* He shook his head, closing the boot, got into his car and drove away.

CHAPTER 1

Have you ever stopped to look at the world around you? Earth's beautiful blue skies with white cloud formations billowing above, the birds flying, trying to reach new destinations due to the changing seasons and climate.

Or perhaps think of the night-time calm, diamond studded as star constellations display themselves majestically on black canvas. We should, as humans, count ourselves lucky.

We, as the dominant species of Earth, may dream of our existence being from another land.

We may feel that we are not fitting into the normal life here on Earth, paying attention to becoming good mothers, fathers, or bosses to our workforces. We have gone to new places, swearing when we get there that we have been there before... our 'déjà vous'. Yet we never for one minute believe that the reason this planet is so foreign to us could be because we are not from Earth at all...

2510- EARTH.

It was January, and the winter seasons had hit hard, with snow falling constantly in Great Britain. The ground had snow up to ten inches deep in places. It was still falling thick and fast.

Fantasia grabbed her son, Orion, clinging to his arm as her feet lost grip in the snow. She looked at him as they walked; he was no longer her little child. He towered above her, his giant frame stood six feet ten inches tall as he powerfully pulled her along towards the shuttle craft, his long, dark hair blowing in the bitterly cold wind.

Fantasia stood over six feet, tall for a human. She wore blue jeans and a blue t-shirt with a rainbow on it. She had short light brown hair and bright blue eyes, which turned paler until they became a silver colour closer to the pupils.

As Fantasia was trying to keep hold of the dog's lead, Shadow was barking, pulling forward, trying to keep his family away from the fencing to the air force base. The black German Shepherd was now the only remaining family pet on Earth. All the other family pets had been relocated already, along with Fantasia's daughter Sky, and her grand-daughter, Emmina.

Fantasia and Orion were not that far behind. Sky had left only months before. With the advances of technology, a shuttle could be in Titan (one of Saturn's sixty-one moons) quite quickly now.

There were no communication systems on Saturn's moon. All ships that landed on their new world had not advanced that far. This left the city, built by academics, stranded without communication beyond the inside of the domes. Earth was seen as unimportant.

The man-made parts of Titan were huge and metallic, consisting of domes built by small robots. Space shuttles were landing, these large aeroplane shaped vehicles with large white double cargo doors, docked at ports, then were soldered together to make gigantic living quarters for the new arrivals. Keeping the methane atmosphere out, it was sealing the fate of all those who had arrived inside it.

"Shadow HEEEEEL!" Fantasia said, giving a pull on the lead. "Come on mate, it's not like a plane, you know. They won't cage you up, or anything."

As Shadow pulled again, Fantasia almost lost balance as she slipped on the ice. Orion dropped the bags, catching her before she hit the ground.

"For God's sake, Mother, can't you get a grip?" Orion turned, facing her, seeing that she was struggling with the dog. His sudden burst of anger disappeared in an instant.

"You never could walk him," he smiled at her, picking their luggage back up and steadily walking on.

"Shadow PLEASE!" This time Fantasia yanked hard on his lead. The dog turned and sat at her feet.

"Thank you!" she began to mumble under her breath. "Stupid bloody animal."

"You really amuse me at times!" Orion said with a

chuckle.

He looked at his mother, noticing how small she seemed. Although in comparison to him nearly everyone appeared small. This was different, her vulnerability stood out as she gazed back. She was leaving her home, the planet she had loved so much. To go where?

Her facial expressions were tired and sad, more than Orion had ever seen her before.

"I do believe you just thanked the dog," Orion said, trying to snap her out of the doldrums.

"Oh…shut it, wise ass. The animal did as he was told, didn't he?" Fantasia said.

They both laughed and continued walking.

As they got closer to the shuttle, a crowd had gathered outside the barrack gates. They began arguing, and shouting broke out amongst them.

Through the noise Fantasia heard a woman screaming towards them, "STOP PLEASE!" she cried.

One of the soldiers walked towards the gates, cocking his rifle. Fantasia and Orion turned to look at what had happened. The woman pushed herself forward from the crowd, getting herself near to the closed gates.

A collective gasp came from the crowd as they witnessed her throwing her child, a new-born baby wrapped in a powder pink blanket, up in the direction of the top of the gates. Aiming over the electric fencing, a spark flew as the child hit the top of the fence.

People stood powerless as the child's little body flew out of its blanket, convulsing, hanging there in the barbed wired for a while as her tiny body burned, then hitting the tarmac, still on the same side as her mother.

The woman let out a scream of terror as she realised what she had done. She ran to her child, taking its burned body from the ground, holding it to her, sobbing, rocking it backwards and forwards. Then she picked it up and wrapped it back in the blanket as others watched in horror.

Turning away, Fantasia could look no longer. Orion

dropped the luggage, running back towards the fence.

A soldier on duty pointed his gun at him and told him to go back. Orion saw that nothing could be done for the child, and he didn't want to antagonise the soldier anymore. So, unwilling, he did as he was told.

"Bastard!" he said angrily under his breath. He quickly composed himself, picked up the luggage and headed back to his mother, who was now crying.

"I don't understand why she did that," Fantasia sobbed.

"She's desperate, like all of those who are being left behind. The Earth is condemned. The planet will be destroyed by fire as the ozone layer, which protected the Earth from the Sun, diminishes. What would you do if you were abandoned here, knowing that all would end soon? She did as any parent would, she tried to save her child," Orion said, as he comforted his mother.

The baggage truck arrived, pulling up next to them as they drew closer to the ship. Orion gladly placed the bags on it.

"The trunk's full of my books and equipment. Have they been put on the shuttle already?" he asked.

"Yes, Sir," the baggage truck driver replied with a smile. "All was placed on the craft early this morning. When you are on board the shuttle, please check that all luggage is present. We can't have you leaving stuff behind; this is the last flight leaving Earth,"

With sadness Orion looked down. He knew this meant that even the baggage handler had no way off the planet, because he just didn't have the skills needed. The academics had chosen but a few, all with achievement.

Orion's scientific skills had saved his life.

Fantasia had also been saved due to her abilities as an academic studying Psychology. The academics took no chances, so thought that if Earth survived, she may be the one who could tell them, even from a distance as far away as Titan, she had a psychic skill.

Putting his hand out, Orion took hold of Shadow's lead.

"Heel boy!" The command was met by the dog

straightaway. "Good boy," he said, as they boarded the shuttle without any more interruption.

*

Orion walked faster in order to keep the dog in line. He had always been faster than most people putting it down to his long legs. He had always been taller and seemed bigger than the average male.

"I really hope there are no other dogs on board, or even worse: cats," Fantasia said. "I did try and request this, but understandably if other animals are here, we can't really complain now, can we?" She looked around. "You know what a disobedient sod Shadow can be, so keep on the lookout and don't let him off. He'll go on a barking spree!"

Fantasia looked around the huge ship, there was nothing other than her own species sitting on seats, picking up books and magazines, preparing themselves for the journey.

Orion looked at his mother's red blotchy face. "I wonder how Sky and Emmina are? They should be settled in by now," he said to her.

He knew that if he changed the subject to something positive, she would soon feel better. She missed Sky and her funny moods: also, the way she would chat constantly. He remembered how much that got on his nerves, but being honest with himself, he also missed his sister. After all, they had been apart for a long time. But mostly he missed Emmina, his niece. She was one of the most precious things in his life, and he spoiled her a lot. He had packages in one of the trunks. There were toys, clothes, and the latest hair accessories, all that an eight-year-old would relish.

Fantasia looked around the shuttle, their new home for the next few months. She surveyed all around her.

This was not like an aeroplane, which had rows of seats each side of a gangway, with busy air hostesses asking if you wanted your flight meal now, or a drink which will cost a gazillion pounds, also giving you instructions about what to do in the case of an emergency.

This was like a flying hanger, with seats in some sections,

12

and luggage in others. With twelve portable loos to the left, which considering there were about 250 people on board didn't seem a lot really. Across the way was a more curious sight: four rooms with baths and sinks. A rota hung on the wall outside, for those wishing to use them.

"Mmm, this is nice!" Fantasia nodded towards Orion, who just shrugged.

They found some seats and sat down; trying to make themselves as comfortable as possible, on what looked like big office chairs, which were anchored down with bolts.

Shadow placed his head on Orion's lap, looking up at him, and making a short whining noise.

"You know boy, sometimes when you look at me, I swear I can almost understand what you're trying to tell me. Unfortunately, if you need walkies, look around, it's a case of where and how. They must have something here. You can't be expected to hold it or not eat for the whole journey. Shall we go and find out?"

Orion began looking for anyone who was not a passenger that could shed some light about dogs, dog poo, and the disposal of it. Shadow trailed behind him, looking slightly miserable and still whining.

As the two walked along, they came across an arrowed sign with the words *'Designated Area Point,'* which took them to a grass patch about twenty-by-twenty feet. Orion saw a fouling sign next to it, a bit like the ones for no fouling on Earth, but without the big red circle with the slash in the middle.

"Oh, that's so funny," Orion chuckled. "I need one of those. I must show Father, I doubt he would have noticed this on his journey."

Shadow whined and proceeded to try to use the facilities. Orion looked around, then took a photograph of the sign with his phone. When Shadow finished, a long robotic arm swivelled out from the corner of the ceiling above the area. It held a poo bag in mechanical fingers. The arm swooped down, picking up the faeces. Orion laughed loudly as the arm then disappeared spraying disinfectant behind it as it returned back where it came from.

"Now that's a crap job!" Orion tittered, as the two walked back to their seat.

"Have you noticed how the framework has been put in place for the buildings, so that it can be attached to the domes on Titan?" Fantasia asked, as Orion took his seat. Shadow plopped himself down at their feet.

Orion looked at the ship: it had markings with drill spots so that foundations could be put down quickly and easily.

"So, what supplies have we brought with us?" Fantasia asked.

"Just some chemical compounds and machinery. I've been experimenting with replication. There is a new machine, which can produce food easily."

"What do you mean produced? How?" Fantasia asked.

"By asking for a certain food or drink the machine will be able to make a copy. It will look and taste like the meal asked for. This seems a bit space aged I know, but it would be helpful while crops and fruits grow on Titan. I believe the glitches in the system are small and think that given a month I should have it up and running," Orion said.

Fantasia was proud of her son. She knew he would miss his life on Earth. He was in the middle of his biology degree when Drakos discussed their need to relocate. "A job's a job," he had said to them. "Orion can get a place at the university on Titan."

"Don't you wish we could be sleep induced for this journey?" Orion asked his mother.

"It will pass. I am just so bored, I will probably sleep through most of it anyway," she said.

"These seats are not very comfortable, but at least we have air conditioning," Orion said.

"Mmm."

"You're already falling asleep, aren't you?"

"Mmm."

Orion shrugged at her, then looked down at his dog, who

had also begun falling asleep. The journey was now underway. The smooth take-off had been and gone long before Orion took the dog for his walk.

"Oh well, if you can't beat 'em, so they say!"

Orion curled up under a blanket he had found under his seat and fell asleep.

~

The months passed without any incidents, and the journey to Titan ended with nothing to remember, apart from the boredom...

CHAPTER 2

When Fantasia awoke, she looked across at the empty side of the bed. The crisp white sheets had become wrinkled where she had tossed and turned in her unfamiliar surroundings. The walls were painted lilac, with the matching bedside table lamp and lampshade. The room was a lot smaller than the one she had on Earth. She picked up her watch from the side table.

"Oh Dam! Dam!" she said angrily. She quickly dressed and ran down the stairs.

"It's 9.30!" she said to Orion, who was sat in the kitchen, chewing a piece of toast.

"Yeah, and?" he replied.

"Oh, just hurry up and let's get to the car."

Fantasia picked up the car keys, and frantically headed towards the door.

Orion chewed down his last piece of toast, grabbed his shoes and followed, struggling as he tried to put them on.

"For God sake, slow down," he said, tripping over himself as he followed her out the front door, one shoe still in his hand, toast hanging from his mouth.

Stepping outside, the metal sky lit up with false lighting, giving day and night effects. Small digital clocks read 9.36am, all placed at the side of the roads as you drove by, so that the people could see and adjust, keeping their sleep patterns as they were on Earth.

The car was a 4X4, a green Land Rover. The vehicles were all heavy duty, due to the rough terrain.

As Fantasia drove off, the two of them looked around, surveying everything as they drove along.

Titan was strange, pods everywhere. All adjoined to one another, making a gigantic metal town. Everything had been built under these man-made tunnels and domes. The whole structure was huge, with no room to spare. Houses and shops were under construction, all squeezed close together.

Robotic equipment on Titan was programmed to construct the buildings on the land; some were building structures with men on board the robotic cranes. Machines were driving electric cables into the ground, adding fixtures and fittings, making the place habitable for the humans who lived in them.

As they looked out of the car window, the grass, trees, and the animals they passed appeared to have a strange anaemic look about them. The sheep had brown faces instead of black. The cows no longer black and white, they were white coloured with liver-coloured patches here and there. Birds were singing in the trees, but not the sparrows or robins they were used to in the UK. Instead, there were exotic birds that looked like they came from the tropical islands on Earth, living on Titan together because the environmental temperatures were suitable for them all. The colours of the birds had faded, paler than Orion could remember from his books and trips to bird sanctuaries.

The cities of metal were all reinforced with a new metal material that neither Orion nor Fantasia had seen before. There were thick panes of glass for windows. Orion looked outside, seeing a beautiful orange/red alien sky; colours caused by the methane in the atmosphere. This was not Earth. The windows of thick glass made vision through them difficult; everything was out of focus.

Temperatures on Titan plummeted outside in the atmosphere, so the systems inside the domes had to be exactly right, with no room for break downs. The human inhabitants would be dead within minutes if the heating system broke down, so electricians here had an around the clock job, monitoring equipment, making sure everything worked efficiently.

The biggest power resource here was the methane, which had been filtered and used to power everything. Titan could naturally produce this, so there was no fear of it running out.

Orion smiled at his mom, still watching the speed dial on the car. "So, you gunna put your foot down or what?" he said.

The car sped away.

~

Late now by half an hour, Fantasia sped up a little more. Her boss was waiting for her. The phone on the dashboard rang out...

Orion picked it up and flicked it open, putting it to his ear.

"Hello, yes, Father we are on our way... Mmm, about five minutes, I think! Look, what do you want? We have never been here before...Okay, yes okay!" Orion's voice sounded irritated. He snapped the phone shut, shaking his head. "For God sake, why doesn't he ever stop moaning?"

Making no effort to reply, Fantasia put her foot down. She too was a little irritated by Drakos's call.

They parked outside a large building that looked like a multi-storey block of flats. Both sighed as they spotted Drakos pacing outside. He stopped as the car pulled into the office grounds.

"You're Late!" he said abruptly to Fantasia as she opened the car door.

"Oh, give me a break!" she said.

"Come on; let's introduce you to the other members of the new team." Drakos ushered the two of them to the building, then through the electronic doors.

Drakos was the team leader, an historian who had met Fantasia on one of her holidays in Egypt.

He stood approximately five feet ten inches, with black hair in a small ponytail. He had silver eyes and a dark complexion, a beard and moustache well-trimmed. He always dressed in black shirt and jeans. He wore a weird looking belt buckle with a design of three moons and mountains on it.

Everyone knew that Drakos was a bit of a character. He was reliable, always on time, if not early for things. He was also a bit of a moaner, but this was something that both Orion and Fantasia were used to after many years. After all, he was Orion's father and Fantasia's partner.

"What, no kiss?" Drakos asked sarcastically.

Fantasia huffed, walking past him, mumbling under her breath.

18

Earth was to be destroyed due to human ignorance; its species had used every energy resource to the full.

An incantation from *'The Book of Demons,'* meant that doomsday would soon be upon the planet.

Drakos took them through the building and then stopped just outside some large office doors.

There were lines of smoky glass panelled windows, dividing the office space buildings, with rows of people sitting at desks. Orion watched fascinated as people sat typing and chatting on phones. He could hear part of the conversations as he passed by.

As Drakos headed down the last corridor, he opened a door and beckoned them inside. As they entered, the room appeared more lavish than the other offices, with plush dark brown carpet and gold wallpaper.

"Oh, this looks posh!" Orion chuckled sarcastically. "What crap taste in décor."

Drakos waited for Fantasia and Orion to sit down and join the others.

He began to speak.

"Hello, you are all acquainted with who I am: Drakos the team manager..."

Drakos began to talk while the others sat looking bored. They had been summoned to find a book, which was all everyone wanted to know. 'What had brought them to Titan?'

Eventually Drakos got to the point. *'The Book of Demons'* has been named the destroyer of planets. Incantations from this book can destroy worlds, obliterating everything living on them.

"Destructive behaviour would happen wherever the book has been opened." Orion said.

"Drakos, I'm sorry, but I do not sense this book is here. It still remains on Earth!" Fantasia said. "Remember I have held this terrible dark book; I have been in it's presence."

"Let's hope you have jetlag, otherwise we have come a long way for nothing," said Drakos, joking.

Fantasia said no more. His ignorance made her want to

whack him.

"Here on my right is Mia; she is from Denver, USA. She emigrated to England, where she graduated from university with a first-class degree. She had begun her master's in research; her subject area was human sciences. She has been on Titan four months now..." Drakos said.

Fantasia began to read the body language and facial expressions of the graduate. Mia was hard to work out at first, obviously hiding something.

She was Asian, with beautiful, long, straight black hair, and she came across a bit pompous. Her brown eyes were slightly bloodshot, but Fantasia put that down to her being a researcher. They sat at computers and read books all their working lives, so it was a burden that came with the job.

Mia stood tiny in comparison to all the others in the team, around 5 feet 6 inches. She wore blue stonewash jeans, a white t-shirt with a white waist length lab coat, which had black, red and blue pens in its chest pocket, which is also part of a researchers profiling.

Thinking of her time at university, she knew that Mia looked like all the other lab assistants. As Mia spotted Fantasia's interest in her, she smiled as if she knew what Fantasia was trying to do, which was delve into her mind.

Mia seemed a bit of a dreamer, she looked in her early twenties. The only information that hadn't been blocked was that she felt hungry and wanted Drakos to hurry up and stop talking.

Fantasia's concentration was broken by Drakos, talking loudly again.

"Sat next to our researcher is Ghost!" he said.

Drakos looked like the man who had just found a rare artefact. Fantasia searched Ghost's profile for information. Unlike Mia, Ghost was an open book; the two sat conversing with one another as Ghost explained who she was telepathically over Drakos's chit-chat.

Fantasia was a little shocked at first but decided to go with it.

"I have no memory of my past," Ghost said. "I am what's known as a shapeshifter. This is the main reason I was chosen, plus my telepathic abilities, like you. Telepathy included, which is why we can talk to one another so easily."

Ghost looked otherworldly. She wore a long flowing robe. Her hair was white silver; her complexion was young; what they could make of it, because she wore a black opera mask, hiding the top half of her face. She seemed to be in her late twenties. Her clothes were an off-white colour, with a cream lace trim around the bottom of the neck and sleeves. She had strange silver patterning embroidered on the robes.

When Fantasia looked into her eyes they had the familiar silver/blue colouring, which stood out under the black of the mask; like Orion's and Drakos's eyes.

"Why are you hiding your face?" Orion asked her, as he began standing up. He was about to head over and touch Ghost's mask.

Ghost did not reply. She just sat silently watching those around her.

"ORION!" Drakos shouted. "We don't need to know. Just keep quiet. I am sure if Ghost wishes she will tell you in her own time."

A silence hit the room for a second.

"I was only asking... moaning git!" Orion said, resuming his seat in the room.

"Ghost is a researcher of the black arts, the occult! She has dealings with magic and has the ability to shape-shift!" Drakos said, trying to surprise everyone. But they didn't react at all, so he droned back into their ears as they turned to look interested at him.

The team gasped with surprise when Fantasia decided to put her hand out towards her new friend...

"Can I?" she asked.

"Yes, go ahead," replied Ghost.

Fantasia put her hand on Ghost's shoulder. As she did, it seemed to disappear through Ghost's body. Even the clothes engulfed her hand. A sudden infusion of feelings jolted into

Fantasia's mind, as sadness and mourning hit her. It was as if Ghost had been searching for the one she had lost, her lover. The ache was excruciating.

Quickly Fantasia pulled her hand away. She felt like an intruder.

"I'm sorry," Fantasia said to her, still feeling the burn from the emotional connection.

"Don't be," Ghost smiled.

They both realised that they had good allies in one another and had already become friends.

"So then…" Orion said, breaking the silent pause. He looked over at the person Drakos had not yet introduced. "Who's this?" he said, a little abruptly.

"Our funding," Drakos said, gritting his teeth. "She has hired us. She pays our wages." Drakos gave Orion a look of disapproval. His son never did know when he was being tactless.

"Sorry, they are always like this, never know when to stop," Fantasia said, turning to look now at the woman sat next to Mia at the table.

The woman was smartly dressed, she looked in her early forties, wearing a traditional black trouser suit, with a white shirt, black patent flat shoes, no jewellery... But again, she had the same silver eyes. This was getting a little strange now, but it could be coincidental, couldn't it?

Fantasia was unsure.

The woman's hair was a strange red, not ginger, but a deep blood red! Her eyes stood out, more due to her vibrant hair colour. Her hand had the familiar scar; one that Fantasia had ever since she could remember, although she had no memory of how it got there. It was a common thing because Orion, Sky, Emmina and Drakos had it too. *'Perhaps it is just a familiar type of birthmark'* she thought to herself.

"So, tell me, why are we here?" Fantasia asked.

Drakos began opening his mouth, but the woman jumped into the conversation quickly. She had obviously heard enough of Drakos's long winded introductions.

"Good morning, I'm Beth." Looking around at the team. "*The Book of Belial* is believed to have been transported onto Titan and smuggled into the city. We are all too aware of what happened to Earth when the book was opened there. It was doomed. So, your mission is to find and destroy the book before it's used and makes our new home a casualty of its destructive powers."

Fantasia was suspicious of her. She began to wonder if she had been brought to Titan under false pretences. She knew why she had to leave Earth. She had left only months before, and the book was still doing a great job destroying mankind there. So, the question was, why did Beth really want the team on Titan?

Beth interrupted Fantasia's train of thought. "I believe that the book has been brought here to Titan to be opened, so that this moon faces the same destruction as Earth," she emphasised.

Fantasia looked down, ignoring Beth's little speech. Then she began to remember.

'Her mind drifted back to another time.
Her house was in Worcestershire, UK.
There she met her friend Phoenix, who had educated her in magic, and helped enhance her psychic powers.
Phoenix was the keeper of 'The Book of Belial.
He had kept it hidden from those who lived with him since it was taken that night in Berlin. He claimed responsibility for the book when he stole it from the shop owner, who had paid for his ownership of it with his life.
Fantasia loved the old man, and his death was a great strain on her life. It affected her, even to this day. She had missed him and his guidance.
The book's power called to her from the moment she had been in its presence, its power emanating like a plague on her soul.
Phoenix stood six feet four inches tall, his hair long and

grey, his eyes pale blue/white because he had become blind through his dealings with the Devil and the black arts.

"So, my white witch... let's see if your soul is truly good, or if you have some darkness within after all," Phoenix chuckled, handing Fantasia the book.

Fantasia took the book home, putting it down on the table and leaving it unopened in her kitchen. It was late so her babysitter had immediately got up and gone home.

Before she went upstairs her phone rang. She picked up the receiver.

"If you need me, all you have to do is call my name," Phoenix said, then hung up.

"Mmm...silly old man," Fantasia said, putting the receiver down. She walked upstairs and got into bed, falling asleep quickly.

As she slept, her house began to bleed, every room inside and outside the walls poured with blood.

The floors spewed maggots, which were seeping through her bedroom ceiling. A strange laughter echoed all over the house.

Fantasia ended up standing on her bed, cuddling into her children.

"Phoenix, help me!" she shouted at the top of her voice.

Phoenix appeared at the bedroom door, floating, oblivious to it all. He looked quite different; his face bulged above his eyes and around his mouth. He had two sets of long white fangs gleaming as he smiled at her.

He clicked his fingers and raised his arms.

His eyes turned black as he shouted: "STOP!"

Fantasia awoke with a start. Everything in the room had gone back to normal, like nothing had happened. It was just a realistic dream.

The next morning, she had marched back over to Phoenix with the book in her hand. She never even looked inside it.

"Have this back you sucker!" she said, thrusting the book

at him.

Phoenix began to laugh. "I came when you called, didn't I?"

"You're an evil old sod!" Fantasia said, now seeing the funny side of it all. Relieved to have the book back where it belonged.'

Her daydream was over, Beth was still talking about the book.

"You do realise the power this book holds, don't you?" Fantasia asked.

"Yes, I am aware you have experienced the book's power, first-hand. You're lucky," Beth replied. Her face turned a little red, as if she had said something she shouldn't.

"Lucky?" Fantasia said, looking angry.

"You have a better connection than we do…its new owner…"

Fantasia interrupted Beth abruptly. "New owner? Phoenix died of natural causes; therefore, he remains the book's owner."

Beth began to argue back but found herself interrupted.

"The legend states the old owner would need to die of unnatural causes before someone new possesses it. Anyone who has done any research into this book would know this," Fantasia barked abruptly.

Ghost stood next to Fantasia.

"True," Ghost said defensively.

Fantasia walked away to calm down.

Beth and Mia sat down with a sigh.

Mia was getting hungry now.

"Mmm, not best friend material then?" Drakos said, walking towards her smiling. He looked at Fantasia, and the smile disappeared from his face. "Oh, you're serious?" he said.

"I distrust her, she's hiding something. We need to be careful. I am sure the book isn't on Titan, I would swear this on my own life," she said.

Drakos looked slightly perturbed and tried to put his arm around Fantasia.

Fantasia caught Beth's face, she looked like she had been caught with her hand in the cookie jar, so Fantasia relaxed and allowed Drakos's arm to fall onto her shoulder.

"Please, Fantasia trust me," Drakos said.

Fantasia smiled at him and nodded, and they went back to the table and sat down.

Beth's face looked relieved.

Soon after this the meeting finished, and they all left the office building, going their own way.

"Think we need a serious conversation" Fantasia said to Drakos.

~

It wasn't long ago that Fantasia and Orion were still on Earth. Now they felt out of place, locked in a metal prison, far away from the home they pined for. No more blue sky, green grass with that fresh mowed smell that used to give Sky hay fever. No more taking Shadow for walks in the park on the hot summer evenings.

Everything here was man-made and wasn't quite part of the evolutionary chain. Man had adapted, but to what?

Humans were living out here on Saturn's moon surface. The moon's atmosphere was freezing cold. Methane air instead of oxygen was lethal; humans weren't meant to survive here.

Scientific advances couldn't help people. The plants and animals that could adapt on Earth couldn't here.

Orion had been working on the food replicators for Titan's colony, it took him only months to perfect it.

All human life would live with a constant fear of the metal domes cracking, letting in the atmosphere from outside. Methane creeping in, destroying all; the loss of every species including their own.

Humans would become like the dinosaurs: extinct!

~

The 25^{th of} December would be time to stop everything.

The Earth ritual of Christmas day, although no longer a Christian celebration on Titan, would remain for everyone to take part in.

Fantasia's favourite day of the year, whether on Earth or Titan. The thought of putting the Christmas tree up the day before, all the decorations, good food, friends giving useless gifts to one another, made her feel warm inside, giving hope that Earth may survive.

Very soon Earth would be gone!

Fantasia sighed. She missed her home. Her mind drifted again; she shook it off. *'Why am I such a daydreamer?'* she thought.

Fantasia stopped daydreaming and joined the others in the front room. This was open planned and adjoined a yellow wallpapered kitchen. The front room area was decorated in red and cream, with a large set of soft black suede sofas, with a huge LCD television in the corner. They were watching a quiz show. Fantasia's mind wandered in and out of memories of Earth and her journey here. She began to gently nod off, feet resting on Drakos, who had as usual drifted off to sleep himself.

Orion just looked at his parents, shaking his head.

"Old people," he said.

Orion turned off the television, placing a fleece blanket over them both. Then he made his way upstairs to bed, turning off the lights as he went.

CHAPTER 3

Travelling the roads of Titan was a challenge, one that Fantasia enjoyed. The trouble was, they moved from hotels to bed and breakfasts; not staying long anywhere in particular.

Fantasia sat in the lounge of a hotel. She walked away from the others trying to search her mind for clues to the books whereabouts.

She didn't trust Beth, or her sidekick Mia.

What would she gain from this?

Not the book, no one would find it on Titan. So, what was this really about?

Shadow sat by her feet and whined, putting his head on her lap as she patted it gently, and began talking to him.

"What's up boy? We're missing something. I know we're going to end up in trouble because of Beth!"

The dog whined again.

Fantasia stood up, taking him outside, and they walked to a dog poo designated area. Then the two of them went back to the hotel again, going back into the same room, only this time Fantasia sat on the floor and the dog lay down cuddling into her legs.

The room was light blue, with painted walls, very plain and clinical. She hated it. The furniture was the opposite, a red wooden table, and chairs, materials like curtains were all frilly and chintzy, with blue velour cushions. It was like something from the 1920's on Earth. The curtains were the same velour material, everything matched nicely in an eggshell blue Hell. Luckily, she didn't have to live there permanently, and had decided to go back to her own house on Titan. She didn't see it as home, even though she lived there. It was a small hotel she had converted and got permission to live in, out of the way from most of civilisation here. The area was still empty.

Fantasia had had enough of all the bull-crap and went to find the others. Shadow followed beside her.

"Drakos! Get up…time to go," she said. "Let's not waste

time waiting for Beth!"

"Wait! Where are we going?" he asked.

"It's time to get a grip with what is really going on. Get the others. I'll meet you in the lobby in ten minutes… Ghost is already with me," said Fantasia, as she walked down the hallway.

"Wonderful, I get to wake up the boy then!" Drakos cursed under his breath.

She smiled at him looking back.

While Fantasia and Ghost headed downstairs, the dog decided to stay at Orion's door and wait. He scratched at it, whining.

"Okay, okay Shadow, I am up!" Orion shouted.

Drakos and Orion met in the hall, which was a relief because Drakos really hated the 'calling and being ignored thing.'

They both headed down the hall together. They met the others who were sat in the café area of the hotel.

Fantasia was drinking coffee. Ghost didn't seem to eat or drink very much at all.

Looking up at Drakos, "you're supposed to be in charge here, so explain why we are on this wild goose chase, looking for a book that isn't here. It's time to stop, before we walk into one of this mad woman's traps!" Fantasia said.

"What?" Orion said, still half asleep.

"We should be looking for something more relevant. Beth knows that the book isn't here and is paying a lot of money to keep us occupied. I want an explanation." Fantasia said.

Drakos looked uncomfortable, wriggling in his chair while Fantasia looked at him.

"The information you've been keeping to yourself; I think it's time for you to open your mouth," she said.

"Okay, but we should make a few enquiries, find our researcher first," Drakos said to her.

Fantasia looked sharply at him, but anything that meant they stopped wasting time would be good.

"Where does Mia live?" she asked.

"52 North Quadrant. It's thirty-five minutes by car." Drakos said, as he picked up Shadow's lead. They all stepped outside and climbed into the Land Rover.

"Okay guys, hold onto your hats," Orion said, as he took the car keys and walked to the driver's side.

Orion put his foot down, so the journey was twenty-five minutes. If Ghost weren't already pale, she would be now. Orion drove like a maniac.

*

Only two of the flats in 52 North Quadrant were occupied.

"Which one?" Fantasia asked.

"52 d," said Drakos, looking back at his crumpled piece of paper.

The flat was on the second floor. No net curtains, but office roller blinds in the windows, keeping the flat private. The building door was ajar, so no problem gaining access. The team walked up a small set of stairs to the second floor. There was no lift in these buildings, so Orion was glad that she didn't live on floor five.

"Do you think she'll be in?" he asked.

"Hopefully not, we could do with a quick look around, see what she's been hiding," Fantasia said, giving Drakos a sharp look. She had been with this man for years, and for the first time had found a reason to distrust him. He seemed to know more than he had been telling, which made her feel quite angry.

They reached the beige-coloured door with 52d displayed on the letterbox. Drakos knocked. Nothing… so he knocked again, this time calling through the letterbox.

"Mia, it's Drakos with the team!"

Fantasia nudged Orion. She spotted the security camera scanning its way down past them, observing everyone.

"Job for you, I believe," she said, nodding in its direction.

Orion jumped up. His giant frame had no difficulty reaching the camera. He pulled hard at the cables, cutting off its power. The buzzing sound faded as the machinery lost its life.

"Okay, now, let's see if she's in," Fantasia said.

Ghost stopped them from forcing the door, stepping through it as if it was water. Concentrating, she turned solid and unlocked the door on the other side, letting the rest of the team into the flat.

"Impressive!" Orion said.

The walls in the hallway were a clinical magnolia colour with an oat-coloured carpet. No pictures or photographs on the walls, just hooks with coats hanging from them. A denim jacket and a cream-coloured mac were spotted. But why she had the mac was slightly pointless. It didn't rain on Titan, everything was inside, even plants were watered by a sprinkler system.

There were another three rooms that led from the hallway. A bedroom with baby pink everywhere, so clean and tidy it was obvious that it was never used. The bathroom was the same.

Then there was the lounge!

"Oh My God!" Orion said. "What the Hell?"

This room was completely disorganised, covered with papers and books. It was so untidy you didn't know if it had a carpet in there. You couldn't see it. There were dirty plates, wrappers from bars of cereal, and sweets scattered everywhere.

"My Goodness, Orion, it looks like your bedroom!" Drakos said, laughing.

"No, my carpet is black with multi-coloured patterns. I saw it when I was last there," he said, still looking amazed at the mess.

"Where the hell do we start?" Fantasia asked, looking over at Ghost, who stood holding her nose.

"How can anyone live in this?" Ghost asked.

"I have no idea. It's like a bloody pig sty," Drakos said.

"Wait! There are daily papers here from Earth." Orion handed Fantasia a small pile of newspapers.

One of the paper's headlines read- *'New PM doing well. Economy boosted as new businesses and higher wages promised.'* Fantasia scanned around for the date: 31st May 2511. She dropped the paper with shock, then scrambled to pick it up again.

"This paper is dated a week ago," she said, handing it over to Drakos.

Drakos did a double take as he recognised the man in the picture!

He then handed the paper to Orion, who hadn't got a clue why his father had reacted so strangely to the front-page article.

Ghost picked up the newspaper.

"Belial!" she whispered, appearing afraid. "Time for us to leave," she said, making her way quickly to the exit.

"Are they coming back?" Drakos asked.

"Yes, we have only minutes to vacate this property," Ghost said.

They made their way to the door, down the stairs and climbed into the car, driving around the side of the building, out of sight. Just in time to witness the open top jeep turning the corner with Beth and Mia laughing with one another, then pulling into the parking space allocated to her.

"When they walk into the building, we need to exit quickly," Drakos said, as he started the engine of the jeep, keeping it ticking over.

"What's the plan?" Orion said.

"Let's get back to the hotel." Fantasia said.

Drakos revved the engine slightly, then put his foot down; hoping the sound of his car wouldn't attract Beth and Mia's attention as they walked into the building. He didn't want them to look back.

"Act normally when they get to us. If they see us leave they'll be minutes behind, so we'll have to look like we've been at the hotel all day," he said.

"What time is it now?" Fantasia asked.

"2.45 pm," Orion said, looking at his watch. "Put the jeep in the hotel garage. The car's engine will be hot, and they will know it has been used recently."

It was minutes after their return before Beth and Mia arrived. They looked frantically for members of the team. As she spotted them, Beth smiled and sighed with relief.

"Is everything alright, Beth?" Drakos enquired, as she came towards them.

"No, not really. I've just driven back from a meeting with Mia and went to her flat. It had been broken into," she said.

Drakos raised his eyebrows in surprise, looking very shocked.

"He's good," Orion whispered softly to his mother. "Too good perhaps!"

"Was anything taken?" Ghost asked.

"No, nothing, but they'd left the door open. It was as if they'd been caught in the act," Beth said.

"Well, maybe they had. Have you asked the neighbours if they saw anything?" Drakos said.

The conversation stopped just for a minute when Mia came over. She looked upset.

Orion was thinking that this was more than likely because someone had been in and seen the utter pigsty she lived in. A real burglar would have left her a fiver to pay towards getting someone in to clean up.

"So, is there any news to tell us? What was the meeting about? Is there anything new to report about our mission?" Drakos said, changing the subject.

"We've found another lead. Crime in Quadrant 39 has suddenly hit an all-time high. It's looking like signs of the book being opened. You'll need to investigate this. You're to meet Joshua at Quadrant 38, on the outskirts of the place. He has temporary living quarters for you. He'll be there at 8.30 am," Beth said.

"Wonder why the crime rate has really gone up?" Orion whispered to his mother. "Does she live there?"

The two sniggered at one another, both becoming straight faced when Beth looked over.

Mia and Beth left, only looking back to smile and wave as

the team got together to discuss their new plan of action.

"So, do we follow the path to certain doom, or go our own way?" Drakos asked. "Either way, we know she'll try to kill us. If we don't turn up, she'll know we were in Mia's flat, and that we know Earth has a new Prime Minister."

"I say we go our own way, I'm not in the mood for a fight. Knowing that bitch, she will ambush us, and we won't stand a chance," Orion said to his father. "Why walk into a fight where we'll be outnumbered and risk our lives?"

They all agreed, packed their stuff, and headed back to Fantasia's house. They knew this would be Beth's next port of call when they didn't show up at the meeting place.

"I have a story to tell you on our way home. Stay with us Ghost, it's too dangerous for you to be alone now," Drakos said.

"Of course, this story will be interesting, my friend," she said, with a smile.

They got into the car and began their journey. Fantasia grinned; she realised now that she could go home to Earth. She would be taking the first opportunity she could, and so would her family.

Orion could start his education again, and Sky would be able to take up her career where she left off.

Whatever they did would be fine to her, just as long as she could get out of this Hell hole.

CHAPTER 4

Drakos began…

"I want to tell you about a planet… in the Mythus galaxy, which is home to a small set of planets, quite a distance away from here. The planet I am going to talk about is called Vox and its inhabitants are Voxians," he said.

"Is this going to take long? I've brought my music," Orion said, flashing his music player.

"Orion, have some patience, this does affect you as well," Drakos said.

"Sorry Father," Orion went quiet.

"A legend claims Angels were sent to seek Demons that escaped into this Multiverse. This isn't about the existence of God, but it's about higher beings who have been sent to protect our Multiverse," Drakos went on.

"So, you're saying that the legend is about the creation of the Multiverse?" Orion said.

"Yes, I am." Drakos looked relieved. "There were many Angels: Gabriel, Michael, Kathos, and others," continued Drakos. "Kathos had been searching for his fallen brother, his name was Belial, he had made '*the Book of Demons*' many ages ago from the tortured souls of angels he had captured.

They sat in silence. This was the very book they had been pursuing, and Fantasia had held it in her hands that night on Earth. No wonder she had felt so terrified of it all that time ago.

The book was evil.

"While searching the Multiverse, Kathos found Vox and its people. The people were peace loving and beautiful. He had never seen such powers. Some had speed, all are telepathic or psychic as they call it on Earth, some could tell the future, others flew in the sky. All the people were harmonious. The Voxians accepted Kathos and his friend, seeing his power as advantageous to have on the planet. Eventually, after many years, Kathos fell in love with the Voxian Princess Ledawna, and in time Kathos became the

Voxians new King. His power is stronger than the Voxians, the longer he remained with them, the more his people adapted, becoming stronger themselves. Kathos and Ledawna had three children, two sons who were named Rellik and Rexus and a daughter, Bethadora."

Drakos stopped talking, waiting patiently for a reaction.

"So, does this mean that you knew who Beth was?" Orion asked.

"For years now I have only heard of her through stories. I became suspicious a while ago, when she kept vanishing and then when your mother took an instant disliking to her. I had no idea that she was the actual Voxian princess, Bethadora, until we went to the flat. She seems to be able to disguise herself wherever she goes."

This explanation was taking longer than Drakos had hoped. He had a lot of ground to cover and had already travelled half of the journey.

Drakos carried on talking:

"Capalia is one of two Islands on Vox. It's the bigger and covers thousands of miles. There are mountains, villages, and a city. But Capalia is covered mainly in forests of trees, where the Voxian people spend their time hunting food. The houses in the villages are large. Like the people, they all vary in styles. The Capalians live in harmony and are very different to the smaller island to the north. Raithar is another matter. The Raitharns aren't peaceful people, they're allies of Bethadora. She rules over them with an iron fist. All the Voxians on this island have to relinquish their powers otherwise face her wrath, and she has no mercy for those who disobey her."

"What's the Raithar Island like?" Orion said.

"No-one really knows. The Capalians don't set foot there; it's just wasteland. Beth took it over with her followers and began recruiting from places like Earth. Humans are weak, not like the Voxians, but she uses them like slaves."

"It's obvious Beth has a plan to take over somewhere," Orion said, interrupting. He couldn't work out where, or who she had as her allies, but this Belial guy certainly came to mind. "Why has the Voxian King allowed her and his brother to do this?"

"He has no jurisdiction there." Drakos carried on with his conversation.

Orion shrugged and felt it would be easier to just let his father speak.

"The land in Raithar became barren. They've little grass and a few trees. Animals there are scarce, so the Raitharns eat any food available to them. We know they won't take over our lands. Lack of food has stopped them hunting, so they have become withdrawn and lazy."

Drakos took a swig of his drink. The temperature inside the domes was hot, and his throat had become dry from talking. He then continued with his story:

"Twice Bethadora has joined Belial in battle, and both times they have failed. Kathos sent Belial back to Hell, but whoever has the book can recall him. The last owner of the book was a German shop keeper in Berlin. Phoenix killed him to own the book. But Phoenix never summoned Belial; he only kept the book safe. He had a second book made, copied, and processed by a publisher. He had this on hand for anyone who wanted possession of it. But the book was fake and had no power."

"So, what happened then? Did the book get found?" Orion asked.

"No-one found the book. It was kept in the attic of Phoenix's first house in Inkberrow, Worcestershire. The house was in the middle of the woods and rumoured to be haunted. This stopped potential buyers, and the house has remained empty. But no book has been found there. Kathos has searched it himself. There is nothing," Drakos said.

The car came to a halt as they arrived back at their home on Titan. They sat outside for a while. Drakos looked in his mirror at the two women who were sat in the back seat, both in silence.

"Is this too much?" he asked Fantasia.

She made no attempt to reply.

Fantasia got out of the car and walked towards the house, a million questions in her head. She had different memories.

Her memories were of a father who died in a house fire. Orion never met him, and Fantasia had been completely alienated by her family. She didn't cry at the news of his death. This made her feel guilty for many years. All of it suddenly made a lot more sense now. It was true she hadn't been a part of this family, and despite the need to fit in with them, Fantasia never did.

They sat down with tea, and Fantasia sat on a chair alone, in full view of the others. She looked at Drakos.

"You've got questions, haven't you?" he said.

"Just a few." Fantasia didn't want to ask them yet, so they sat talking about Beth for a while.

"Why did she want us here? What's Titan got to do with her gaining power?" Orion asked.

"I can help with that," Ghost said. "I checked the newspaper from Earth. Look at the article again closely. Who's in the background?"

The newspaper was pulled from Fantasia's pocket. They had taken it while hurrying out of the flat. The picture of Earth's new Prime Minister was shown around, there stood in the background were Beth and Mia.

In Beth's hand was the fake second book!

Fantasia recognised it immediately. It may have been a copy of *'The Book of Demons,'* which Phoenix had made but it still sent a shudder down her spine, it had one difference, the cover was brighter.

Suddenly a black metallic tint appeared on Fantasia's face.. But as quickly as it had appeared it disappeared again.

"Her memory may take time to return," said Drakos.

Out of the blue Orion stood up with a smile on his face. "I'm a fricking alien!" he said, as the realisation suddenly hit him.

The others laughed at him as he danced about, making a complete prat of himself. The questions began:

"So, what does this mean? What about all those years we've spent on Earth? What do our species live on?" Orion asked.

"Not cheese on toast!" Drakos smiled at his son. "We are hunters, usually of the animals in the vast forests of Capalia. We feed from their blood."

"Cool! Like vampires?" Orion said.

"No, not like bloody vampires, those creatures aren't anything like the human stories. Let's not complicate things right now with more species that aren't our concern. We're living, breathing people," Drakos explained.

"So, is everyone here Voxian?" Orion looked at Ghost.

"Orion, sometimes you're so subtle. Yes, we're all Voxians, even Ghost, who I believe is a very rare shapeshifter. I have no idea why she's like she is, but I'm hoping that once we're back on our own planet things will improve for her, and she will be able to become solid again, if she wishes. I'm sorry, Ghost, for talking about you when you're here in the room, but we all know how hard it is to get information across to Orion sometimes. He can be such an idiot considering he is so intelligent," Drakos said.

Ghost smiled at them, saying nothing, she had been lost for such a long time. The thought that she had a home was quite a relief. She had been searching for a long time for a place she could belong.

"What could be that bad that I would abandon my life on Vox and my family?" Fantasia asked.

"Let's talk more later. You look exhausted," Drakos said to Fantasia.

"Let's have some food. You can sit down and watch your favourite film," Orion said, fetching a pack of frozen cheese and tomato pizza from the freezer and switching on the oven.

Suddenly Fantasia had an outburst "What? Do you mean I have to drink BLOOD?" Fantasia said, as she began to sob. She looked dismayed. She had absolutely no recollection of anyone or anything.

Drakos got up and pulled Fantasia from the chair and sat

her on his lap. He realised that she was finding it hard to accept. He didn't want to tell her yet that she had wished to alter her memories.

"I know it's hard to believe that you aren't who you thought you were," Drakos said, as he held Fantasia's hand. "Come on, have some pizza! It'll be okay. Have something to eat. You'll figure this out once you have all your memories back; I promise you."

Fantasia felt safe and warm in his arms. She stayed there for just a while longer.

Tired, she began eating her pizza, but gave up halfway through, leaving it on her plate for Orion to eat.

She got up and headed towards the stairs. "Night," she said, and then walked up the stairs to bed.

CHAPTER 5

The star ship hovered above the atmosphere of Titan. It looked like silver liquid mercury. Its engines were silent, the equipment on board was so sophisticated it could remain unseen by the occupants inside the metal city. No radar system inside could pick it up, as it cloaked and disappeared.

The star ship's pilot Comet stood six foot six inches, with mousey brown hair, and was very handsome. His facial features were almost perfect, except for the slight skewed angle in his nose, like it had been broken. His muscular body was dressed in blue jeans, a red t-shirt with a long black leather coat, plus boots on his feet that looked like he had dressed for a night out at a metal club.

The Voxian crew came dressed like some of the people from Earth.

"Comet, please give a destination, we need to teleport." Safire said.

"There is a point just next to Fantasia's home; it looks like an empty warehouse," Comet said, turning towards Kathos for his approval.

"That'll do nicely. Be prepared to teleport." Kathos said.

~

Orion was still elated from knowing his true origin. He couldn't believe he had spent all that time thinking he was a giant amongst little people. He had lived with the nickname 'Lanky' throughout his life. People in the street would always have to state the obvious: *"Look at him! Isn't he tall?"*

Orion sat smiling, giving out a chuckle occasionally. "I'm a frickin' alien!" he said.

He decided to go and find his father, who had sat in the kitchen reading the morning paper *'The Titan daily.'* He wanted to ask more about his species. There was still so much he needed to know.

The kitchen was small. It had bright yellow wallpaper that Fantasia didn't like very much. But on Titan there wasn't a lot of choice yet. The kitchen units were made of oak, with black marble tops. Nothing special to her, so she hadn't made much effort when designing the decoration.

Drakos looked up at Orion. It was wonderful finally talking to him about their home planet. Fantasia would be fine once she realised that this was a good thing.

"Father, surely there must be consequences for us living as humans all this time?"

"Maybe, but nothing that won't return. You see, we didn't think you would be living as a human for quite this long."

"Tell me, what's it like on Vox?" Orion asked.

Drakos put down his newspaper. Orion could see he was in for another long story.

"Capalia's wonderful. Mountains like the Swiss Alps on Earth. The Lord Warrior of the mountains is a great leader; a giant even by your standards." Drakos laughed as he pictured his friend. "He has three sons around your age. I'm sure you will all be great friends."

Orion acknowledged his father with a small nod.

"Capalia city is the busiest place I've ever seen, with line upon line of high-rise shopping malls, to die for. It also has a Lord Warrior. He's very calm and intelligent, and has a beautiful daughter, Azaya. I don't want to tell you too much. I want you to see for yourself," said Drakos.

"Tell me about my family. Who was my biological donor? Why did Mom leave him?" asked Orion.

"Saul was evil. He was violent and disliked by the other warriors. Fantasia was a rebel in her youth. She went against Rexus, her father's wishes, trying to show people that Saul was not evil. In the last fight to destroy Belial there were many casualties. Unfortunately, Saul was one of them. He and Bethadora had been plotting with the enemies of Kathos, who is your great, great grandfather, and the King. Fantasia's Brother, Kaos was also a casualty of the war, killed by your father's betrayal," Drakos said, looking grim.

"So that's why Mom never talks about him. What a complete waste of space!" Orion said, looking a little angry now, with a momentary flash of metallic black on his face.

"The reason why your mother doesn't talk about him is because if you remember, she has no memory of that life at the moment." Drakos reminded him. "Kaos was Fantasia's closest friend, her brother, so she blamed herself for his death. She was infatuated with Saul."

"So, what happened next?" Orion said, showing no empathy.

Drakos continued his story.

"After the death of Saul, Fantasia wanted to leave the memories behind. He had been caught in the crossfire of fighting between Kathos and Belial. His death was welcomed if you understand my meaning. He couldn't come back to our people; they would never trust him again. But we couldn't let him free either; he could fight on the side of our enemy once again."

"So, you'd have killed him anyway?" Orion asked.

"Yes, I'm afraid so, Son," Drakos said, as he got up from his seat, giving Orion a pat on the shoulder.

"This is gunna be a long day," Drakos said, looking upstairs.

Drakos turned to Orion, and said: "Do you think your mother will come down soon? I just don't want to disturb her; not unless I have to."

"Why would you have to?" Orion asked him.

"Mmm, because she has visitors coming. Your great, great grandfather, your aunt and her partner Comet. I am finding it difficult to communicate with their ship, it's probably cloaked." Drakos said.

Orion gulped his toast; he was about to meet his real family!

"So, what are you going to do about Mom?" he asked.

"I need to talk to her, today, as soon as possible. I am going to put the kettle on and make her a cup of tea, then hope she wants to know more. She'll be shocked if she isn't forewarned first." Drakos said.

Orion agreed. "I think it might be a good idea if I go out for a walk with Shadow."

Drakos nodded and went off to put on the kettle, just as Fantasia walked downstairs and entered the front room.

Orion left, calling his dog who followed.

"So, tell me more." Fantasia asked, flicking the channels over on the television, not really watching anything. As she sat down on the sofa, the breakfast news was on.

Drakos walked over to Fantasia, taking the remote from her. He flicked off the television and put the remote back down on the arm of her chair.

He retold the story, but this time with a lot more detail. Fantasia sat and listened.

He began to worry; she didn't seem to remember her life on Vox.

Drakos had hoped she would, but he was sure actually seeing them may be the trigger she needed.

"Saul was an evil man! He betrayed his family, and his lies helped to assassinate Kaos." Drakos said.

"My poor Brother," Fantasia said, looking dazed. It looked like she recovered some of her memories. She looked at Drakos, waiting for more.

"Kaos was ambushed by Belial's warriors. He didn't stand a chance," Drakos said.

"So, what happened next? Please continue, I'm fine honestly!" she said.

"Saul was discovered. Kathos and Comet realised a little too late but gave chase. They found the hateful man before he could cross the borders. Belial stepped in and attacked Kathos. Comet found Saul spying from behind the trees in the forest, so he took out his sword and cut off his head. Then he burned him, his head thrown into the fire so that he could never double cross anyone again." Drakos paused looking at Fantasia's puzzled face. "I should perhaps mention that if our heads survive an attack, we can grow our bodies back, although they are weak for some time afterwards."

"That's just unreal! You've got to be joking, Drakos?" She got no reply "You are, aren't you?"

Drakos said nothing. He lifted his right eyebrow, smiling.

"Kathos believed that you were so grief stricken you couldn't live on Vox. So, you chose to live on Earth, and Kathos put your memories way back in your subconscious. You wanted to be with your children on Earth."

"I asked for this. How? I mean, how did he take away my memories? " Fantasia asked, surprised.

"He's a supreme being, so it was simple. Kathos believed you would never get over Saul's betrayal while living on Vox. He gave you a farewell kiss and wished you the best. Rexus, your father, on the other hand was devastated, but believed you would be back soon. Your mother, Genesis, was distraught also, she didn't want you to leave. She had lost her son and then you left with her grandchildren. She thought life would never be the same but clung to the hope that you would come home." said Drakos.

"What will happen with Emmina? She is only half human. Will she be okay? Will they be coming with us?" Fantasia asked, panicking at the thought of her daughter and granddaughter being left behind on Titan.

Orion waked in right at that moment, followed by Shadow.

For a moment Fantasia watched him as he entered the hallway "What do you think about it all?" she asked.

"I'm happy. I only wish you could remember more," Orion said, as he stepped into the room, Shadow closely followed, gave a deep moan as he lay down on the carpeted floor.

~

The Voxians teleported from the ship to inside the warehouse behind Fantasia's house. They sent a message to Drakos, telling him of their arrival.

Drakos left the house to greet his family, leaving Orion and his mother to talk. Drakos hadn't told Fantasia that her family had arrived.

"Comet," Drakos said, greeting his friend as he got close to the building.

Safire stood in the warehouse doorway. She was curvy, with black hair. She was around six feet tall; her elegant slender figure made her all the more attractive, you could tell she was Fantasia's sister.

Both Safire and Comet were extremely enigmatic and beautiful.

Safire was wearing a pair of black trousers, with a white loose fitted blouse. She looked smart. Her coat was red, with a strange swirl of black patterning. Her makeup subtle, her face was unblemished with cherry red lips; seductive.

Drakos had failed to tell Fantasia about her older sister. But it would appear to have made no difference anyway.

Kathos smiled at his friend. "It's good to see you, Drakos." He held out his hand, pulling Drakos in closer for a friendly hug.

"Your Majesty!" Drakos bowed, but Kathos shook his head.

"No, my friend, we'll have none of that. You've taken care of my family for me, and I'm profoundly grateful."

Kathos stood over seven feet tall. He had a bright glow around him. His pale complexion and strawberry blonde hair gave him a presence; his hair, shoulder length, which he never tied back, looked shiny and healthy. His clothes were like Comets, black stonewash jeans, a yellow t-shirt which didn't clash, it was coloured like a banana milkshake. He wore a long black leather coat and rockers boots on his feet, which he picked up on one of his visits to Earth. Kathos had said that rocker platform boots were the first sign of human intelligence as well as their sense of style.

The Voxians had walked the Earth since the beginning of the planet's life. They were an advanced race, so knew how to fit in undetected.

~

"Have you finally remembered something?" Ghost asked Fantasia.

"Yes, but nothing much. I don't understand."

"Perhaps you'll need to see it to believe it?" Ghost said.

"Perhaps I need to see Kathos," she answered.

"What will happen to the family I have on Earth?"

Fantasia said, a little worried.

Drakos interrupted as he entered the room. He took her hand.

"Fantasia, the memories are there, they've just in the back of your mind. Your Earthly family were a bunch of self-absorbed people that you don't need to worry yourself about any longer. Kathos didn't want you to think you were alone on Earth, so he gave you new memories and people who should have been there for you. Your real family are here, and when you're ready they're waiting for you. Your sister, grandfather, and brother-in-law are not going to pressure you. Your mother and father have remained on Vox, they didn't want you to be overwhelmed. They want you to be happy to see them," he said.

"I want to meet them and get my first blood sandwich." Orion said, chuckling.

"All in good time," Drakos said.

"I need Sky and Emmina here," Fantasia said, a little unsure.

"We'll fetch them," Drakos said.

Drakos and Orion left the house, got into the four by four and drove off.

Fantasia began to pace up and down the front room.

Fantasia needed to adjust to the news. "I think I'm beginning to remember; I remember a place where we all used to meet, a large house on an estate. Does it sound familiar? Do you think it's a memory?" Fantasia said.

As she turned to look at her friend, Ghost smiled at her. "Yes, by the look of those fangs, I believe you do remember," she said.

Drakos returned with Sky and Emmina. They'd been told the Voxian story before they arrived. Sky, like Orion, was happy that her height had been explained, and the idea she was alien pleased her as much as her brother.

"In answer to your questions mother, yes, we're coming with you, and yes I'm happy that the humans are still there." Sky said.

Fantasia smiled.

"So, tell me, what now?" Fantasia asked Drakos.

"Now, if we're all present and correct, it's time to meet and greet some of your family."

Drakos signalled for them to follow him. They'd been nervous about the meeting, but happy to have questions answered. Fantasia wanted to see if all her memories returned once she saw her family again.

"This is cool," Orion said, excited.

"You think this is cool? How do you feel about being royalty?" Drakos asked.

"WHAT?" Orion staggered a little. Sky began laughing, seeing the funny side of being royal.

"Kathos is your great grandfather!" Drakos announced.

Orion suddenly remembered something…

"I am not leaving without my motorbike," Orion piped up.

"It's okay, we'll take it. We can teleport solid matter to the ship. Coordinates compute more precisely when close. I don't think you'll ever use it on Vox. It's, what shall I say, slow!" Drakos said.

"I'll use it," Orion smiled. "Even if it's just to get me from A to B."

Drakos smiled at his son as they went to meet their family.

~

As Drakos walked down the steps of the house on Titan, Kathos, Comet and Safire stepped out of the warehouse building just across the street. They walked towards each other, as Fantasia began to remember. It was like a computer running through a program.

"So, how do we calm a pissed off Voxian? What if Fantasia isn't that happy to meet them all again?" Ghost whispered to Drakos.

"Oh, she will be, it's very obvious how close they all were!" Drakos said.

Kathos approached, and Fantasia turned 'battle-mode.' She had a black metallic tint on her face. Her fangs glinting brightly in the false daylight, but not in anger; she could now control it. Her family looked at her with the same black tinted faces. All were the same.

Kathos walked passed Ghost, and she looked a little star struck. Kathos looked at her, and she bowed in respect at the giant man.

Kathos glowed, while Comet and Safire followed behind him. All watched Fantasia, except Sky who was picking up Emmina. She had begun to cling to her mother in fear. She was used to Orion, but these people were bigger than her Uncle, so she was surrounded by very tall strangers.

Then, Kathos put his hand on Fantasia's forehead, he whispered something in an old language.

Something they were not expecting happened.

Fantasia put her arms around her grandfather. As she did, her face returned to normal; she smiled happily.

"It's okay, I remember!" she said, running and hugging her sister and brother-in-law.

"Fantasia, we're so pleased to see you. You're coming home, aren't you?" Kathos said, as he put his arms out and caught her as she sped back to him.

"Yes, Grandfather, of course," she said.

"Safire, I'm so happy you're here," Fantasia said.

Safire smiled and grabbed her sister from Kathos, hugging her for a while. "Oh, I have missed you so much. Mother and Father stayed on Vox. They await your return with great anticipation." Safire spoke with excitement.

"I wish I'd never left; it would have been better to grieve at home," Fantasia said.

Kathos grabbed her hand. "It doesn't matter, you're here now."

The family went back to the house to talk through everything that had happened to Fantasia and her family, and all that had been happening with Belial since she was absent.

"So, does that mean everyone tall on Earth is Voxian?" Orion asked, going off the subject.

"No! Although some people on Earth are," Comet replied.

"What about my college friend, Chris?" Orion said.

"Yes, He's one of your father's warriors, from the Capalian Mountains, along with Raidar," Comet said. "Drakos is Raidar's First Officer!"

Fantasia began to smile. "So how is our Lord Warrior leader?"

"Why don't we go back to Vox? You can ask him yourself," Comet said.

"I want to know more about our people," Orion said.

Kathos patted his grandson on the shoulder. "It takes our ship just twelve hours to get to Vox. Believe me; it will give us plenty of time to answer your questions. It'll be better when you get onto your own planet. You will be able to see and ask as much as you like."

"Wait until you see your house," Safire said, as they all walked out of the hotel only ten minutes later.

Orion turned and whistled. Shadow came running, his beautiful shining black coat and his big paws padding through the house one last time.

Kathos called him "Shadow, you look well."

Orion looked on in amazement, the dog hated every stranger alive. Shadow approached Kathos, sat next to him, and then he lay on his back, showing his belly, wagging his tail as Kathos rubbed him. They were old friends.

"Wow. Shadow has never allowed strangers close to him before," Orion said.

Kathos smiled but said nothing. He lay on the floor with the dog, and hugged into the dog's body, stroking him. It was as if they were talking telepathically.

"Shadow's not a German Shepherd; he's a Voxian wild wolf. He just looks remarkably like the breed. When he gets home you'll see what I mean," Kathos said, smiling.

"Kathos sent Shadow to guard and protect his family. He has done an excellent job for us," Comet said.

Safire looked at Orion. Her nephew was a baby when he left Vox. She knew he would have no memory of Vox, so his Voxian family would be getting asked a lot of questions.

"So, how many wolves are there on Vox?" Orion asked.

"We've only a few on Vox. They live in our forests and tend to hunt with us. Shadow is rare; he was the first pure black wolf we had ever seen. His mother was a silver coat and his father a red. He had been abandoned on the boarder's edge. Drakos found him and rescued him and his family. Kathos picked Shadow out of the litter when he was a puppy and tamed him. At ten weeks old he was no longer wild, so Kathos gave Shadow to Drakos to bring to Earth and give to you as a gift," Safire said.

Orion called his dog. Shadow immediately got onto his feet, happily running back to his master.

"You're a Voxian then?" Orion said. "So that's why you're such a chump!"

The others laughed and began to pick up the luggage and equipment they were taking with them, including wheeling Orion's motorbike into the warehouse.

Orion was impressed. He turned for one last look at the place he had grown to hate.

"Good riddance to Titan," he said, walking in the warehouse.

To be honest, Fantasia felt the same. She had not been here long, and she hated it: No blue sky, no fresh air, just a giant metal Hell.

Safire put her hand on Orion and Sky's shoulder and pressed a small button strapped around her wrist. It looked like a watch, with a large digital face. They all teleported outside the planet, into the waiting spaceship, still on standby outside Titan's domes.

Comet closed the ship's massive doors behind them, a sound of air being released as the room cleared and filled with oxygen, the ship moved slowly away, leaving the atmosphere of Titan behind them.

"Titan really does look amazing from out here." Orion observed.

"You could always stay !" Sky joked.

"Nah, you're alright." Orion laughed.

"What about my guinea pig, mommy? I can't leave him

behind, he'll die!" Emmina grabbed onto Sky's hand.

"It's okay, Emmina. We'll go and fetch him for you. It'll take seconds. Tell Comet where he is, and he will teleport him here."

Emmina looked a little panicked "Will he explode?" she asked.

"No sweetheart." Kathos assured her.

"Thank you, Grandfather." Emmina hugged into him.

The ship stayed where it was, a locator found the tiny animal. Emmina watched with fascination as her new uncle plotted in co-ordinates and the animal appeared on the ship in its cage.

"It's okay, don't worry, you're on a spaceship!" Emmina put her hand in the guinea pigs cage and stroked him gently.

"This is going to be very cool. We don't have animals like this on Vox; he'll be rare," Comet said. "He'll love his new home. It's much better than here. He will get fresh air, for one thing."

Emmina smiled, picked up her Guinea pig cage, putting it somewhere where it wouldn't slide backwards and forwards.

"Okay, is there anymore?" Safire enquired.

"Yes, there's something else detected in the house, actually three or four things upstairs." Comet scanned again. "Definitely something big; human size," he said, reading the information coming up on the screen.

"These aren't more animals, there's a Voxian signature, Comet," Safire said.

"It looks like there are other Voxians in there!" Safire turned off the scanner and looked at Kathos. "What now?" she asked him.

Kathos thought for a moment, looking at Fantasia and Comet.

"It's Beth," Fantasia said. "She has warriors with her."

"In my home! I can't believe it. What a monster!" Sky stood up, ready to go back.

"We should leave her," Safire said. "Is there anything in there that's valuable to you? Remember, you don't live there anymore. You have your own house on Vox, and the usual things like TVs are already there."

"No, I haven't had time to get anything that's of value to us. Even photos here I don't really want to keep. I can't see Emmina's school photo being of much value to her, she hates going to school, it's full of snobby bullies," Sky said.

The ship's engine hummed.

"Hold onto your hats," Safire said, as she pulled the lever in front of her. The ship made a small noise as it lifted off from Titan's surface.

"Okay, take one last look at your Titan Hell." Safire smiled at Fantasia. The look on her sister's face was wonderful. She was so happy to be going home to Vox.

By the look on the rest of her family's faces, they too were relieved and happy to see the back of Titan.

CHAPTER 6

Sky hated the idea of Beth in her house on Titan: It was intrusive. The thought made her blood boil.

"It's okay. Sky don't think about it. Remember, you'll not have to go back there again. It was never much of a home. Your place is not on Titan, it's on Vox. I'm sure everything there will be exactly the way you want it; if not straight away, within weeks of you living there," Fantasia said with a smile.

Emmina was completely oblivious to her mother's stress, happy playing the learning game with Kathos. He was teaching her how to levitate. She was happily copying him, and no one seemed to be amazed that she could do this; they were aliens, so anything was possible.

Kathos laughed loudly, as she wobbled from side to side at first. Emmina tried to gain balance, and after a few attempts, she did easily.

"Hey, Sky, your daughter's a fast learner; look at this," Kathos said.

Sky just looked on, staring blankly, still in another world.

Orion was with Comet, and they were both discussing the structure of the ship; the metal it was made of, and how it was something he had never seen before. Orion was intrigued to know more about the metal which was virtually indestructible. The metal was called Votiam, and he was told that the only thing that could damage it was something made of a stronger version of the same material.

"So, what gives it the mercury look?" Orion asked.

"Well," said Comet. "It's like Mercury. Only you can turn it into a solid form. It can be used to build almost anything; it's extremely versatile. In battle, enemies believe us to be an easy target. They fire at these vessels, thinking bullets will go straight through, hitting whoever is inside. But they don't, they bounce off it. It's quite amusing to see the shock on their faces as bullets they've just fired ricochet off the side of the ship."

Orion was astonished. He sat next to Comet contented as

he took in all the new information.

Fantasia was sitting with Sky, and Safire had joined them.

"Don't you need to fly the ship?" Sky asked.

"Oh no, it knows the way home; believe me," said Safire.

Safire looked at her sister; she was the same now as the day she left. Her time on Earth hadn't aged her. She looked in her mid-thirties still, as if time had not touched her since she left Vox.

Fantasia looked exquisite.

Voxians don't age quickly unless they suffer considerable pressure. They grow quickly as children, going through puberty like humans. But once this is reached, the aging process appears to slow down almost to a stop. They are immortals, well almost.

"So, tell me, what's my home like on Vox?" Sky asked, trying not to worry about her house on Titan.

"It's lovely. I have photos. Would you like to see?" asked Safire.

"Yes, please!" Sky felt excited, Titan fading fast from her thoughts.

"You may be a little shocked. We don't have small houses, they're all quite substantial in size," said Safire.

Safire opened a small notebook computer and began pressing buttons. She was looking through the photographs on it. "Ah, here we are." She passed the computer to Sky. "Press the down button for more. I'll explain to you whose house belongs to who, as we go through them."

"Okay!" said Sky with a nod.

Sky looked at the first picture. The house was modern. The front garden had giant gates, with grass and a lot of playing space. There was a swing, slide, and a big playhouse for Emmina. The outside décor was white with black beams. The theme remained the same on the inside. She was a big fan of Stratford-upon-Avon, UK, when she lived on Earth, spending a lot of time there with friends and family.

She began to scroll down the pictures. They were of empty rooms. The downstairs hallway was long and thin, it led her to a stairway with thick, oak banisters.

"Okay, if you press the red button on the side, you'll find a list of décor. You can change your house virtually to how you want it, choosing furniture as you go along. When we get to Vox it'll be as you have chosen. Anything you don't like can be changed for the things that you do. Some food shopping may be in order as well." Safire smiled at her niece.

"Food! I thought Voxians didn't need food?" Orion said.

Safire and the others laughed.

"Of course, we do, we only hunt perhaps once a month, twice if we have been off world and caught something bad. We don't carry our technology with us, if it was found we may end up causing problems with some civilisations."

"What? So how do we pay for all this?" asked Sky.

"We don't have money on Vox. Our society works only to benefit one another. That means we've no greedy people making money off the backs of those who are differently skilled, like on Earth. We're all proficient here, as you'll soon see."

Sky looked confused.

"We've a system: You're credited the items with a card; the card has no limit because we have no need. Our people build and replace the items as they're taken from storage. Then we produce more goods.

"Wow! So, no poverty on Vox then?" Orion said very impressed.

"No, we have no poverty. You'll receive what you need when you get home," Safire said.

Sky looked blankly at Safire. She couldn't believe that this was true; these people were so advanced they didn't need money.

"So, what motivates the Voxian people to work?" Sky asked.

"If people don't make the products, they can't have them. Although we do have some specialised items, these are made by skilled designers. Most things are made to last and can be modernised. This system works for us. We're happy and peaceful. Our race suffers no greed. We believe having things, made by hard working craftsman is better appreciated. Struggling to make a living, being paid too little, is not a good way for planetary survival," Safire said.

"So, when I get there, will I have a job?" asked Sky.

"Oh yes, of course you will. It'll be with animals, learning and speaking their languages. Animals always know when you care for them," Safire said.

Fantasia was looking forward to getting back to her job. She was the leader of the seventh faction of mountain warriors and helped train the females. She hadn't been able to train for years. She believed she was too stiff and out of shape for any training and would have to get her rhythm back very quickly, which would be hard.

"What's my job?" Orion said. He was listening to his aunt and mother's conversation. He walked over to them.

"Warrior!" Kathos said, as Emmina lost concentration. He jumped forward and caught her as she fell from the air.

Emmina laughed, running from Kathos's arms back to her mother. She was happy to be with these people, feeling loved more than ever.

"What else can you tell us about Vox and our people? The world sounds like a paradise," Sky said.

"It is really compared to some, I'm sure," said Comet. "Like all species in the Multiverse, we have our problems. For instance, we have Beth: She took over the Raitharns, and gave them a terrible life. The land is barren, and she exiles the powers of her people in honour of her love for Belial. Hoping she'll win favour with him by making him the only power over her people. Kathos has captured and exiled Belial to Hell many times, then he is summoned again by '*The book of Demons*' and the 'war bringer' re-appears back in a new place to cause chaos."

"So, although Phoenix owned the book, if stolen others could still say the incantation?" Orion asked.

"Phoenix had a lot of power, but even a copy of the book could be used to bring back the fallen angel!"

"You must understand that Kathos has no jurisdiction in the north, but under Kathos's rule there should be no poverty. He feels responsible for the people of Raithar, because at one time we all lived as one." said Safire.

"That's crap! Couldn't anything be done for these people when Belial was captured?" said Orion.

"No, we couldn't liberate them fast enough. As soon as Belial was in Hell, evil incantations were performed by Beth, and he was back on Raithar in minutes," Comet said.

"In all honesty, Beth will probably know the incantation off by heart by now." Kathos said, looking a little sad.

Safire could sense the tension, so got up from her seat.

"Anyone in need of refreshments?" she asked.

"Unless there's some serious cheese on toast on this ship, I may have to go hungry. I don't believe my body would take blood or meat until I introduce it all slowly, I've been a vegetarian since I was about 4 years old." Orion said. His stomach growled loudly, and he rubbed it.

"Orion, we've all sorts of food here. Cheese on toast though. Well, you may have to help us with this, as it's not usually in our dietary requirements," said Safire.

Orion went with his aunt, smiling, proud of who he was, and still totally ecstatic to be non-human. Going to his home planet would be wonderful for him.

"So, how long have we got left before we reach our home planet?" Orion asked.

"It'll be five hours before we get to our nebula," said Kathos. "I'll open the shields. We've no fear of approaching our planet. Unlike Earth, our Sun is on the opposite side of the galaxy. We're quite a distance from it. It doesn't mean we live on a frozen planet. I'll show you when we get close enough to see," Kathos said, smiling.

Orion followed his aunt towards the kitchen area, speaking to her as they went.

"Where were we? Ah yes, cheese on toast," Orion laughed.

The two went off. They were gone for a while. When they

returned, there was Voxian deer blood for Drakos, Fantasia and the others. Sky opted for noodles with Emmina, and, well we all know what Orion had. 'Cheese on toast.'

The chatting continued, and time passed very quickly. The Mythus nebula came into view. The Voxians wanted to show off the planet to Sky, Emmina and Orion.

The nebula looked beautiful. Its colours of green and blue all intertwined with a bright red centre, looking like a giant eye in the star encrusted Multiverse. As they sped through, there were three enormous planets that came into sight.

Kathos smiled.

"The planet to your left is Vox," Kathos said.

As they came closer to the view screen, the planet looked like Earth, a giant ball of blue water. Instead of having many islands on it there were just two, one large and one much smaller.

"Look closely, you'll see there are three moons around Vox. Two inactive, but valuable to our solar system." Then Kathos pointed, "This one is volcanic. It gives our planet daylight, but also this moon provides our planet with power for heat and energy. Its heat can be felt even now as the ship enters the nebula's atmosphere." Kathos pointed at the massive yellow and orange moon, which stood out due to its brightness. It could easily be mistaken as a sun.

Kathos looked at the interest on their faces.

"If you look to the far distance, at the bright light just over there." Kathos pointed to a shining white orb in the blackness. "That's our actual sun, it has little effect on our planet, but it does send the occasional weather burst to us."

"No problems with sunburn then?" Orion piped up.

"None." Kathos replied.

Orion smiled and looked out at his home planet, his love for space was going into overdrive with this brand-new solar system.

Kathos pointed south, to another planet that seemed to be covered in a mass of white gas.

"This planet is called Isis. It shares one of our inactive

moons but has some contact with this nebula's sun. It spends a lot of time in darkness, due to that shadowing planet next to it."

Kathos pointed to the largest planet in the nebula.

"Isis does get about five hours daylight on average in spring and four in the winter but can be a little longer in the summer. It can vary to maybe six or seven hours."

Sky and Emmina said nothing, just took in the view.

"Is there any sort of population on Isis, Grandfather?" Orion asked.

"Yes, I'll explain all this once we've landed. They're not a bad race, but we try to keep our involvement with any species restricted," Kathos said.

Kathos stared at the viewer for a while and then started to talk again.

"Now for the last planet. This one shares our volcanic moon like Earth, with a solar system surrounding it. However, it's of some interest to us; Reptilia, the hottest in our nebula, is closest to our sun."

"So, does this mean the sun determines the weather on this planet?" Sky asked.

"Yes, it gives Reptilia, its wonderful terrain, covered in rain forest, thunderstorms are really interesting, some can be quite catastrophic. Being closer to the Sun means the weather there is tropical. We have never disturbed the peacefulness of the planet, so we can't actually say for sure what it's like on the ground." Kathos said.

"Who lives there?" Orion asked.

"Reptilians. These aren't creatures that we've had any contact with, in the past. What we do know is that their DNA originates from Earth before the humans evolved there. We believe that, like all species in new environments, they've evolved on Reptilia, and may look different now," Comet said, looking at Sky.

"So, they're Dinosaurs!" Sky said, a little excited.

"Well, in a way, I suppose they could be called that, although they're very different from what I've seen in books on Earth," Comet said.

"I know this seems a little frightening right now, but I'll teach you the Reptilian culture and language. We'll need good allies, and I believe that they'll be an advantage," Kathos said to Sky. "So, what can you tell us from your knowledge of these creatures on the Earth? Will they make good allies?"

"I think it'll be a case of wait and see, Grandfather," Sky said. "The Dinosaurs of Earth lived amongst each other. There were a lot of different species. Some enjoyed eating the greenery, while the others were fighting and eating one another. If I'm not mistaken it was a meteor that triggered an ice age, wiping out this species."

"This doesn't mean that this version of the species is fighting or eating one another," Sky said'

"How did the creatures evolve? Why did they evolve? You can't tell me that they just appeared here," Orion asked.

"They had been taken by one of my brothers, Galileo. He witnessed the meteor hitting Earth," Kathos said. "The rest is unknown. We must be able to negotiate with other species, even if they remain neutral in this war. I need to know that we can at least try to talk to the others and persuade them to look at what Belial is, and not be taken in by our enemies," Kathos said.

"A war?" Sky said surprised.

Orion and Fantasia looked other now interested in the conversation.

"I'm sorry to say that this is looking like a possibility, I am sure that this is what we are faced with, so Fantasia, you have arrived just in time." Kathos explained.

Kathos was sitting at the navigation computer, pressing the keyboard that produced the ship's landing coordinates on the display unit.

Comet and Safire took their seats at their own computer posts on the ship, as it rapidly approached Vox.

"Okay, no need to buckle up; our ships have exceptionally smooth landing gear. The most that you'll notice is touchdown, which will happen about ...now," said Safire, who looked over at Fantasia.

There was a very slight bump like a car going over a small pothole. The ship turned into the hanger and came to a halt.

Fantasia looked excitedly at the rest of her family. She grabbed Emmina's hand and walked to the ship's door, which slid open, and steps appeared.

The fresh air hit their faces as they went through the exit. Standing at the top of the stairs, the place looked familiar to them. Like Earth.

"It's just so wonderful," Fantasia smiled, breathing in the fresh air. "Home. I can't believe it; I am actually home."

The family went down the steps, it was like stepping off an aeroplane on Earth.

Birds in the sky stood out with bright colours all displayed. They looked magnificent, with bright reds and blues, some even glowing.

Rexus, Genesis and Ledawna waited patiently, standing by the side of the ship, excited to see their family at last.

Kathos approached his wife, kissing her lightly on the forehead.

Fantasia ran quickly to her mother and father, hugging them, breathing them back in. Calling for Orion and Sky to bring Emmina over.

Excitement felt by all.

A bright red limousine waited for them. The hugs and the tears at the limo's doorway were over quite quickly. The family got into the cars, driving away.

A meeting was planned in the main Manor House, where Ledawna and Kathos lived.

"What kind of animals live here? Emmina asked.

"Apart from the deer, we have many small creatures that live in the edges and underground, but you will need to watch your fingers because they have fangs and bite!" Safire laughed.

Emmina looked surprised.

"You're such a beautiful little girl, Emmina." Safire said.

"So, there are no cows then!" Emmina said.

The family laughed.

"No sweetheart, no cows, just deer." Safire said.

"Where are we heading?" Sky asked.

"The Manor estate to begin with. We all live within walking distance of one another. If you're all too tired from your journey I'm sure we could take you home in the car later," Kathos said.

Kathos sat back, letting the newcomers take in the planet and the views: They were stunning. There were snow-capped mountains that went on for miles, with large houses sat on them. Forests appeared as they spied other landscapes, and then beyond them a mass of green fields. People in villages were walking up and down the streets, just getting on with their daily lives.

Kathos was proud to be the King of such a beautiful planet.

"Oh My God, this is just perfect!" Sky grabbed her mother's arm and gave it a squeeze. "They're actually watching us. None of the animals seem to be running into the road as the car passes, which is just fascinating!" she began to chuckle, finding it all amusing.

"You'll be pleased to know that all the animal information you want to know is waiting for you, plus a new educational computer system is set up for you at home. You can study animals to master's degree if you wish to. Emmina has already been enrolled in school. The first car will pick her up Monday, two days from now," Safire said.

"Do I have to wear a school uniform?" Emmina said, looking a little fed up with the thought of school.

"No, school uniform isn't important. Learning and playing is." Safire smiled at her niece.

On Earth and Titan, she found school boring. She didn't really learn anything overly exciting, and at eight years old she had a lot of abilities that the children of Earth didn't, she just thought they could do exactly the same and her extra powers were normal, it never came up in the classroom or the playground.

"So how long do we have before we get home?" Orion asked.

"We're about fifteen minutes away from our village, then there is about another ten minutes to the Manor House. That's at this very slow cruising speed." said Ledawna. She smiled at her grandson.

Ledawna saw his future in her visions. He would be the bringer of great changes to her family, but she wondered if he realised his own ability.

CHAPTER 7

MANOR ESTATE

A large set of black iron gates suddenly appeared through the fields and the trees. They opened to reveal a large country estate, and the driveway to the main house was in sight. It looked tiny, just in view as they looked down to the end of a vast winding driveway.

"Here we are, home sweet home," Kathos smiled.

Both Orion and Sky looked on in surprise.

"So, you live here Grandfather?" Orion asked.

"We all live here, this is the King's Estate," Kathos said, proudly.

A while later they pulled up outside the main house. The car came to a stop.

Fantasia was home at last.

"Do we all live in this house?" Sky asked a little confused.

"No, I live here with your great grandmother. There are more houses dotted around the land," Kathos said. "There's no differentiation on Vox. The people see us all as equals. You're a princess here, Sky, but you will be greeted as everyone else. We don't need protection because there is shared wealth and happiness. This works well, and we respect our people. You'll make a lot of friends here."

The family stepped out of the car and walked into the Manor House together. The hall was huge. The large mahogany doors opened from the steps of the building.

A middle-aged man stood on the other side of the doorway, wearing a traditional suit. He began talking to Kathos as he stepped through the door: About meetings and schedules for everyone, the minute the family entered the house.

"Good morning Francis. How are you this morning?" Ledawna asked.

"All is in order, and thank you, I am very well," said Francis, in a very British accent.

"Francis is our personal assistant. He was trained on Earth in 1992," Ledawna told Orion and Sky.

Francis bowed to the newcomers, and then vanished into the kitchen area.

Walking into the hall, Orion glanced around at the black and white checked flooring, following it with his eyes into the centre of the room, where stairs with huge wooden banisters led around to the bedrooms of the house.

There were many rooms on the top floor, all with mahogany doors matching the stairs and banisters, with a bright red luxurious carpet running up the stairs.

In a large frame on the stairwell hung a photograph of Kathos, Ledawna, Beth, Rellik and Rexus.

"I'll show you around later." Kathos said.

Safire and Fantasia both took the family into a large lounge. It looked like an old ski lodge. White walls with old beams of dark wood across the ceilings, an open fire burning brightly with lamp lights around the walls. Tables and large sofas with comfy chairs, cushions, and bean bags, scattered in no particular place.

In the middle of the room stood a carved coffee table. Under that a massive rug of fur, white and fluffy, giving the pine flooring a warm and comfortable look.

"You're to meet my warrior leaders here. Raidar and his sons will be here, and so will Hyedan," Kathos smiled.

"Do we have many warriors?" Orion asked, looking impressed.

"We've all sorts. After the meeting we can discuss your ceremonies of life, they will distinguish your place here," said Kathos.

~

Hyedan and Elen arrived first, with their daughter Azaya.

Orion looked at Azaya, her white-blond hair, and pale beauty. Nothing like the girls on Earth he had dated, his instant attraction to her was incredible. It wasn't love at first sight as such, but something damn close.

Azaya was around six feet tall. Her hair shone in the

daylight, making her pale complexion and blue eyes stand out. She was slim, wearing black jeans and a white t-shirt with a black Celtic pattern. Orion couldn't help but stare. She stared right back.

As Orion's eyes shifted to her mother, Elen was wearing a long blue flowing gown, which shimmered in the light. The same blue eyes and blonde hair as her daughter, but with a very small hint of grey, glistening as her hair touched the light in the room.

Orion turned to Hyedan, who was almost as tall as him. His hair was white, and he had a stern face with a short beard, red with wisps of grey through it. He wore a green cloak, with Celtic type patterning in a gold embroider. The cloak opened revealing his white silk shirt and grey slacks. Orion couldn't help thinking that he looked like a character out of one of his Tolkien books. Incredibly old fashioned, his face was authoritarian.

"Hyedan can you remember my granddaughter, Fantasia?" Kathos asked.

Kathos signalled at Fantasia as she stood up to greet Hyedan, the Lord High City leader.

"These are my children. Orion my son, and Sky my daughter," Fantasia said.

Orion stepped forward, putting his hand out to shake Hyedan's hand.

Hyedan stepped back, not knowing what to do, placing one hand on his cloak, where his sword lay sleeping underneath.

Orion realised his mistake immediately and stepped away, backing off.

"I apologise," Orion bowed. "It's an old Earth tradition I've been brought up to follow. It's known as a polite welcome. Let me show you," Orion said.

Hyedan came forward again, putting out his hand in greeting. Orion took it and shook it firmly.

Hyedan began to laugh.

"That is a very strange welcome indeed, my boy,"

Hyedan's deep voice bellowed. He chuckled with laughter.

Orion relaxed, getting comfortable now with these new people, as three more men appeared in the middle of the room.

This time they looked more like the missing link!

Giant 'Neanderthals' with mohawks!

"Must you always be late?" Kathos smiled, taking the hand of the older man, and shaking it. "This is Lord of the mountains leader, Raidar!"

"All a bit of a mouthful if you ask me, just call me Raidar." He said to Orion and Sky.

Kathos's face seemed to light up at this man's presence, like his best friend had just entered the room.

Raidar looked on as his hand was shook in greeting by his King. It was obvious that, like Hyedan, he had no idea what the handshake was about. But because it was his leader, he allowed it.

Orion had never seen a man so large. He was at least seven feet tall, and much wider than Orion. He was not fat; he was solid muscle. He had short black hair that was shaved on both sides. His mohawk just lay in one long line in the middle of his head.

His cape was black with red stars and with the three moons of Vox on it in golden embroidery. Unlike Hyedan's aged clothes, Raidar wore combats in a khaki grey green colour, a black t-shirt with a hand holding a flaming torch, with the words *'Blood, Fire, War, Hate,'* under the patterning.

His large, blue Voxian eyes met with Orion's, and he grabbed Orion's elbow, pulling him forward in greeting.

"You'll be an awesome mountain warrior, boy," Raidar began saying loudly. "If we're to do battle with the devil, Belial, we must first give you the power." He chuckled at the look on Orion's face, which appeared confused!

"For Goddess's sake stop scaring him, he's new here," Kale said, as he walked over to his father. "Hello Orion, I'm Kale, son of Raidar. We've been assigned the post of mentor, while you're learning the ropes here. This is my younger brother Halen, and we're both happy to meet you."

Both men bowed in greeting.

Kale, a tall slim blonde male, stood over six foot. He looked more like Azaya's brother than Halen's, but a tell-tale glint in his eyes, and the white blond mohawk, gave him the look of his father.

Kale wore blue jeans, a two-toned red and black long-sleeved t-shirt, blue trainers, with one of the laces hanging loose on the floor.

Halen on the other hand was the image of his father. Not quite as tall, just under seven feet, with the same mohawk in thick brown hair, and his electric-blue eyes which were piercing through his dark complexion, like bright beacons of blue light.

He wore the same sort of clothing as Raidar: Combats, only his were dark green. His t-shirt was black and said, *'machine f***ing head!'* on it.

Orion knew he was going to like this guy. He had the same t-shirt himself from his trip to the Download festival on Earth. He knew the band were awesome.

Sky was instantly hugged like a long-lost friend by all the visitors. It was great. She took an instant liking to everyone. "My kinda music!" she said, as she pulled away from Halen. "So, you're into rock?"

"It rules!" Halen said, as he began playing air guitar, making a strange noise.

Sky smiled at him, shaking her head.

"Let's conclude our meet and greet. We can all continue to celebrate, or go home, if you wish," Kathos shouted amongst the noise.

Kathos sat down with Orion and Sky, explaining what the ceremony was for. They listened, contented to be a part of it. Both agreed that they wanted to be a part of the Voxian people and learn their culture.

After the meeting, Sky was taken home. It was on the right-hand side of the Manor. A large building which looked a little like a black and white beamed barn conversion, it had grassed lawns with roses growing around it. She was pleased when she stepped inside with Emmina. Everything she had asked for was in place.

Her cupboards were full to the brim with food from Earth, which was always a good thing for her, having Emmina who could eat as much as any adult.

~

Fantasia crossed the sandy coloured slabs laid in the yard from the front of the Manor to her walk home.

As she entered her house, everything was warm and comfortable. Her memories came flooding back; her love of the house, and gardens surrounding it. Just being at home again after all this time suddenly made Fantasia fight back her tears, as she filled with emotion. She picked up things she had left behind so long ago: Photographs, trinkets, and a picture that Sky had drawn for her when she was very small. Looking around at the familiar sight of her home before she dragged herself from it, because of circumstances that were beyond her control.

As he looked around, Orion could see familiar things his mother had owned on Earth. She may not have remembered consciously, but her subconscious must have had some memories, because she had similar things in her home when he was a child.

"So, where's my room?" he asked, looking at the black and white hall floor, and a stairway that was almost identical to the one in the Manor House.

"You don't have a room here. You have the conservatory. It looks a lot like an annex, and it's just through the French doors there," Fantasia said, pointing.

Orion turned to a pool area (at least that was what he thought it was). It had window upon window, a giant conservatory, with lots of light coming in with a skylight above. Then the biggy, as he got closer, he could see a large telescope, it was the one from his room at home on Earth, pointing out into the Voxian starry night.

"Cool it's all light and bright, but how am I supposed to sleep in here?" Orion asked.

Fantasia walked into the conservatory room, it had everything he could need in it.

"The windows are designed to turn black in the need of privacy," Fantasia said. "Look here, you have a dial that controls it." She began pressing a remote control, and the windows went lighter and darker.

"Your inventions from Titan and Earth are here. So is your bed, and any other familiar things we thought you would like," she said, pointing to a large cupboard space.

"If you want anything else, you've a computer system there," Fantasia said, pointing to the desk and computer sat in the corner. "You do understand that you can go onto the shop-programme? Even better, you may like to see more of the city after your ceremony tomorrow. In which case we can go shopping." Fantasia smiled.

CHAPTER 8

CEREMONY

The ceremony would take place at midday.

Tradition was that Voxians went through this in order to gain true status. Fantasia had been explaining that the pentagram birthmark they had on their left hand was a way to adapt and infuse powers with one another.

Orion and Sky both wondered what this would mean to them.

"In battle, you can change and use things around you to your advantage. If you touch someone who has the power of speed you will then adapt their power, meaning you will become faster." Explained Fantasia.

The Voxian ceremony of adulthood is carried out on or after a Voxian's eighteenth birthday. As children their skills are still developing. The power of adaption is part of every Voxian's skill set.

~

Orion was dressed in a black, two-piece suit, with a white shirt, no tie. He said he wasn't going to wear one. He was moaning because he had to have his long hair up.

Sky dressed in a lilac-coloured long gown, and her long black hair was platted with lilac ribbon and flowers woven through. She looked wonderful, much to her displeasure.

"Good luck, Sis!" Orion said, as he hugged her for the first time in years. He could see how nervous she was, and that she wanted to get back to her black tomboy look.

"Thanks, I need luck...What the Hell is this about? Am I going to find out I'm Queen fool or something?" The two laughed at one another and carried on getting ready.

"Just want my everyday look back. It takes ages to perfect the scruffy tramp look!" She smiled at her brother.

Orion laughed at her comment.

Unlike Earth, the disruption of telephones ringing was replaced by telepathy. The Voxians could just talk to one another from long distances, no telephones required, (or as Orion would joke, *hearing voices*).

After years talking with their mouth the family all found the telepathy a bit difficult.

It took over one hour from the Manor House to the city. The cars for the family were already arriving in the yard.

In spite of their powers, the cars were a Voxian tradition.

"We've got to leave very soon. Is everybody ready?" Fantasia called loudly.

The first limousine to pull up outside the Manor was white. This one was for Kathos and Ledawna. The others followed in all colours. They looked like a rainbow, a royal crest on the front of them.

The crest was a large set of white angel wings, a crown of silver and a Voxian sword.

Sky's limousine was pink because she knew it was Emmina's favourite colour. Kathos had left Emmina a gift, boxed in pink with a big lilac bow around it on the car seat. The label read *'for our little granddaughter with love. XX.'*

Emmina screeched with delight as she pulled on the bow, and opened the package, which contained the latest Voxian doll.

"You must thank your great grandfather and grandmother when we reach the city. That doll's incredibly beautiful," said Sky.

"I will Mommy, I promise." Emmina clutched the doll, which had blonde hair that cascaded down in a mass of ringlets, and a porcelain face. She wore a pink dress with a lilac sash of ribbon around her waist, and Emmina couldn't stop hugging her.

As the cars filled, and the family began the journey to the city, all were talking in excitement. All except Orion and Sky, who just looked like they were about to go on trial for a crime they had not committed.

When the cars pulled into the Royal Circle in the Voxian city, Emmina ran to Safire and Comet, the doll waving in the air with pride. They had saved her a seat, and had bought her a nice, shiny pink three-moons robe, with flashes of silver through it, which made it glisten in the daylight.

Orion and Sky walked nervously over to Kathos, who had now taken his place at the head of the circle in the large arena. Ledawna had chosen to sit next to her family, but there were another two empty seats each side of Kathos. When Orion and Sky scanned the whole picture, there were two seats in the circle, alone, and for all to see. Sky just knew they would be for them.

Looking down from the main circle, they could see a strange pentagram pattern. It looked like a devil's trap, or something to raise some dead people. Only, the symbols and writing were in English, and at each of the five points of the pentagram it said: *'Honour, Peace, Truth, Strength and Protection,'* and in the centre it had the three Voxian moons.

"Is this evil?" Sky asked Kathos, as she looked at her grandfather a little worried.

"No! Do you believe you're Demonic?" he chuckled. "This is our sign of protection, and the sign of our powers. You'll understand as the ceremony takes place, my darling. Please try to concentrate on what you have inside yourself," Kathos said, putting his hand on his chest.

Orion took hold of his sister's hand, and they walked to the seats together in the centre of the lower circle. It was like a gladiator arena, with thousands of people sitting around waiting for a fight, only with decorations, ribbons, and streamers everywhere.

"Well, it looks like the whole of Vox is here," Orion whispered to Sky nervously as they took their seats, noticing that all were watching them in the middle of the lower circle.

As they sat down, the crowd cheered and began stamping and shouting a chant: 'BLOOD, FIRE, WAR, HATE!'

All the Voxians in the arena changed. Their faces became bulged, with a tint of metallic black which transformed on their skin, and they grew giant white fangs.

Sky tried her hardest not to freak out, until she turned to Orion, and he looked the same. Sky touched her face, her face felt different, as she touched her mouth she felt her fangs. She couldn't help thinking that it was cool, she was the same too.

The circle went silent!

Sky decided to go with the flow, and soon Orion did the same. The two were shouting and stamping with everyone else, the power of the chant was like magic flowing within them. They felt like they could take on the Multiverse, their strength seemed undefeatable.

They began to focus. They noticed that Raidar and Hyedan had both taken their places next to Kathos on the platform, at the head of the arena.

All three leaders glowed with Kathos's Angelic powers covering them.

Kathos's wings spanned white and large at the back of his white robes. Then his face glowed with silver light; he looked like nothing in this world could defeat him.

An all-powerful being that was God-like.

"We ask for the protection from all those on a higher plain, to keep our two newcomers safe from harm," Kathos said, as he began holding his arms up, in prayer.

"We ask this of you, Galaxia."

The whole congregation replied by repeating his words: *"We ask this of you, Galaxia."*

Raidar stood forward. "We ask you to guide our warriors onto their true path and enlighten us to their vocation on our blessed planet. We ask this of you, Galaxia."

Again, the congregation repeated this.

Then it was Hyedan's turn. "Be their guide. We ask you to grant them strength and honesty, to help develop their skills here, see the beauty of our world, helping only to preserve it. This is our law. We ask this of you, Galaxia."

The congregation repeated.

"All must now close their eyes in prayer. We must thank our Goddess for the blessings she has given us: Our homes, our world of peace and tranquillity, our ability to protect those who are vulnerable, our love of all creatures. This we give thanks for," Kathos said, and then he paused, and the congregation all replied: *"Thanks be to our Goddess."*

Orion and Sky had been buzzing with power now for a while. They had tried to focus on the crowd and find Fantasia and Emmina for a little touch of reality.

The glow from the three leaders energised Orion and Sky as they stood in the arena looking around. The entire crowd glowed with the same light.

As the ceremony seemed to pause, Orion had a vision. He could see stars. He could see himself battling as a warrior in the mountains, his life map revealing his sword of hope. The power surging inside him made him scream out: "BLOOD! FIRE! WAR! HATE!" But now he had gruffness to his voice, which sounded almost like a growl. The congregation replied: "BLOOD! FIRE! WAR! HATE!"

Sky did not turn to see why he was doing this, because she too had her own visions: Walking amongst the animals, through forests and trees, all calling to her, and she understood them. She bore no weapons. She had the power to control and communicate with animals from all over the Multiverse. She felt them all calling to her as she screamed: "BLOOD! FIRE! WAR! HATE!"

Again, the congregation copied by chanting her exact words loudly back to her as she powered up.

The glow then dimmed. The power hummed to a slight buzz inside Orion's and Sky's chest, as the ceremony was ending.

The arena went wild with chants and celebrations for their two newcomers.

Kathos, Hyedan and Raidar came towards them. They smiled proudly.

Kathos touching both Orion and Sky on the shoulders, standing in the centre of them both. Hyedan turned to Sky, offering a hand and Raidar doing the same to Orion, as the two took their leaders hands. The crowds were in uproar. Streamers, fireworks, and music bellowed from the stands.

"I feel like I could run for miles. I can do anything: Walk on water, fly. What is this all about?" Orion asked Raidar.

"You feel this way, Orion, because those powers are a part of you. It all comes naturally. As you train, more will be revealed to you. You are a strong warrior who will only get stronger as you learn," Raidar said.

The ceremony was over.

Sky looked for Emmina. This must have frightened her half out of her wits, she thought. But as she spotted her, she saw Emmina was peacefully asleep in Comet's arms, Comet hugging her in close to him.

They all walked back to the cars.

"Is she okay?" Sky asked, smiling.

"Yes, believe it or not she slept through the whole ceremony," Comet laughed.

"We are talking about the child that while on Earth slept through a 7.9 earthquake!" Fantasia said, as she passed them both and got into her car.

Comet followed Sky back to the pink coloured limo. He then carefully placed Emmina on to her mother's lap, as she sat in the back seat, quietly closing the door of the limo, trying not to disturb the sleeping child.

"Sleep tight, our perfect one," he said, as he went back to Safire and they headed to the royal cortege, All heading back to the estate.

CHAPTER 9

RAITHARN-NORTHERN HEMISPHERE VOX

The sound of heavy metal music played loudly on Beth's car stereo as she raced towards the hills in her red convertible, her hair blowing freely in the wind. She smiled, knowing that where she was going, her older brother would be waiting.

Her face changed as her mind began to swirl and her concentration on the road was interrupted.

Beth's smile left her face as she heard the all-powerful voice of Belial. Beth was afraid.

"Yes, my Lord, I'm on my way." She paused as the voice of her master spoke to her telepathically. "No, nothing will go wrong. I will persuade Rellik this time. He knows what's good for him if he doesn't want to suffer any more torture, I'm sure of this."

Beth went to say more, but the voice was gone. Message communicated, and that was all.

CAPALIA – SOUTHERN HEMISPHERE VOX

The warriors meeting was at 7.30pm in the Manor, all making plans for Belial's capture.

Kathos turned to Fantasia.

"We need to rescue the humans from Titan. Their own planet will need them. We must make those who are still on Earth aware of the danger to their planet. Give them the choice to join us in battle." Kathos said.

"We also need to find the traitor Rellik!" Raidar said.

"Rellik a traitor? Is he allied with Beth and Belial?" Fantasia said, mortified.

This was extremely hard to take in. Orion and Sky were oblivious, but the rest of the warriors hung their heads in sadness.

"He was taken by Belial after he killed Radonna..." said

Comet.

"Oh Goddess, why did he do that? She was a peacekeeper. Radonna wouldn't threaten anyone," Fantasia said, fighting back her tears.

"Without her, Rellik was emotionally destroyed. When Beth came to Capalia to talk, we believed that she had finally seen the light. But instead, she had been sent by Belial," Comet said.

Comet approached Fantasia and handed her a box of tissues.

Safire frowned and sat with Fantasia to comfort her.

"Rellik is a great loss to us. Beth set her trap... part of the plan was for Belial to kill Radonna. Rellik fell apart at seeing his one true love die and while he was in an emotional state they took him prisoner, turning him evil, if he hadn't been turned, he would have found a way to be home by now, so we can only assume the worst." Safire said.

"We've not seen or heard from him for many years. It seems obvious that he has become one of Beth's soldiers. I have no telepathic link to him, although he may just have given up on life altogether," Comet said.

A sudden look of anger came across Fantasia's face.

"No... They could never turn him, he's way too strong for that," Fantasia said, gritting her teeth.

Fantasia began to concentrate with her mind's power. With her powers back, her left hand began to glow silver blue, and the pentagram star ignited, Fantasia put her hand to the floor, electrical bolts flashed from the ground, gaining power as her eyes lit electric blue as the pulses of energy entered her body.

"I can find him..." Fantasia said. "If the two of us join forces, Comet, this may work. If Rellik had become evil, he would still answer me, to try and damage my powers," Fantasia said, looking hopeful.

Comet joined in doing the same. Both of the warriors were about to join their forces of power to adapt, and then stopped.

Safire grabbed her sister's arm.

"Fantasia, STOP! You will put both of your powers at risk. Then you would both be lost. Mind-traps are impossible to break, you may become possessed. What would we do without you? Any outside communication to help us establish Belial's next move would be gone." Safire said.

Kathos agreed with Safire. He had to trust that Rellik's capture would be settled once they had dealt with Belial and his followers.

The two warriors powered down again.

"I'll find another way." She said to Comet.

As the Manor started to fill, familiar faces began to appear.

Fantasia was amazed when Raidar was the first to arrive. (He would be late for his own funeral!) He had a lot to say and looked fired up and ready to go. His two sons, Halen, and Kale had followed him inside.

Orion's eyes shifted across the room, as the beautiful young woman stepped in through the door. Azaya and her father arrived, so from that point on, Orion didn't notice anyone else enter or leave.

Azaya held her hand out in polite friendship.

"Good evening," she said, as she moved towards him. She smiled as he stood silently shaking her hand continuously, not letting go.

"Orion, I think that belongs to me," she said, after about thirty seconds.

Orion's eyebrows rose with surprise. He realised and pulled his hand away.

"Sorry," Orion said, turning a nice shade of red.

Fantasia was in the front room, still meeting and greeting, people said how glad they were she had returned from Earth.

She bowed politely as they spoke of Kathos and Ledawna, and their misfortune, grief, and the traitor, Rellik.

Fantasia made no comment about Rellik. She believed he was no traitor but had to prove it before saying more.

The house was full by 7.45pm, and the doors were closed.

Shadow lay curled up next to Orion. He was busy looking on with suspicion, letting out small growls of warning to the new arrivals. That and chewing on his 'balls.'

"Steady boy," Orion said, patting his dog, who had risen to his feet several times. Shadow twisted himself around, lying down again, going for his usual nap. But every time someone got up, Shadow's eyes would open, and he watched their every move.

Kathos got up, his towering body glowing, and his wings tucked into his back. The people attending the meeting, even after all these years, still looked at him with admiration.

"We need to search for *'the Book of Belial'*. I know this will be a big task, but as Fantasia has connections to it, it should be easier to find again." Kathos said.

Fantasia had an idea where she would find the book, she would need to search Phoenix's old house first, but it was more than likely in France with its guardian, Victoria, she was Phoenix's earthly daughter.

"So, what's your plan? How do we get the book back?" Kathos asked her.

"It won't be easy. It will just be the case of beating Beth to the book. Remember, once they get the information that I am moving towards Earth, they'll know we're going for the book. I need to make plans and be in and out of Victoria's loft before Beth can get a fix on me," Fantasia said.

"Phoenix was a highly intelligent man. When you sent him to find the book, he had kept it hidden from Belial," Fantasia said.

"Phoenix was loyal. He gave up his home here to live an Earthly life. Even though he must have missed his family and home, he stayed there so he could protect the book until you found him again. Linking me to the book meant that if he had died before you located him, you would still find it," Fantasia said.

"Giving me time to retrieve it," Kathos said.

"Yes Grandfather," Fantasia said.

"So, what now?" Comet asked.

"We need to get the book, with as little disruption as possible," said Fantasia.

This meant she would be attempting to get the book back herself.

The room fell quiet, but not for long.

"Next is for the humans on Titan and on Earth to be told of Belial's invasion and planned destruction of their planet." Kathos said, looking at his warriors.

"Send envoys to them both. Explain who we are. Explain they have been tricked. These people need to be aware of what they are facing, and it needs to be done quickly," said Hyedan.

Raidar interrupted. "What a crock! These humans are suspicious of everything. Do you think a giant fanged alien stepping into their territory would be seen as friendly? You're taking the piss! Leave them. We can fight the battle without their help, and win."

"I'm saying that a peaceful attempt to communicate with the human's would be better," Hyedan said.

"For Goddess's sake man, humans have no backbone!" Raidar replied.

Hyedan knew there was no point in trying to talk, while Raidar just didn't have any other intention but to go in all guns blazing.

Raidar began pacing, which was nothing new.

Orion and Sky watched as the giant's face turned 'battle-mode.' His fangs stood out like white jewels on his face. Orion began to feel nervous. This guy was gigantic, even by his standards. He didn't want to argue with him.

"The humans are weak, misguided fools who have let a fallen Angel take over their planet. Do you really want them fighting on our side? Well, do you? Screw that...do you know what this species is like...? A bunch of suspicious, unkind morons who have no power. They fight with nuclear weapons, which destroy their lands and kill their own kind...Why the Hell would we want them fighting with us? They would probably turn on us in the middle of the battle, and go on to Belial's side," said Raidar angrily.

Orion got to his feet. "STOP! That's rubbish. We lived as

humans for many years. We know this species, and they're not all suspicious and weak!" he said angrily.

Raidar stopped and looked. Orion was also bearing his fangs. The discussion suddenly became heated, turning into an argument, so Kathos stepped in.

"Before your verbal exchange of views, and things become violent, Hyedan has a point. But so does Raidar. We can't just walk in; there must be some other way. Any useful suggestion that would actually help the situation?" Kathos said.

"Yes, let them die!" Raidar stomped to his seat, sitting back down in a huff.

"Fantasia and Drakos, you decide the best way to get the book. I entrust this mission to you, and whoever you wish to take with you," Kathos said.

"Yes, Grandfather." Fantasia got up to leave the room.

"Orion, you and I will head off to Titan to speak to the people there. Hyedan and Raidar, you will do what you do best...train your warriors, and when Orion and Fantasia get back from their missions they'll join you," Kathos said. "Sky, your job will be to study hard, find out all you can about Reptilia and the Dinosaurs."

"That's what I do best, Grandfather," Sky said, standing up to leave. "If you'll excuse me, I'll get started."

Sky headed back to her house on the Estate. She looked back to see Shadow following her, but not because he didn't want to be with Orion, she was the first one through the door, and a dogs got to do what a dogs got to do.

The meeting ended. The warriors then enjoyed a couple of hours drinking, talking about how plans would go, and about the 'what ifs.'

They all quietly dispersed in the early hours of morning and went to their homes.

"Do we have a lot of these so called 'meetings'?" Orion asked Raidar and Halen, as they considered teleporting home.

"We don't crap without having a meeting. But hey, you'll soon get used to our ways!" Halen said.

Kale, his father, and brother, teleported.

Orion watched as they vanished.

Orion smiled. "God, I'm gunna love it here. It's all so frickin' awesome."

CHAPTER 10

'THE BOOK OF BELIAL'

Drakos knew the walk home only took minutes and decided to make no eye contact with Fantasia at all.

Orion went the back way into his own house, leaving his parents to talk.

Capalia city shopping was put off, just for a little while as other things on the list were much more important.

"You're going now, aren't you?" he asked, as they stepped in through the front door.

"Yes," she said.

"Alone, I suppose?" he said.

"Sorry, Drakos, but yes."

"There's nothing I can say to persuade you otherwise?" Drakos said.

"No, you can't persuade me to change my mind. Now let it go, I'll see you soon," she said.

Fantasia put on her long red and black jacket, then picked up her sword. She placed it under her jacket on the left-hand side.

Fantasia teleported.

"She's picked teleporting back up fast enough!" Drakos mumbled to himself, impressed.

He walked through and sat in his large library. He began researching Belial. This was not a battle the Voxian people could take lightly. They would need to be prepared for anything.

WORCESTERSHIRE IN THE UK.

So, Fantasia teleported to the loft, which was small and cramped, filled with old books and letters, she found a letter dated from when Phoenix had still been alive, there was an address for Victoria in France, Fantasia took this and placed it folded in her coat pocket. She saw things from Phoenix's army days, things from all countries that he had been assigned during his time in the war.

She passed a box that looked like it had been handmade, carved in mahogany. She noticed it straight away. The two figures carved into it were Kathos and Belial.

"Oh, My Goddess!" she whispered. She had seen this box a thousand times before but had never known what the picture carved on it was, she looked inside, the box was empty.

The box had been made to protect those who had the book, it had been lined with an incantation so that the book could not be detected when inside it.

Fantasia grabbed the box. Her next port of call was France.

A small villa, in Calais, beautiful, the village was quiet and the air pollution-free.

The cottage she appeared in front of had honeysuckle growing up and around the door, concrete whitewashed walls, and roses around the garden, which made the whole place very picturesque.

She had heard Phoenix talk of Victoria but had always assumed she lived in the United Kingdom. Calais, therefore, was a surprise.

The cottage was just off the coastline. Fantasia could hear and smell the sea.

Phoenix would talk about the world war. He had escaped the enemy, coming ashore here. Victoria's grandmother Mary had hidden him from capture.

Fantasia knew that, unlike Phoenix's empty house, this was occupied. Her sense of the book was strong here. The cottage she stood outside was a lot older than the house she had just left in the UK.

She stopped, and then teleported into Victoria's loft. This was large and high. It had enough room for Fantasia to stand up in and was full. There was an old rocking chair, and large cases and boxes, amongst other sundry things.

Paintings of relatives queued on the floor, with eyes that seemed to follow her around the room. The whole place was like a horror film. She imagined foraging wild children hiding in corners, ready to jump out.

"Creepy!" Fantasia whispered to herself.

Tip toeing around the large attic, she searched until she came to an old tea chest in the far corner, on the right side of the attic. Discarded near the top was a large bundle of items. One was wrapped in a black cloth. Fantasia began to move things around. She removed the cloth, and underneath was a bundle, wrapped in a gold-coloured silk cloth.

She had found it!

Fantasia could feel a strange, vibrant power through her fingers.

She grabbed the wrapped book and hurried over, putting it into the carved box from Phoenix's loft.

As she was about to teleport home a noise came from the floor below.

She heard a whisper...

'Murder...' it said.

Nothing more than a creepy whisper, but it made the hair on her arms stand on end.

She could hear the whispers of Beth's Vardu allies as they entered the room where Victoria lay sleeping.

A shifting of cloth as their feet slithered across the wooden floors, and a slight hissing sound, as they changed from their spirit forms to solid flesh, then a loud piercing scream.

Then silence...

Fantasia knew that she was too late to even attempt to save Victoria.

She had to get out with the book before they realised that she was there. It sounded like there were at least ten creatures on the floor below, and Fantasia knew they were too many for her to fight alone. She couldn't risk the loss of the book now, so she teleported herself back to her home on Vox.

She had been only minutes. Drakos hadn't even chosen a book to read in his library yet.

The look on her face told him she had just had a lucky escape. But he left her for a few seconds, just to give her some time to compose herself, and get her breath back.

Fantasia put the box on the desk in the library. Drakos smiled at her, and she smiled back.

"I take it that was a close call?" Drakos asked her.

"I would say, pretty damn close," she said, trying to compose herself a little.

"Who or what did you encounter? Is the girl alright?"

"Afraid not. Beth's stooges got there before I could do anything to help her. It was quick if that's any consolation. I didn't stop to introduce myself, there were too many for me to handle alone. I guess Beth's Vardu must have picked up my trail and planned to jump me. Luckily, I was too fast for them," she said.

"That really was a close call then," Drakos said, impressed.

Fantasia sat for a moment. "Next thing will be to make sure the book is unobtainable."

Fantasia couldn't rest, she had been pacing since she had got back home.

She felt unsafe with the book on her property, but wanted to tell Kathos all was well, and the book had been hidden safely.

She picked up the box with the book inside and teleported.

The next day as they met, Kathos asked if the book had been dealt with. Fantasia gave a smile and a nod and nothing more needed to be said.

TITAN

"We're going to teleport. No point in being detected," Kathos said, looking at Orion. Kathos picked the keys up to Fantasia's empty house on Titan.

"Where are we going to start?" said Orion.

"Maybe you could suggest a good place? We need to try not to make any fuss!" Kathos said.

"When you say fuss, you mean without a fight with Beth and her fanged zombies?" said Orion.

"Yes, I suppose I do." said Kathos.

"Grandfather, what exactly are these creatures like?" Orion asked.

"Like nothing seen before. The Vardu are swollen and bloated, like a human body found dead in water. Their eyes are red, with no pupils, and when they cry it is tears of blood, like they're bleeding on the inside. They make a hissing sound as they come up from the ground in groups. It's like gas being released from a pipe. They have fangs on the top, and bottom rows of teeth, sharp, jagged and yellow, usually with age, and the smell of decaying flesh is overwhelming."

"Where are they from?" Orion asked.

"The creatures have been allowed to reside in the dark caves of Raitharn. Their planet was destroyed long ago, so they go from place to place in our Multiverse, hunting for blood to consume. They keep living at the expense of other lives. The truth is, they're an alien life with no home; they just prey on the weak." Kathos said.

"What else can you tell me?" Orion asked.

"They are almost silent, faster than any creature I have ever come across in my many thousands of years. A sudden sadness fills their victim, like they will never be happy again. Their will to die becomes so strong their victims freeze and are filled with sadness. As they bite with their many fangs, and drain their victims of blood, the Vardu become solid, almost human looking, and for a split second you could mistake them for a person, which legend says they were once, many centuries ago, before they turned," Kathos said.

"Jesus Christ! They sound frickin' dreary!" Orion said.

"Dreary? Well, yes they are. But once bitten, if the creature hasn't killed its victim already, you have the same life as they do. Belial loves the Vardu, they're like living Hell all wrapped up in a cold human form," Kathos said.

"What about our species, Grandfather? Have they ever turned us?" Orion asked.

"No, I believe they have neither the method, nor the inclination, Orion. Voxians are far too complex a being for a mere Vardu to even get near. It would take something very special to turn us into anything," he said.

The two stepped from the Manor, where Comet was waiting for them, they teleported.

"So, tell us what you can about Titan?" Comet asked.

Orion spoke about the moon's atmosphere. It didn't take him long. Then he began on his favourite subject, the smell that lingered in even through the domes; *'the smell of cow dung!'* was how he put it.

He spoke quickly giving the basic information.

"I'm hungry!" Orion said, stroking his stomach like a small child.

"What do we do for food here on Titan?" Comet asked him.

"We either shop at a supermarket, or we use the food replicator," Orion smiled.

"What type of food do you like?" Kathos enquired.

"Well, I love cheese on toast, beans on toast, macaroni cheese, and bread, plain on its own" Orion said.

"Hmm, that's pretty bland," said Kathos.

"Why? What do you eat, being an Angel?" Orion asked.

"Me? I don't have much of a problem. Being an Angel, I don't actually need to eat, but do enjoy trying different foods from other places," Kathos said.

"So, is there something wrong with me? I have Angel blood as well. Why do I get hungry?" Orion asked.

"Now, that's quite an interesting question, because you're not just Angel blood, but Voxian as well, and they- EAT! Mind you, you haven't really tried any of the food on Vox yet, have you?" Kathos asked Orion.

Orion sat thinking about this. No one had eaten human food that he had noticed. He was not inclined to eat until reaching Titan.

"Maybe it's the different atmosphere. We should talk about this perhaps when we haven't got to consider other things," Kathos said, looking now at Comet for help.

"Maybe we can discuss this later, after we get inside,"

Comet said.

The men were standing outside the converted hotel. Nothing appeared to have been disturbed.

Orion went straight to the kitchen. He walked straight over to the replicator and pressed some buttons then he said the words: 'Cheese on toast!' it took him only seconds. He made plenty of food and drink for his guests. He sat down in front of the television, switching on the DVD player, the film was *'Dracula,'* with a cup of tea and a massive pile of cheese on toast.

"Good times," he said, mimicking one of his favourite Earth comedians.

Kathos and Comet just looked at him, and then began to eat. The strange film was about a vampire, Vardu, with only two fangs. He was in love with a human. The Vardu would rip this woman apart. They could only find such romanticism funny.

"I wonder what a Vardu would make of all this?" Orion asked.

"They're living dead. I don't think they do have much in the way of thinking; they just have the instinct to feed," Comet replied.

They all settled down eating, watching, and laughing.

Tomorrow they began their stressful mission on Titan.

CHAPTER 11

Orion felt strange to think that Sky's house was invaded, yet the old hotel he had lived with his mother and father had not been touched.

Kathos, Comet and Orion left the building, on their way to find Orion's friend.

"You say there's a newspaper office nearby?" Kathos asked.

Orion nodded at his grandfather.

"We need to get the humans home as quickly as we can." Kathos said.

"Titan has computers and the internet. My idea is simple and quick: A newspaper article. We have both the physical and the technical communication then," Orion said. Orion took out the newspaper article he had kept from Titan before, "this should prove that Earth has not been destroyed yet."

"The date will need to be highlighted Orion." Kathos said.

Orion had picked up his mobile phone from the table in the front room, he began to punch in some numbers as they walked. He waited, not pressing the call button just yet.

"Last night I managed to contact my friend from college, Stuart," Orion said. "He's working on *'The Titan News'* in the press office. He will be of some help!"

"Is that who you're contacting now?" asked Comet.

"I'm hoping he's alright. We can meet him at the office this morning. I'm going to ask Stu (Stuart) to place an article in the dailies of Titan," Orion said.

"How big is the population here, Orion?" Kathos asked.

"Titan has a population of around two million. I can assure you that, between all of us, we can get the article distributed, highlighting the date on it in bold, with a circle around it if needs be. The news will be distributed, one way or another, and seen by the people who live here, but either way people here read, either on their computers, electrical devices or in print." Orion said.

"Those who don't read this article, I'm sure, will be told

by those who have. The only problem we have is Beth and her Vardu cronies," said Comet.

"Yes, I'm afraid there is a complication in our plan. I have been advised this morning that Belial has taken ownership of all of our press offices. He won't be too happy when we use his businesses to inform everyone, which in a way is ironic," said Kathos.

"Ah...That is just too bad, but no one here as seen Belial really, he wasn't Prime Minister in the UK when we all left. He is on Earth and as no jurisdiction on Titan. Okay, I will go to Stu first, giving time to get organised." Orion said.

"We should contemplate getting to work on this. I'm sure we can help your friend. All we have to do is set up the article and get out of there before we're seen. We can take your friend, Stu, with us..." Comet said.

"That's a solid plan. I'm sure he would be happy to get away from here." Orion was walking away, he turned back "If I need you, I'll call you." said Orion tapping the side of his head. "A nicer idea would be for you to warn me if Beth turns up."

"Looks like you may be getting used to telepathy." Kathos said, with a smile.

"No, but it may be better than trying to scream from the press office!" Orion said, sarcastically. "Can you please get the list and go back inside, if we can get the packing done we can make a quick exit if need be."

Kathos and Comet went back into the hotel with the list given to them by Fantasia. They had a list of books from Drakos, whose words to them were: 'I'm never going back to that crap hole.' So, they needed to pack them all.

Orion got into a black and red Land Rover he couldn't really use his powers here; people would probably notice. It was one of Drakos's jeeps left here, he had already taken his motorbike to Vox. He wasn't happy to be back on this iron Hell. This time he hoped to persuade Stu to leave with him, he believed it wouldn't be too hard...

Orion pulled up outside the press offices but could see

93

immediately that something was wrong.

The place appeared abandoned, and the offices silent.

They were in a large factory building, which usually had the noise of chatting and computer key boards tapping coming from it.

Orion walked through a door at the side, which was left open slightly, then he heard a... "PSSST!" Orion looked around, but he saw no one.

"PSSST! Over here!" came a familiar whisper.

Orion turned to see Stu. He was bundled under a mass of netting and old disused magazines. He looked filthy, like he had been there a while.

"What's going on?" Orion said, looking around. No one else was in the building. It stood empty.

He went over to his friend.

"What are you doing here? You look like something the cat sicked up!" Orion whispered.

"I've been hiding out here all night," Stu said, running his fingers through his untidy hair. "Yesterday this chick turned up wanting to see the editor. She had got some strange looking guys with her. They were weird man, all toothy and fangy. They were just too creepy for me, so I hid. These dudes walked into the editor's office, and just grabbed him, the editor! She snapped his neck, like breaking a stick," Stu said, shaking his head.

Stu looked terrified. Orion understood what he meant. The Vardu scared the heck out of him and that was without him actually encountering one, and he was a Voxian.

"Mate, are you okay?" Orion asked him.

"I think so. I didn't want to hide but, man, it was too late for my editor, he was dead. I just did a runner. Didn't see the point in trying to fight her and the strange fangy dudes. She looked like a bodybuilder. The things that were with her, man, they appeared up through the floor like, from nowhere!" Stu began to panic as he described the scene in the press building.

Orion looked around. The computers were switched off,

blank screens everywhere, it did look spooky. Every move they made in the building echoed.

"So, what do we do now?" Stu asked.

"I'll call my grandfather here, and uncle. All this could be too much for us two to take on. And if Beth comes back we need to be ready to fight her. Look at this article!" Orion said.

Orion handed over the newspaper and showed Stu the front page. He was speechless and angry. He had left a lot behind on Earth, including members of his family. He had no idea what to say.

Stu bowed his head, looking extremely saddened.

"It's okay, Stu." Orion put his hand on his friend's shoulder to give him some comfort. "We can copy and distribute this picture to everyone. Will you be able to gain access to all the computers still? We can help you the reboot system again. We'll even help to distribute the papers."

"Thanks, man," Stu said, half smiling.

"Most of the equipment here is already sorted. We just have to take the article and add it to the computer systems here." Orion pulled out a small device from his pocket, it was a USB.

"No lid as usual." Stu laughed at his friend. Orion always lost the lids off these things.

"Is Beth, err...? I mean the buff woman; is she still around?" Orion asked.

Stu shook his head, still staring at the photograph he noticed Beth.

"Dude she's here!" Stu said pointing at the picture.

Orion nodded.

Kathos and Comet arrived surprisingly fast, both by foot.

Stu just shrugged it off, thinking they had been with Orion in the first place, so they couldn't have been very far away. But Orion smiled and shook his head, quite glad of his friend's ignorance.

"Beth has been here," said Orion. "She's killed the editor and left no workers. The Vardu have probably killed them all by now. We need to pull together and help get this printed and distributed around Titan."

"Okay. Let's get the article for the web sorted out first. A lot of Titanian dudes use a computer for news. This has to be our first priority. It's the most used method for spreading information." Stu said.

Comet and Kathos looked at one another. The young man's language was causing them slight confusion.

Comet leaned towards Orion. "What's a Dude?" he asked.

"We're dudes. We're what are known as his fellow man!" Orion said.

"Is this English?" asked Comet.

"No, it's just slang talk!" Orion smiled as he answered.

Comet looked even more confused now. "But how can it be cool if no one else can understand it? No offence!" he said.

"None taken, Comet," Orion laughed.

Stu walked back over putting his mobile back in his pocket, after talking on his phone. He was shaking his head. "That's just so wrong, man," he said.

"What is? What has happened?" Kathos asked.

"The built chick warned our reporters that the paper was her property. She told them to leave. Then she said they could never come back here, not without being punished," Stu said.

"So, we can't rely on a reporter coming then?" Kathos said.

"No, man, they can't come back here, they were too scared. This Beth chick said they know where their families live. She threatened to take revenge if they see anything written with their name in the newspapers again. They'll be killed. You know; done over, Dude!" Stu said.

"Done over?" Comet looked in confusion at Orion again, who then made a cutthroat sign with his finger across his throat. Comet got that immediately.

"It looks like it's up to us then. We have to make this right and get the news out on the streets quickly, man!" Stu said. "For Earth!" He put his fist in the air as Orion looked on.

"Dude, sometimes you are such a drip!" Orion said.

The friends all shifted into action. Stu wrote a particularly good article: '*Are the people of Earth alive and still out there? By Stu Jones.*' He missed out his slang language, like 'Dude' and 'chick'. In fact, the article proved why he was on Titan in the first place. He was very obviously an academic, despite his jibber jabber, as Comet now called it.

Stu e-mailed the news article out to all he could, for fast delivery. He posted the article on every social networking site he could find. Hoping that people wouldn't think it was a hoax.

Stu, made a daily newspaper, and called it: "*EARTH NEWS!*" Putting the day's date, which was 12th February 2512.

"Oh, My Goddess! February 2512! We've only months to prepare and conquer Belial," Kathos said.

"We already have our own warriors in training. We will be okay, Kathos," Comet said.

Stu had begun to pick up on the conversation. He still just shrugged and carried on regardless.

"You must explain that the pods can be separated from the domes; that they will be able to programme the computers and robots to carefully reverse their work, then they can travel back to Earth. It may take a while, but they should be back in time for us to recruit those who wish to help fight. They must be careful that they are well sealed in, before separating," Comet said, as the words were added to the article by Stu. He nodded, saying nothing.

Stu was fast. He had articles, survival tips, information for computer reversal programming and recruitment details, all placed in the small five-page paper. It was only two hours later, and he had managed to prepare everything. All in colour. It looked very professional.

"How many papers do I print?" Stu asked, jumping on to a forklift truck, loading massive coils of paper to the machines, with Orion's help.

"How many do you think we can distribute?" Comet asked.

"I have called on the factory drivers to deliver the papers.

Press distribution is about twenty thousand daily, will that be enough? I can deliver some myself if you need me to, and two trucks are coming to take papers further afield," Stu said.

Kathos was impressed by this young man. He felt afraid of what could happen to him if left behind, yet still he had helped them to get the message out to his fellow man.

"Stuart?" Kathos said.

"Err...? Stu, if that's okay, Dude," Stu said.

"Stu, have you ever considered that other planets have inhabitants?" Kathos asked.

"You mean green aliens 'n stuff?" Stu replied.

"Well, not quite...but...Yes!" said Kathos.

Orion stood smiling again, shaking his head in amusement as Stu was talking to Kathos, their planet's King. If only he had realised he was royalty, he doubted Stu would be speaking to him like an everyday person.

Kathos and Comet understood why it was so important to save Earth. Not just because it had been home to their long-lost family, but they kinda liked this guy as well, so as Orion had said there must be others.

The was something about the human race that made saving it worthwhile. They may not have strength, and be as powerful as the Voxian race, but there was something that made them like the Voxians. Stu had spirit, despite his weaknesses. He was still willing to risk his life to help his friend and his species, and he was just one man.

"If we asked you to fight by our side to save the Earth, would you want to?" Comet asked Stu as they worked.

"Sure thing, Dude. The Earth is our mother. She gave us life and sustains people. As chick planets go, Dude, she is pretty awesome!" Stu replied.

Comet looked at Orion, confused again.

"That means yes!" Orion said, laughing.

Kathos and Comet could not help but laugh at the language he used. It was easy to understand once you caught on. It was about what replaced what. They knew he had the intelligence to talk properly, but he had more fun using slang.

"Another question for you, Stu. Would you come back to our planet with us and train with our people? We want you to stand as good a chance of survival as possible," Kathos asked.

"YOUR PLANET... Dude... JUST A SECOND!" Stu said, a little panicked.

He looked at Orion, and the panic just vanished from his face. He shrugged his shoulders. "That figures! Sure, why not? When do we go?"

Orion smiled at Kathos. Stu would be safe from harm with the Voxian people. He was a brave man and would be a welcome addition to his family.

"So, Orion Dude, you're an alien?" Stu said, finding it all very funny now.

"Hmm. If you're coming to my planet, Stu, actually you're the alien! As for Titan... we're all aliens," Orion replied.

Orion began giving Stu a quick rundown of Vox and his people as they carried on working.

Stu suddenly realised that the reason his friend was so big was because he was from Vox, and not Earth. A resounding "Dude!" was respectfully said.

Orion was a fighting machine from another planet that had been sent to help save his planet, but Stu saw Earth as Orion's planet as well.

"Man, this is just so cool!" Stu said, throwing the printed papers now into the back of the waiting vans that had arrived at the door of the press offices. "Voxians, I can't believe this. Did you know all along?" he asked Orion.

"No, I basically reacted like you when I found out. After all, we're quite an awesome species. If I had been from a naff planet maybe I would feel different, but we are pretty cool on Vox, Dude," Orion said, now using the same slang.

The drivers of the four vans got out and asked which district they wanted the papers to go. Stu pulled out maps of the quadrants, and the areas to drop the papers, that would be safe from Beth.

Stu and Kathos climbed into the back of the one van, while

Comet and Orion jumped into another.

These human drivers were risking their lives just driving the papers to the destinations. The Voxians hoped that none of them would be caught handing them out.

But news needed to reach the people who lived on this god-forsaken moon.

As they pulled away, the doors began to shut on the vehicles.

Kathos shouted: "Meet you back at base camp!"

The others nodded in agreement, and the vans moved off.

"Base camp. Dude, where is that?" Stu asked.

"Fantasia's makeshift home," Kathos said, smiling.

Stu shrugged. He knew that this guy could be trusted. He was different from Orion. There was something, but he just couldn't put a word to it.

Orion watched as the van with Stu and Kathos drove away. He really hoped that this would not be the last time he saw him.

Kathos would not let anything bad happen to him. He would do all that he could to keep Stu safe from harm, but these Vardu creatures of Beth's were a bunch of sneaky morons. Orion turned to Comet, and they began making plans to distribute the rest of the papers.

CHAPTER 12

After hearing the news, the humans wanted to be back on their own planet to help with the fight.

A meeting was made and discussions and plans to begin the reversal of the computer programmes so that those who wished to leave, could do that.

Some wanted to stay, mainly the scientists that had begun the Titan project, but Kathos and the others stayed long enough to be sure that all went smoothly and no interference from Beth occurred.

Which luckily it didn't. she would be so angry when she discovered the Titan project had in fact failed, worse for her so would Belial, he would make her pay for this somehow.

Kathos and his warriors left, once satisfied that the humans had everything under control and would leave the same way they had got there.

They were told of Beth and her threats, so that they would be aware that their enemies could strike at any time.

~

Stu befriended Comet, who had taken him to Vox to stay with his family. Comet found him fascinating and wanted to show the other Voxian people why he believed that humans were worth saving.

The next meeting at the Manor was planned for the next day.

The next morning, Kathos made his announcements from the lounge at the Manor.

"Time is short. I'm happy to tell you that the people on Titan are now in their ships heading back to Earth." Kathos smiled at Orion. "Although some scientists have decided to stay, resealing the domes again once the population who wish to leave have gone. Most humans opted to go back to Earth. Now, won't that be a shock for the British PM?" Kathos said.

Orion looked content with the news, smiling dreamily to himself.

"BLOOD, FIRE, WAR, HATE!" the warrior's cry of

battle was loud and clear.

All went quiet, but not for long as Ledawna joined her partner in the centre of the room.

"Belial has many allies. The Voxians from Raithar have had most of their powers taken away. Belial insists on being the stronger power, this is the way to prove loyalty to him. The Vardu appear to be very few, I believe there are around 1,000 of them," Ledawna said, speaking softly to her people.

She sat down and then Comet stood.

"I'm here to introduce one of our first human allies," Comet said. "He's called Stu to those who know him well. Please, Stu, step forward?" Comet gestured towards him. Stu was quite tall as humans go, but he still looked small in the land of these giants.

Stu got up to his feet a little uneasily, and Raidar grumbled something in a low voice. Comet stepped over, still gesturing to his friend to move to the middle of the room, until all could see him.

"This man showed bravery, courage. He helped us spread the news of Earth, putting his life at risk to make sure everyone on Titan knew that they were able to go back home. Stu did this under the threat of being killed by Beth and her parasitic Vardu followers," Comet said, looking at Raidar.

Raidar moved towards Stu. As he did, Stu stood his ground as Raidar towered over him, putting his giant face right into Stu's.

"Dude, I have personal space issues!" Stu retorted. "Back off a little!"

Stu had been told how to handle Raidar by Comet and Safire before the meeting. He stood firm and confident.

The look on Raidar's face was terrifying. He snarled at Stu, who still stood his ground, not taking his eye off the big guy for one second.

"What are you? What help can you be?" Raidar snarled even more now. "You're weak against Vardu soldiers, and we..." Raidar gave a loud chuckle. "Well, even if we had no powers, we would be able to snap you like a twig," Raidar growled as he began backing off, but only slightly.

"Dude, chill out, I'm not weak. What if your enemies have humans fighting on their side? Will you be able to justify killing them if you are as powerful as you say...? I'm not your enemy!" Stu said.

Raidar looked amazed at this man's nerve.

"I'm not saying we would kill them, idiot. I'm just stating a fact. I could fart and break your neck at the same time." Raidar put his face closer again elongating his fangs.

Stu still stood his ground, wafting his hand over his nose. "Man, that would be stinky! He said.

The warriors laughed.

Except Raidar, who growled a bit louder.

"So, what, Raidar? Do you want humans to keep out of the fight? Just because we aren't as strong as your Voxian people are?" Stu said back, angry now.

Raidar was shocked. That this man had the guts to stand up to him. He had to admire that.

Comet stood next to Stu, trying to calm the argument.

"See, I told you," Comet said to Raidar. "They may not have our strength, but I believe that there are many humans who are strong willed enough to fight with us. With training they would be able to fight for their planet if they wish to!"

Raidar turned, smiling at Comet.

"Yes, I can see why you like this idiot now," Raidar said, sitting back down in his seat. "I just hope you're right. I'm willing to train this species, but it will have to be without Voxian warriors. They're too strong for the beginners now. If they wish to live to fight Belial, we'll have to build them up, introduce them into the fight slowly."

"Thanks, my friend, I'm so glad you have seen their potential," Comet said, stepping away with Stu.

Again Ledawna took to the centre of the room.

"Now for a journey never made before. Sky, have you finished your study of Dino logic?" Ledawna asked her.

"Yes, Grandmother, I have," Sky said.

"Okay, we're going to travel to Reptilia," Ledawna said,

smiling at Sky.

There was a gasp of surprise in the room. They had left this species alone since the beginning of time. Why were they approaching them now?

"As we all know, we've a psychic and physical link with our pentagram stars. This means if we touch other allies, we can adapt their abilities to ours. What we want from the Reptilians is their armour." Ledawna said.

The warriors in the room showed displeasure at her suggestion, wondering if they would need more protection. The suggestion was ridiculous to them.

Ledawna waited for the room to quieten again.

"They're descended from the Earth's Dinosaurs and have evolved. We're hoping they are intelligent enough not to see us as prey. Hopefully, they can be persuaded by Sky to ally with us in the fight," Ledawna said.

"Now that's gunna be awesome!" Raidar laughed as he looked around the room at all the shocked people. "Well, it is, these things were deadly in their time."

The warriors all looked at the only person they thought would know. Stu's shoulders shrugged, the only knowledge he could remember was from school.

"Dudes, I believe that some Dinosaurs were the deadliest of the carnivore species, they would eat the plant eaters. This was before the Ice Age killed them all off!" he said.

Sky was excited that she would be facing Dinosaurs. But when she seemed a little nervous, Orion went to comfort her.

"Talk to Dinosaurs...Why would I want to do that?" Sky asked nervously.

"Don't worry, we'll protect you. I don't think you're going there alone," Orion said.

Kathos hugged Sky into his side. "You'll be just fine," he said. "You're allowed to take as many of our warriors with you as you wish."

Sky thought carefully. She knew humans had evolved, so was sure the Reptilians would have done the same. She had researched them well, but only as dinosaurs on Earth.

Even if they hadn't evolved, she could speak their language. Also, she would be happy for a chance to see these creatures in the flesh. That's if they didn't try to eat her.

"It would be an honour to help, Kathos. I'd like to take Rexus, Orion, Kale, and Halen. They're all good strong warriors. I'd also like to take Genesis and Ledawna, with their ability to calm the situation, if needs be," Sky said.

"Is that all? I'm sure they will be happy to go," Kathos said, turning to the younger warriors. "Will you be happy to accompany Sky to the planet?" he asked them.

"Yeah...why not?" Halen said.

"I'd like to go as well, Sky," Comet said. "I may be useful in locating the species when we're on the planet. I believe it's full of jungle."

"Okay, but we need to limit the size of our team. We don't want them to believe this is a full-blown invasion, do we?" Sky said.

"This is your mission, Sky. You're completely in charge. I know you have studied hard since you have been here on Vox. I'm happy for you to make all the decisions about how this goes," Kathos said.

"Thank you, Kathos. I will be proud to represent our people," Sky said.

Kale whispered to Orion. "Is this going a bit over the top?"

"Hmm, have you just met her? She is over the top!" Orion whispered back.

The two warriors sat down beer in hand as the subject came up about Stu, he wasn't one for a big fuss, so Kathos handed him a talisman that shone green if danger was approaching, it was given in a presentation for all his sacrifice whist on Titan, it gave him extra strength and would help with his defence of the humans.

CHAPTER 13

CAPALIA CITY SOUTHERN VOX

The shops in the shopping centre were floor upon floor of goods to choose. The buildings stood sixteen storeys high in some places.

Orion looked at Stu. The two of them smiled, and just walked through the doors, into what they saw as shopping heaven: Games consoles and computers, everything they'd left behind on Earth. Gadgets and silly gifts. You name it, the boys had seen it, and they were only on the ground floor.

Orion found shoes and clothes that fit him. He didn't have to stretch them; he didn't have to wear them in. No problems with holes in his crotch, and they had jeans that would not ride up his legs and be too baggy around his waist.

"Oh yes, black baggy jeans. There is a God!" Orion said, joking with Stu.

"Oh, there's a God, mate, his name is Stu!" he laughed.

The friends all began playing about, trying on all sorts of things: Hats, EMO wigs, more hats and old man shirts, playing with golf club holders. Halen found himself getting the latest video game, along with Stu and Orion. They all picked up the latest consoles as well.

"Hey, having this credit thing is great!" Stu said to Kale.

"Yes it is, but try not to get too crazy, save some for another day. Just remember that we have to get it all home and it has to fit in the car." Kale said.

With shopping over, the boys all went to meet up with Fantasia and Drakos.

Drakos had loaded himself up with a horror novel, and a collection of horror DVD's.

Fantasia had been shopping for clothes and shoes. She didn't find a lot but was happy just to have lunch at her favourite restaurant again.

"So, where are we going next?" Orion asked his mother.

"You boys have been training, haven't you?" Fantasia

asked.

"Yes, of course we have, with Raidar," Orion said. "Why."

"You need your first defensive weapon. We need to take you to choose your first swords," Fantasia said.

Kale and Halen left, they had to get back to training, both wished them good shopping and teleported.

"Swords! How awesome is that?" Stu said.

The boys put their hands in the air and slapped them together.

Orion looked back over at Stu his face contorted with pain.

"Oh crap! Sorry mate, was that too hard?" Orion said, taking his friends injured hand. "I'm really sorry. Do you need medical attention?"

"A bit!" Stu said cringing; trying to shake off the pain, but it wasn't working.

Fantasia immediately took Stu to the car and fixed him up with a bandage.

Orion looked at Stu with a guilty face.

"I'm sorry, mate," he said.

"Dude, its fine. Think it's just a sprain, don't worry about it," Stu said, patting Orion on his shoulder with his good hand.

They all picked food from the menu and then ate, when finished they stepped outside the restaurant. They began to walk down the street.

The buildings just kept going. It was one massive department store after another. There was furniture in some, clothes in others, and so on.

The buildings stayed huge, and the path seemed to go on and on, until Orion spotted a small shop which was just there suddenly, out of the blue.

Between all the other massive skyscraper buildings, the shop stood just one floor in height, with a large picture of a unfamiliar map of space in the window, with a telescope standing in it. The door was blanked out with a dark blue curtain.

Orion thought for one split second, as he passed it, that the stars on the map moved.

But they couldn't, could they?

As he passed the shop window, he saw a man, whose face peeked from behind the curtain of the shop.

Fantasia pulled Orion past.

"You can go back there once we have got your sword. I think you'll be interested in who owns the sword shop," Fantasia said, pulling him a little harder.

They went a little further, and another small shop appeared in the distance. This also stood out, mainly due to its smaller size.

This shop had two floors and nothing in the window, or at the door. When Orion and Stu looked inside, there was a plush yellow and blue carpet on the floor, with an old-fashioned beaded curtain in multi colours on the doorway inside the shop.

Drakos smiled at the boys. He could see they were curious. A man stepped from behind the beaded curtain.

"Oh, it's Hyedan! So, he's the man to see about weapons. Why doesn't that surprise me?" Orion said, smiling.

CHAPTER 14

<u>SWORD SHOPPING</u>

The family and Stu entered the small shop, and the bell rang out that was hanging above the door. A shop keeper appeared from the beaded multi-coloured curtain, and immediately smiled at Orion as he saw him.

"Ah, Princess..." he said to Fantasia, turning to look at her. His voice was deep and quiet. "I see you've brought your son." His face lit up with surprise. "And what's this, a human warrior?" he approached Stu, gliding towards him.

"Yes, he is," Fantasia said, as she watched Hyedan shake Stu's hand. "Stu, can you remember our city warrior leader?"

Stu looked on nervously "Yes, I believe I can." He said.

Orion was about to ask how his wife and daughter were, out of politeness, when Azaya walked into the room through the beaded curtain.

There she stood in all her beauty. Orion smiled awkwardly, going slightly flushed. He was rendered speechless for a few minutes; he then managed to compose himself enough to smile at her properly.

Azaya, on the other hand, was not shy. She walked up, individually hugging and kissing them, one by one. Orion was the last, of course.

Hyedan stood watching for a while. He walked through the beaded curtains and into the next room, gesturing for them all to follow.

"This is my exhibit room. I would like you to see a few rare swords I have," Hyedan said with some enthusiasm.

Stu followed excitedly.

Orion was still recovering from the kiss he had just been given by Azaya. He was still smiling, and scarlet faced, rubbing the spot on his cheek with his hand. He had gone into a temporary daydream.

"ORION!" Fantasia said, digging his side with her elbow.

Fantasia grabbed his arm and pulled him. He snapped out

of his daydream immediately and began to follow.

"Just keep up," Drakos said, looking back at Azaya, who had found it all very amusing.

Hyedan had also seen the funny side. He whispered something to Azaya, and then said quiet loudly: "Now stop misbehaving."

She grinned at her father playfully, then began to swish her long skirt, which was deep purple velvet with black lace. She wore black lace fingerless gloves, and a black lace top. Orion couldn't stop looking at her.

Azaya left the room for a few minutes to bring the warriors drinks and make them feel welcome.

In Vox, a sword was the most important thing anyone could have. Hyedan felt honoured to supply their weapons, but he did own the only sword shop in Capalia.

He wanted the new warriors to feel that they could take their time and look carefully.

They all entered the room at the back. It was plush, with deep red carpeting and curtains. There were several glass cases, all with four swords on display, beautiful and well-made masterpieces in their own right.

Hyedan picked up his first sword out of a locked glass cabinet.

"This sword is the traditional Voxian sword. The blade is silver," he said.

The hilt was white, carved with a pattern of three moons and a distant Voxian sun, with a traveller standing on a mountainside. The two boys had never seen such craftsmanship on a swords hilt. But let's face it, not many normal earthbound men own swords. It had a gold trim at the edge of its silver blade, and when it was handed to Stu, he couldn't believe how light it was. It weighed next to nothing.

Stu handed it over to Orion, who took a step back and began to swing it in all directions, jabbing and keeping it steady in his hand. It was natural for him to use it.

Hyedan looked impressed as Orion aimed at some targets that had been set up in the room, and never missed one.

"Orion, perhaps you would like to consider this?" Hyedan said as he walked to a higher plinth and took out a sword which sat alone in its case. It had a gold trim on its blade, and writing on it...

*For the man who will stand up
for those who are weaker.*

The sword was engraved with a cream picture on a red hilt. It had the Earth, the Sun, and in the distance the Mythus nebula. Decorated with gold leaf trim, it was just outstanding.

When Hyedan handed the sword over, it was like a feeling that Orion had never experienced: A rush of warmth entered his body, and the sword felt like it was suddenly a part of him.

Orion could feel nothing but the sword. It was like it had been there all the time, sat in his hand. But it felt lighter than air.

"I think this one likes me," he said.

"I think so too," Hyedan said, looking at Fantasia.

"This sword was crafted by our own King, your great grandfather... Kathos," Hyedan said, smiling at Orion.

Orion carried on swishing it through the air.

"It was to be used in the fight against Belial. I believe that Kathos never thought it would find a user, because he had made it so specifically. He'll be so pleased to know that you, his own great grandson, bonded to it," Hyedan said.

"It's of a big importance then, this sword thing?" Stu said. "King Arthur comes to mind, not the legend, the cartoon!" Stu smiled at Orion, who pointed the sword in his direction, mockingly.

"Yes, swords are important. You'll find one just as worthy that will suit you, my boy, I promise. We've a lot more to look at yet," Hyedan said to Stu.

Stu carried on searching the cases. Suddenly he came to a stop.

"This one! I mean, can I try this please?" Stu said,

pointing to a case next to him.

"Yes, of course!" Hyedan smiled.

Hyedan pulled out the sword from the case. It had a silver blade; the hilt was a picture of a Voxian deer running through the forest, with a hunter giving chase. It was white mother of pearl, making it look a little anaemic.

Hyedan handed the sword to Stu. He too felt the same warm feeling as Orion had, as the sword accepted his human hand.

"Perfect," he said.

Stu did what Orion had done. He played with the sword, swinging it. He was just as natural with it as his Voxian friend, and again the sword was like a part of him.

"Orion!" Hyedan said. "A gift."

Hyedan handed over a large blue velour box, Orion happily took it and opened it immediately.

Inside sat two small handheld swords and a holder that would attach to him, so he could carry them around.

"Thank you sir," he said admiring the silver edged blades.

Orion put his finger on the edge, his finger began to bleed the second it touched the blade but healed again immediately.

"Be careful." Hyedan said.

Stu laughed "You're still the kid that no teacher would ever trust with scissors!"

The two men walked over to the counter to put the exchange card through the till.

He could now go into combat, and train with his warrior friends.

They all thanked Hyedan, Orion waved at Azaya a little red faced and they all left.

CHAPTER 15

CLOSE ENCOUNTERS OF A TELESCOPE SHOP

Walking back up the street, the shop with the telescope in the window came back into Orion's sight. He was still playing with his new sword when Drakos suggested he put it away as they were in public. So, he gave it to his father to put in the car.

Orion couldn't put the sword into its scabbard because he hadn't brought his coat. He wore the one Phoenix had left him, it was an old jacket in red and black. Phoenix had packaged it for Orion only weeks before his death.

Orion would play pirate in it when he was a child and hide all sorts of treasures in the deep pocket on the inside of it. It got ripped, so Fantasia recommended he put it away, and she would sew it for him. He had put it in a beautifully designed box and had forgotten about it until now.

Orion quickened his pace. It was only seconds before he was outside the map shop again.

Orion was looking through the shop window, staring at the telescope from outside, studying the maps that moved. Orion stood watching as stars exploded and comets moved through the map. He was impressed.

Orion stepped inside the shop alone.

The shop walls inside were dark blue with golden stars painted on them, badly. The windows to the outside world were on every side, big and very bright, letting every bit of light in the shop possible. So having a dark night sky on the walls just didn't really have a lot of effect. It was strange because, over the painted night skies were row upon row of poster holders, all full of maps that moved. All the different galaxies; Andromeda, the Milky Way, were there, and so was Mythus. It could be fair to believe that everywhere in the Multiverse seemed to be covered.

Orion pushed the door, and a small bell rang, he stood admiring the maps in silence.

The door at the side of the shop opened, and an old man walked through it. This shocked Orion; because this was the first time he had seen anyone who looked older than about thirty on this planet.

Orion watched as the man approached him, still saying nothing.

The old man stroked his long white beard, looking extremely interested in Orion. He wore a long, dark blue cloak. He had exceptionally long white hair, that went right down his back, hitting his posterior. All that was missing was a pair of rounded silver rimmed glasses and a wizard's hat. He could have been Merlin's double, from the stories of the round table.

"Good day young Orion, what can I do for you on this bright afternoon?" the man asked.

Orion stood staring. This man was like looking at a cartoon character.

"Can I help you?" The man insisted, smiling now, trying to prompt conversation with Orion.

"Oh, I apologise. I'm looking for three items," Orion said, a little red faced.

The old man put his hand up to stop Orion from speaking "No apology needed my boy... Let me see, ah, yes I've a good quality telescope, a map of both Earth and the planets around it. Also, a map of Mythus, like the one in the window," he said, smiling mysteriously.

"I...I'm sorry, I didn't catch your name," Orion asked, very confused.

'How the Hell did this guy know all of that information, even his name?' Orion thought.

"Hello Orion, I'm Mallick, the keeper of the maps of the Multiverse and of Vox, and I'm the best friend of Kathos," Mallick said, bowing with a large grin.

Orion gave the man a look of disbelief. His scientific brain went into 'reject the information' mode. Could this be madness? This man was now even claiming to be a 'Map keeper?' Well, I suppose he is really, Orion looked around the shop.

'Trouble is,' Orion thought, *'am I supposed to play along and be nice? Or should I just say what a croc? Nah... Be nice, after all, this guy is bigger than me!'*

"I'm a lot older than I look; I came here with your great grandfather, Kathos, many years ago. I'm from the planet of spirits. Hence I age slowly, but obviously your great grandfather doesn't age at all," said Mallick, trying to give Orion an explanation.

"I guess that explains a lot Mallick, it's good to meet you. Now, can you find maps that are ten feet by ten feet. Is that possible?" Orion said, a little unsure.

Orion tried to play down what the old man was saying, changing the subject quickly. Senility he thought 'maybe.'

"Oh yes, of course it is. Where are you planning to hang them?" Mallick said.

"On the ceiling area of my bedroom," Orion said.

Mallick laughed. "You've a bedroom?" Mallick looked curiously at Orion. "I do apologise, I forgot that you spent your childhood on Earth. It must be strange for your family to see you sleep."

Orion smiled at Mallick. "Yes, I think after years on Earth, I've the habit. It doesn't make me feel any more or less energetic. I'm already feeling on tip top form right now, although we all slept when we lived on Earth, including Mother."

Mallick gave a laugh, finding this news a little amusing.

"Oh boy, call me Mal, everybody else does. You wait and see, the longer you spend here, the more your power will build. I can help you a little later down the line, when you've discovered all you can about your abilities," Mallick said.

"Thanks, Mal, I look forward to that." Orion said, letting Mallick through to get to the counter.

Mallick wrapped the moving maps, and the telescope was boxed. He suggested that Orion get someone to help him carry it, but Orion shook his head; he was okay. He picked up everything he had bought and carried it out of the shop.

Orion turned back.

"One thing before I leave," he said.

"Yes, of course, anything!" Mallick smiled.

"The maps constantly move. Can I ask how?" said Orion.

"Ah!" Mallick looked like an old philosopher as he put his finger in the air. "Well, we have map makers who travel through the different solar systems, mapping out and photographing the different galaxies. You should ask Raidar's oldest son when he reappears here. He can tell you about everything; after all, that is his line of work. The skies are ever changing; the stars, comets and other Galaxies debris move about. We can change the maps digitally on computer systems, so once you've bought one, you will never need to update it. We do that for you." Mallick leaned further over his shop counter. "With our technology, we can put any new information on the maps, and it will remain changing as the skies do. Did you know that the only reason you can't see stars in the daylight on Earth is because..." Mallick was then interrupted?

"Yes, the daylight is too bright for them to shine through," Orion said.

Orion exited the shop and left to meet the others.

Walking down the silent streets, Orion headed towards the car.

Stu met Orion outside the shop and the two men turned and began to walk back to the car, everyone was waiting for them there.

Why the car you ask, well, Stu hated it when the others grabbed him by the arm and teleported, he said it made him feel sick.

"Find anything interesting?" Fantasia asked.

"Not really. Bought a few maps, new telescope, met Mallick!" Orion said, smiling at Stu.

"Nothing too exciting then?" said Drakos unaffected, shrugging.

"Nothing we couldn't handle," Stu said.

The boys climbed into the back of the jeep.

"Tell you what, Father, I think you should drive." Orion said sarcastically dangling the keys at him.

Drakos snatched the keys, shrugged and began moaning about the youth of today. 'Lazy bleeders' he called them, while the others looked at one another smirking. At least Drakos was consistent; they could always rely on him to moan.

Orion started copying his father, saying what he was saying only just after Drakos said it. They all started to snigger.

"Orion, you can stop that right now," Drakos snapped.

The car fell silent.

Drakos turned and started the engine of the jeep. The men smiled at one another, sniggering just a little, but quietly to themselves now.

"Home James!" Stu said.

The men laughed again. Drakos shook his head, and they headed back to the Manor Estate.

CHAPTER 16

REPTILIA

Sky awoke, feeling the buzz of excitement.

She wanted a look at the island from a bird's eye view. The team flew above the planet, and then they decided to land the ship in the vast forests of Reptilia.

As they looked through the ships window. There were buildings, mainly large wooden huts, with huge window frames letting in sunlight. The team noticed some of the huts and brick buildings were hidden by thick undergrowth.

Comet made contact when they landed, to his surprise it was also in Earth's English language. They could only guess that this was because they had originated from there. The Voxians spoke English for convenience, usually when around humans, but they spoke many languages; whatever was required.

Comet spoke softly to the new species through telepathy, which these creatures seemed very comfortable with.

"For the Goddess's sake, you're not telling them something corny like, 'we come in peace,' are you?" Halen asked.

"Shut up!" Sky said quickly, knowing that Comet would need to concentrate if he wanted to talk to the alien 'Dinos'.

A sudden silence fell over the ship, as the team waited for Comet to speak, and let them know what was going on.

"They're waiting for us, in the great hall. It's one of the brick buildings..." Comet said.

"You mean, that great hall over there," Halen said, pointing.

There in the thicket stood a massive red brick building (even by Voxian standards), with windows that went from floor to ceiling. From the outside, the windows were tinted black, and the lights inside could barely be seen from the outside. The door was a cherry mahogany, or what looked like it. The handle, from this distance, looked iron, plain and uncomplicated.

"It must be like an oven in there," Orion commented.

The warriors took a walk over to the hall, through the forest of trees.

The ship cloaked. The warriors had no idea what they could be facing, so they didn't want to chance the ship being confiscated if things went wrong.

Rexus grabbed a backpack with some supplies.

Ledawna and Genesis carried a peace offering for the leader of the Reptilians. It was flowers from the Capalian Mountains; they had the healing ability to mend cuts that were deep and infected.

Kale, Halen, and Orion were the first down the forest path. They carried their swords in their coats, hands firmly resting on the hilt.

Comet and Sky just followed them down the path, hoping they wouldn't end up in a fight if the Reptilians saw the swords as a threat.

They stood outside the building; the large double doors towered above them. They did a head count, and then just stood there, waiting.

"What now?" Halen whispered, "Do we knock?"

"No, they're already aware of us, and want us to enter," Comet replied.

"How the Hell...?" Halen said.

"Just take my word for it, Halen, please!" Comet insisted.

"Okay, but this may be an ambush!" Halen replied, looking very suspicious.

"Hmm...No, it's not an ambush!" Comet said as he stood at the door, hands on his hips. He began to wonder why they had brought the mountain warriors with them in the first place, always ready for a fight, even if there wasn't one to be had.

They could be, 'fight first, ask questions later'.

"Come in, my Voxian neighbours," a female voice spoke as the door opened. "You're welcome here; all are welcome.

Please enter."

The warriors walked slowly through the door. As they entered the hall they looked around like lost strangers. The room was gigantic, with only the one doorway.

There in the room stood different varieties of Earth's extinct Dinosaurs.

They were quite different than the pictures and skeletons found on Earth. They stood on two legs and were taller than the Voxians. The Reptilians had a lizard-like appearance. Only their facial features showed any sign of their type of Dinosaur genealogy.

There at the back of the room, three Reptilians stood.

The first was descended from a Tyrannosaurus-Rex. His facial features were all teeth and a giant mouth. He stood approximately fifteen feet high and wore a black cloak with a drawstring around his neck. He was huge.

Standing next to him was a thin, lizard-like female. She was elegant, standing at about ten feet tall. Her cloak was red velvet with white trim, and a long, golden draw string.

Upon the female's head sat a crown, jewelled with diamonds and rubies.

"I think it's pretty obvious who she is," Kale whispered to the other two.

Next to the female stood a Brontosaurus descendant. Again, his face was lizard-like. Standing on his two feet, he looked about thirty feet tall, but could have been taller, it really was hard to tell.

You can now imagine the size this room had to be.

The female gently walked towards them. She gestured to meet her halfway.

"My name is Bellazard. I'm Queen of all you see. This land is ruled by me." She turned her head. "To my left you see Deathladon." Bellazard pointed over to the T-Rex. "And to my right, Callouradon." She indicated to the Brontosaurus descendent.

Both males moved forward in greeting, bowing to the Voxian visitors.

"I am Sky..." she said, bowing back.

"We know who you are, my darling. But did you really believe you could visit our land, and we wouldn't detect you immediately?" Deathladon said, laughing loudly.

"No, but..." Sky said nervously.

Comet put his hand on her arm to assure her she was still alright.

"We knew you were coming here before you took off from your own planet," Deathladon said.

"That's amazing. How?" Halen said.

"Like Comet, we have the ability to hear telepathically from a distance," Deathladon said.

"So, you knew of our plans before we arrived? What do you think?" Sky asked.

Bellazard stepped to the front, gesturing for Deathladon to back off from the visitors just a little.

"We're aware of Kathos and respect his people. We were becoming extinct on Earth. When it got to the last few of us, an Angel called Galileo rescued our ancestors. He was the brother of Kathos. He brought us here to this planet." Bellazard smiled at Sky. "We were the first in this nebula. Closely followed by the Voxian evolution. Isis also evolved. We've kept our distance, and our technology is slow. We still travel by foot, but now have the ability to walk tall."

Bellazard stood next to her second in command Deathladon. "We would be happy to help your fellow man in the fight to stop the Dark Angel Belial."

Bellazard turned to her commanders looking for their agreement.

"Well, that was easy!" Sky said, laughing, a little more confident now.

The three Reptilians smiled in agreement.

"That's scarily happy!" Halen joked, looking at their giant teeth.

Kale and Halen were still standing guard in the room when the warriors were asked to join the Reptilians in a meal. After a few stories, they all began to sing and dance. It was all very civilized, but it also felt quite surreal.

The Reptilians began to sing of a 'time of dragons.' The words were about a fearless leader 'Layottae' Queen of the gates, guardian of the Multiverse, the beautiful white scaled protector of all.

The Voxians became used to the new species very quickly and were pleased they'd taken the chance to make them a part of the alliance.

The Queen clapped her hands as the hall filled with uncooked meats like wild boar which occupied the Reptilian forests and blood to drink. No Voxian would turn down such a meal. The feast began. It may have been unusual to the Reptilians to eat with a new species that had dietary requirements like their own, Although Voxians ate cooked food as well, they really did prefer the taste of wild animal blood, so they were all happy to see the Reptilian diet.

As they looked around the tables, a large platter of vegetation sat in the middle of one. Sky noticed that very few there were herbivores, but they had survived and evolved like the others.

Now Sky had a new problem; how to get these large Reptilians onto her planet. She contacted her great grandfather to see if he had any ideas.

The Reptilian combat training was important, as the two species needed to learn how to use their skills of combat alongside one another.

Sky was told that Belial would attempt the fight on Vox, or on Earth, both of which have the same type of terrain.

"Grandfather, I think we have a problem!" Sky said telepathically.

"What is it?" Kathos said.

"The Reptilians are bigger than anticipated. Transporting them to our planet by spaceship is impossible. I'm worried about their health, travelling this distance in crapped conditions would be detrimental. We'll have to travel back and forth many times to get their warriors to Vox. Some are just way too big to fit," Sky said.

Kathos said nothing. He was thinking of a better way for them.

"I have it!" he said. "I'll find Galileo. He transported the Reptilians many years ago. If he did this, he surely could do it from Reptilia to Vox. Or even give us information on how we could do this ourselves."

Kathos walked away from the computer. He needed help from Galileo, and to find where he was at this present time in the Multiverse. Kathos closed his eyes.

Silence...

"Brother I need your help..." Kathos called to him.

Galileo was quick to respond.

"Heaven's above Kathos, do your people have the power to teleport?" Galileo said.

"Of course, was that the power you used from Earth?" Kathos asked.

"As angels our power is endless, but your Voxian people could do this just as well." Galileo explained.

Kathos thanked his brother, then he returned to the viewer.

"I have all the information we need from my brother to teleport them. It's a difficult job to do, but not dangerous. Go back and speak to our new allies. You will need to explain to them that the warriors must be altogether in one place for the teleportation to Vox. They'll need to be in an area big enough to take them all," Kathos said.

Sky was pleased, this meant that the visitors would be in Vox before the ship.

All was explained, and it was decided that they would have to find a good clearing for the teleportation, whilst arguing who would return with the ship.

"It's okay, I know just the place," said Callouradon (Now nicknamed Cal).

Genesis went back to the ship with Bellazard. She was too wide for the ship's door. Genesis smiled touched her arm and teleported her inside.

"We are many. I will bring four-hundred of my finest with

me, leaving some to protect our own planet, and the young ones." Bellazard said.

"Thank you, that's very generous of you," Genesis said.

All agreed with the Reptilians, and the Voxian ship took off with some of the warriors on board. Comet had stayed behind, offering to wait, and be transportation for the Reptilians. Orion and Sky also stayed behind, to help.

Bellazard was glad she had contact with their neighbours. It was possible that the Voxians may help advance their technology if they wanted them to.

The Voxians could help the Reptilians build ships and use better materials for houses, all an advantage to their species. A small price to pay for this magnificent species' loyalty.

"Comet, Orion and Sky thank you for staying behind and supporting us when we travel. I know our ancestors came to this planet for survival needs, and perhaps we're doing the same coming to Vox. Well, after all, if Belial can attack one planet's species, surely ours would eventually be a target as well," said Bellazard.

The other Reptilian warriors all agreed with her.

Bellazard was the wisest Queen. Her people all admired and adored her, as the Voxians loved Ledawna. To them she was incredibly beautiful.

~

Kathos arrived on Reptilia, which caused a stir amongst the Reptilian people. All came to watch as the Angel stepped in to help those in need once more.

"Your colour is brighter than your brothers." Bellazard said.

"He is of a darker complexion than I." Kathos explained.

They began to chat amongst themselves about prophecies.

This Angel was beautiful, the Reptilians began to say. He had a glow around him, and the power was warm, his presence was gentle.

Kathos shut his eyes and began an incantation. His arms rose from his side. Comet grabbed onto Deathladon, and the creature placed his newfound friend onto his shoulders.

Kathos clapped his hands together, but they made no audible sound. The Reptilian warriors and Voxians were gone.

The other Reptilians cheered, as if they had just seen their first magic trick.

Well, I suppose they had.

CHAPTER 17

The Voxian warriors seemed a little disturbed at first at the sight of the new species size, but it took only a short time before the Voxians, and Reptilians had settled in together.

"What is the first thing you want to do while here on Vox?" Kathos asked.

"May I suggest hunting" Deathladon said to his newfound allies."

"Excellent idea. The Voxian deer are extremely fast. It'll be good to run off some steam. Does anyone else want to come with us?" Comet asked.

Comet explained: "Voxians hunt their food. Firstly, our bite has saliva which acts like a sedative, making the deer submissive. We feed from them, hearing their heartbeat as we do, and we stop feeding as it slows. The deer is then allowed to recover, unless the animal is too old the Voxian hunter will then allow it to die. We don't need to feed often; it all depends on the person's size. The bigger Voxians, like Raidar, will have to hunt around four times a year. The species has no cravings for blood, we could live on fruit and vegetables if we wished, but we feed to keep our powers strong, and because we like it."

The Reptilians looked at Comet impressed.

The hunt was on only a few minutes later, It took the Reptilians only a short while to grasp the methods, but of course they could not hear heartbeats, so had to go for their best guess. Laughter and the shuffling of the trees could be heard from outside the woodlands. Goodnews was they managed to keep all the animals they encountered alive.

TRAINING.

Bellazard and the Reptilians settled quickly into their life on this planet, as they could hunt here whenever the mood took them. It became a good life for the Reptilians, only killing prey that had become old or weak for the meat eaters.

Bellazard was in charge of the Reptilians training for combat. Raidar still took charge in the mountain terrain, and Hyedan helped with adaption of warriors in the city.

"Warriors, tomorrow we must all gather together. The women don't fight with us yet." said Comet.

Deathladon turned to Comet. "What does he mean?"

"If we train together without some preparation it'll turn into a session of uncontrollable rough sex, which is great if we had the time, but not what we're aiming for," Comet said.

Raidar smiled. The Reptilians looked a little disturbed at the picture painted but made no attempt to reply.

"Sorry," Comet said. "We didn't mean to offend you. Rough sexual activity helps us keep fit. The stuff that keeps us on our toes. Our women enjoy the soft touch and the emotional connections we have, but only on the odd occasion... Let's just say we're a passionate species!"

"Sticks and stones might break our bones, but whips and chains excite us," Halen laughed.

"Really?" Deathladon grinned.

"In other words, we can get a little extreme with one another," Fantasia interrupted.

"I understand, but please explain why Comet felt the need to go around the subject? We have sex too and are consenting adults, otherwise there would be no Reptilians left!" Deathladon said, shaking his head. "I believe we're all over the age of sexual consent here, you know; adults?" he said to Comet.

Comet felt himself become embarrassed. Orion and Halen began to laugh, but quietly.

"Okay, we like rough rumpy pumpy!" Raidar said loudly to them all. "I don't know, I get a bit embarrassed, like Comet, and the whole world laughs. Nothing wrong with sex talk, but perhaps we could save our explanations until after training." He was becoming a little impatient.

Everyone tried to hold the laughter, as they could see Raidar was in a bit of a mood now. He began grumbling under his breath.

The warriors settled down and began organising themselves to train.

"Okay, Fantasia, we trust you'll be training at the lakeside with the women?" Hyedan said.

"Yes," she said.

"Raidar, what are you doing?" Hyedan said.

"I'm training my warriors to abseil down rocky mountains. Nothing too big to begin with. We also need to climb fast, without damaging one another," Raidar said.

Hyedan was impressed. Raidar was gigantic; one of the largest of the Voxian people, yet agile enough to fly. Raidar's abilities seemed to hold no boundaries.

"I'll teach those who are coming with me 'connection'; the art of using one another for fighting. It's a wonderful way to escape your enemies, and to keep your partners and allies safe," Raidar said.

The Reptilians looked confused.

Hyedan went to Callouradon. "May I?" he said, touching the Reptilian's arm. Hyedan grew reptile scales, like the skin of his Reptilian friend.

"Now, that's pretty strange, Hyedan," Raidar said laughing.

"I'm Vox-tilian!" Hyedan joked.

The warriors smiled at the new look. The Reptilians looked on in amazement as Bellazard approached him.

"I'm so impressed. So, can we become like you? What else will 'connection' do?" she asked.

"It'll do this!" Hyedan said, as he touched Callouradon's back. He closed his eyes and concentrated.

Cal opened his mouth. He had grown giant white fangs; two sets, one next to the other, like a Voxian.

"Okay, Cal concentrate hard. Think of moving from here to there," Hyedan said, pointing.

Callouradon teleported. He vanished from one place, reappearing in another, but only small distances.

"Now, that's power... " Hyedan said, looking at the others. "This will get stronger with practice!"

"I guess the Reptilians are staying to train with you?" Raidar said.

"No! I wish to follow the mountain warriors if I may?" Deathladon asked.

"Then you follow Raidar, Deathladon. While you, Cal, can follow Hyedan to the city. I will stay with the female Voxians. I'm sure they can teach me a lot!" Bellazard said.

~

Shadow spent lot of time hunting. To keep himself fit and healthy. He'd grown bigger, gaining body mass and weight, finding that he had many abilities. Even his skills to talk had improved.

Orion had heard Shadow's telepathic speech a few times now. It was a shame that he still thought it was in his imagination.

So, Shadow decided to try and communicate with someone who realised he could talk, like Comet or Ghost.

'That's it!' Shadow thought, today he would approach Comet before he started to train. Surely he would realise that wolves have powers of telepathy.

Shadow ran from the forest and went to find Comet.

Ghost hadn't been around for a while. Perhaps she had found something or someone to keep her busy or was training in the city. She didn't exactly have to let anyone know.

The lakeside looked beautiful, surrounded by forests of trees, all secluded. The water gave off warmth, which made it easy to meditate (also very easy to fall to sleep). Fantasia sat in front of her warriors and began to meditate, instructing the others as she did.

"Clear your minds, count backwards from fifty. Think only of the numbers. See only the blackness. Sense the warmth and beauty around you. Breath in fifty, breath out, breath in forty-nine, breath out..." she said.

Bellazard's mind began drifting, seeing trees, and in them sat her lonely wolf friend. His eyes shone brightly, gazing out at her. Then she began drifting even more. She began to focus, thinking clearly, as her eyes flickered for just a moment.

The Voxian female next to her touched Bellazard lightly. As she opened her eyes softly to see why, she was floating high above the middle of the water, in the air.

Fantasia watched as Bellazard suddenly lost her concentration.

"No, Bella, stay relaxed. You're perfectly safe," she said.

Bellazard looked around her. All the women were floating with her, just taking in the sight and smell of the water and enjoying the feeling.

Safire turned to Fantasia, and then they watched the newest member of their family experience her first connection with the Voxians.

Bellazard felt wonderful.

As the women levitated, they all touched the Reptilian, contacting her skin. They became scaled as Hyedan had earlier. Bellazard smiled. "Am I doing that?" she asked. The woman next to her nodded, and they just drifted back into meditation. She had never felt so rested.

Bellazard knew that she would be doing more amazing things as the training progressed, and she couldn't wait. Her new friends were the greatest allies she had ever made.

~

The city was amazing. Cal watched as the warriors lined up in the main square. They all stood in a line. They began a routine, thrashing swords and swinging them, barely missing one another, with such precision that they would stop literally millimetres from each other; even in massive crowds.

"I want to do that!" he said, as the warriors stood lined up together.

"It is a type of Akedo, a martial art from the ancients of Earth." Kale explained.

"Let's get you kitted up!" Hyedan said, as he brought out a large samurai sword. Its hilt was carved with a Reptilian standing, sword held high in victory. The Reptilian looked like Cal. Hyedan had made an attachment for the handle, so that the Reptilian could keep hold of it with his giant claws.

"Now I'm impressed!" Cal said, taking the weapon. "Do I need a sword?" He spread out his claws, showing them to Hyedan.

"Maybe not, but I thought you may want one anyway," Hyedan said.

"How did you know?" Cal said.

"It's my business to know the needs of those who'll join the fight with us," Hyedan laughed. "And you, my friend, wanted a sword."

Cal picked the sword up and felt its power. It was lighter than he'd expected and was easy for him to hold.

"How did you do this?" Cal asked.

"I've done this job for a long time, my friend. I know how big you need the hilt to hold it properly," Hyedan said.

As the city Voxians began to train, they jumped around, swinging acrobatically, climbing up buildings, and into an alleyway. Cal was not confused by all the commotion. He found that he could also use his body mass, but it was different to the Voxians. He began throwing them high. Everything to the advantage of the soldiers while they practiced. They flew in the air, thrashing swords, hitting targets placed in very high positions.

Hyedan could see that those who didn't have flying powers would find Cal an advantageous friend to have.

~

Raidar began the trek up the tallest mountain.

Deathladon found it a little hard to keep up, so Raidar, looking at his large ally, walked back to him.

"This is the hardest training. You would do best to let me fetch Comet; he can adapt your speed, and it'll help you if you can maintain a connection with him," Raidar said.

Deathladon nodded in agreement. He carried on trekking up the mountain terrain.

Comet was at his side in seconds. With one small burst of energy, he jumped up high, and then touched Deathladon's shoulder. He passed Deathladon, and smiled, shouting: "Come on...Keep up!"

From that point on Deathladon did just that. His body began to heave with power.

His breathing slowed right down, and he began travelling at an incredible speed. He passed Stu, who was also training in the mountains with his young friends.

"That's it; let the old Reptilian beat you young men. I thought you were fit!" Deathladon chuckled, as he went by.

"You carry on...we'll meet you at the top!" Halen shouted. The boys all began laughing, then touched Orion's shoulder, and their speed went from fast to incredible. They shot through everyone. They looked like a whirlwind as they sped by and were all standing at the mountain top in a matter of minutes.

Deathladon just carried on at his new faster speed. "This connection thing is fantastic," he said to Comet.

"It's handy when you need to get somewhere fast or protect others from death. It gets you away very quickly, and of course helps catch those feisty little Voxian deer!" Comet said.

Comet had reached the top of the mountain now.

"They're faster than a wild rabbit, which by the way we tend to kill and eat a lot of. But let's face it, we would be overrun with the little devils if we didn't," Comet laughed.

Comet and Deathladon both stood next to the boys, looking on as the rest of the mountain warriors as they began to arrive.

The training went on.

~

Weeks later the training sessions became more frequent, and a lot easier for all.

The males and females began swapping from city to mountain. They trained so that all terrain could be used in the battle against Belial. If there was to be a fight, then they would be ready for it.

The women went back to the lakes for one last session, before they began their battle training. All happy that they could train together, they'd missed their friends and family.

The training was hard without the opposite sex there to help spur on aggression.

"Why would you be sexually attracted to one another before, but won't be now?" Bellazard asked Safire.

"Ah, we still are. The training teaches us control. We gain more when we have practiced combat apart. We use an adaptive connection when having sex, but it's used in a different way. We're extremely rough with one another, but it doesn't harm us," Safire said to Bellazard. "Once we've precise control over our abilities, we are able to use the aggression to protect the vulnerable."

Fantasia stopped the conversation, raising her hand.

She looked into the trees. "Ssssh!" she said to the women with her.

Safire sniffed at the air, and turned to look at her sister...

"Bethadora!" Safire snarled.

Safire began to run, pulling her sword from her long coat. Fantasia was right beside her.

Bellazard felt sudden anger, and the need to do something, anything, attack her enemy. But her mind told her to hang back just for a while.

Suddenly Orion, Halen and Raidar appeared out of nowhere, swords held high as they stood waiting.

Raidar growled. "Stand to the left of the trees, Halen. She may double back and attack here."

"Yes, Father," Halen spun in the air, his giant body agile like an acrobat, spinning off the tightrope and landing perfectly at the end of his show.

Orion sped around the lake borders, listening, and looking all the way around. He was back in only seconds. "Nothing," he said.

"Then we wait for the girls," Raidar said, standing his ground.

Safire appeared first. She had a human man with her who was struggling to get free.

The man was big for a human, with a lot of muscle; what the humans called a bodybuilder type. She threw him

133

forward. He staggered a little as if he had been pushed, and began smiling at the other women, ignoring the Reptilian...and the Voxian men.

Raidar began growling saying under his breath: "Bloody humans!" He growled a little louder, but still the man didn't even acknowledge him.

"Ladies!" He began to approach them, as if he was picking them up in a bar. "Let's be reasonable, I had a job to do and was happy doing it. You are all so...Hmm," he said.

Their attention changed as Fantasia came back. "Nothing," she said. "Gone before we could catch her. What an animal!"

The two sisters looked at the human, still trying to chat up the other women.

"So, what are you doing here?" Safire asked him. "What is your name?"

"I'm Phil, ladies, and this is your lucky day, a dream come true. I was just doing a spot of spying for my mistress when you spotted her. She left me so she could get away," Phil said, still being very cocky.

Fantasia began walking away, ignoring him. He was just her decoy and not all that bright.

"What shall we do with, hmm...him?" Raidar asked, pointing in Phil's direction.

"Just kill him!" Safire said, showing no interest.

Fantasia shrugged at Raidar and walked away as well.

Phil didn't have a chance to protest. With one slash of his blade Raidar finished him. Human or not, he had allied with the enemy, and that wouldn't be tolerated.

"Okay, so, dinnertime I think," Raidar said, not even showing any sign of guilt.

"Beer and Blood?" Halen asked his father.

"Son, you read my mind!" Raidar said, laughing.

CHAPTER 18

Night-time came in Raithar, the northern side of Vox. Beth stood upstairs as she gazed out of the window of a huge house. She stood upstairs. It had bare floorboards, peeling paint and damp window ledges. The house had been empty now for quite a while.

Beth had killed the old woman who had lived there. She burned the woman's remains in her own garden. The charcoal stain was still there amongst the grass and flowers.

The room had peeling wallpaper and the pictures on the wall were of the deceased woman's family and friends.

She began to peel and pick at the blue paint on the windowsill through boredom; bits dropping on the uncarpeted floor.

She waited for her master. He made her do evil things, but she couldn't help it, she had to obey him. Anything he asked, even when she knew it was wrong, she would do it for him with love.

She looked up, staring at the stars, and waited.

Cold suddenly hit the room, a frosty breath that made the hair on the back of her neck stand on end. She cringed; her whole body immobilised as she felt his presence. Her Lord and her love...Belial had arrived.

Beth looked at him, his dark eyes hypnotic...evil.

"Is it arranged?" His deep voice whispered in her ear, lacking any sign of feeling.

"Yes, My Lord," she said to him.

Beth shuddered. She wasn't allowed to show any signs of weakness. Any nervousness would lead to violence.

"When are you going to see the traitor? He must be executed. There's no point keeping him alive, he's of no use to us," Belial said.

"I understand...But, My Lord..." Beth said.

She was cut off there. Belial swung her around to face him, slapping her face hard. Then he threw her onto the hard wooden floor.

"DO NOT interrupt me!" he said, as his eyes flared red.

Beth cupped her hand on her cheek. It stung, and her lip began to bleed. She hated him so much, but she also loved him. What was she doing here?

Beth knew better than to get up, so she stayed down on the floor until he had disappeared again. She then waited a while just in case he came back. Getting to her feet, she walked over to the chair in the room. A chest of drawers sat next to it. She pulled open one of the drawers.

Getting out a cell phone, Beth began dialling...

"Hello, yes, I'm leaving in the morning. I trust all is well?" she said to the prison guard with no emotion in her voice. She hung up, putting the phone back in the drawer, and went down the stairs and out of the house.

Beth thought she had better go hunting, even if it did mean crossing the border. There wasn't a lot left to hunt on Raithar. The forests spanned over thirty acres, and the deer there were few. Normally she could find herself a few rabbits, or smaller animals, but the little creatures bit and went into a type of frenzy when caught. Beth killed them before feeding, it was easier than just letting them go again, because they were so small, and the supply of blood was so little.

She had got away with crossing into Capalia earlier, she would try again.

She began to sprint, her speed picking up. She was in the forest and near the boundaries of Raithar only minutes later. She went towards the cliffs edge, the sea a huge barrier between her and Capalia, making out the thick forests and seeing the mountains as she gazed across, her home was still there somewhere.

"Capalians, who do they think they are?" she snarled and went to turn away, maybe tonight was not the right time to step into enemy territory.

She caught sight of two bright, red eyes looking at her from across the sea. It made her stop dead in her tracks. The figure just waited in the thick of the forest. She shivered nervously, turning her back on the Capalian spy.

Beth turned around again quickly, but the small lights had gone.

"Flynn?" she whispered. Her heart sank with disappointment, and she sighed, walking away.

She didn't want food anymore. Her heart began to ache for her lost love.

~

The air was clear, the night sky warm and full of stars. Gazing over at the Raitharns forests, Flynn sighed as he took off across the water. It glimmered underneath him. He had to give Beth one last chance.

The giant man landed in a small clearing in the forest. He felt a little afraid. If he was caught, he would definitely be signing his own death warrant.

"Beth...can you hear me? Beth!" he whispered, but there was no reply. "Please, Beth, I need you to come home with me."

Still there was silence.

Flynn sighed and looked down at the ground. He couldn't understand why she wouldn't talk to him. He had seen her standing on the cliffs edge. He gave one more look around the wooded area. He turned, leaving again, heading back towards Capalia, looking back only once. He saw the figure of a woman peering out from the trees. He knew then that he had lost to the Demon. Belial had taken his one true love, leaving Flynn with his broken heart that could never mend.

Beth fell to her knees, feeling wretched, as she watched Flynn disappear into the night. She sobbed uncontrollably, knowing that she would never again be able to hold or kiss him.

She would remain yearning for the one man she had truly loved and lost for the rest of her eternal life.

~

Raidar, Halen and Kale had settled down for the night. They were watching a comedy about a girl vampire meeting a human boy.

"What a pile of absolute rubbish! Humans don't get it, do

they? Nothing in the Multiverse would make anyone screw around with a Vardu, they're dead! You would have more chance of screwing with a stuffed animal! Not that I would...I mean, yak!" Halen stammered as his father came in to the room, and just gave him a strange look.

Kale laughed. None of them felt comfortable talking about sex. Halen had turned red and looked back at the television.

Raidar pretended he heard nothing, walking past smiling to himself.

The lights were off, but a noise outside made the two brothers jump from their seats.

"Intruder!" Kale whispered.

The men raised their swords and stood, prepared to fight, as the intruder stepped closer. There were footsteps coming across the pathway.

Raidar stood next to the door, waiting for it to open.

"I didn't manage to sneak up on you all then. Not even when you're watching..." he turned and looked at the television. "What the Hell is that?" Flynn caught sight of the film. "Oh, for the Goddess's sake guys, it's a chick flick?" he said.

Raidar laughed. His face brightened the second he heard the familiar voice.

"Flynn, you're home. How the Hell are you?" Raidar said, taking his eldest son's arm, pulling him in for a hug.

His brothers jumped into them both, dropping their swords on the hallway floor.

"Hey, that's no way to treat your weapons!" Raidar said. The boys picked them up and put them away.

"Sorry Pops." They both said in unison.

"This calls for people...people and celebrations!" Kale said, using his telepathy to contact Orion. "Man! I know it's late, but PARTY!"

"Cool, do I spread the word?" Orion asked.

Raidar butted in. "Tell your grandfather that the prodigal son has returned. There is much partying to be done. Spread the word, the beer is already flowing!" Raidar shouted excitedly.

Orion had never heard Raidar sound so happy. He found it a little scary. The big man smiling at something would be enough to make anyone run away quickly.

"Bring our human friend. I'm sure Flynn will be pleased to meet him; the man honoured with our powers," Raidar said.

"Okay, I will give him a call!" said Orion.

"Cool!" Raidar said.

Orion headed off to tell the rest of his family.

When he got to the Manor, Comet and Safire were already there with Stu. Comet had heard the good news and was gathering those wishing to go. The mountain house was a good hour away for those who could not teleport, (Meaning Stu, who didn't like it).

"Jeep, I believe, will be best for the terrain. Raidar lives on top of the mountain!" Comet said.

"Let's make tracks then," Stu said with excitement. He had never met a map maker before.

"Does he have wings, like Kathos?" Stu asked.

"Well, yes and no, he has large black Devil wings, and deep red eyes. He looks more like a Demon than Belial does," Comet said.

"Dude, REALLY?" Stu said, looking a little nervous.

"No, his wings are white, like Kathos, but his eyes can glow red. I do enjoy how gullible you are, Stu," Comet said with a chuckle.

"Dude! Don't joke like that," Stu said, relieved.

~

Heavy metal music blasted throughout the house, even before the guests arrived. The place filled quickly.

All were introduced.

Flynn thought Stu would be an interesting ally to train with. It would be nice to meet the human.

Shadow was first to appear. He turned up at the house, before going off to guard the perimeter of the forest.

As far as Shadow was concerned, Beth had made the mistake of coming to Capalia once. He wasn't going to let her in a second time. He had heard a pack of wolves on the west side of the forest. They would be handy in a fight, and could give warning of spies coming on the island

Ghost turned up as the second guest but stayed in the background.

Memory from her long forgotten past seemed to be edging its way back. She recognised so much of Vox; it was a permanent déjà vu. Nothing was clear, and no one seemed to recognise her. She kept wearing the mask; not realising that it would stop people identifying her. She had it on for so long now; it had become a part of her.

The party went on until the small hours of the morning, then crowds began to disperse at around 4.00am.

Kale and Orion went off racing one another, in the mountain terrain, on quad bikes. Halen and Raidar had begun arm wrestling. Stu and Flynn walked through the large garden. It was lawned, with roses and hedgerows. Flowers and colours all greyed in the dark skies. Flynn was talking about his job as map maker, asking Stu about how he felt being on a strange planet.

"Is there no sand or deserts here? I haven't heard any mention of lions and tigers here either," Stu said.

"We have tigers; they're further afield in the jungle terrain." Flynn pointed. "Just beyond the mountains. Vox is a big planet, my friend, big enough to share with all species."

Stu was impressed.

"We took some from Earth when the species started being hunted by humans. Their numbers had been getting less. Kathos doesn't like the survival of the fittest stuff! If it faces extinction, we'll try to help it to survive," Flynn said. "I believe tigers and lions survive here in their thousands."

Stu's eyes were closing as sleep was winning, even as they walked along.

"Let me take you home. We tend to forget that man needs to sleep. I'll tell my father we're leaving, and I can have you home quickly," Flynn said.

As Flynn went back inside, shouts of goodnight came

through as others also left, the party dwindling down slowly but surely.

Flynn came back from the house, grabbing Stu around the waist, picking him up from the floor, as if he were lighter than a feather.

Like an eagle, Flynn just took off from the ground, his white wings extending. Wobbling a little at first, as Stu struggled slightly in the shock of being just taken.

"This is awesome, man!" Stu shouted.

As they flew, he dreamed of telling the friends on Earth how he had a friend who could fly. They would never believe him.

"Dude," he said, yawning.

Stu stared at the scenery around him. It was breath-taking. He was at his front door in minutes.

Flynn bowed, leaving immediately, bidding a goodnight to his new friend.

Stu was in bed and asleep shortly after that.

CHAPTER 19

Beth's red sports car raced through the countryside of Raithar. As she gazed over the hills she could see the prison building on top of a hill, huge, wired fencing surrounding its grounds. She knew that today was the day. She would persuade her brother to come with her, and fight on Belial's side.

As the car raced closer to the building, Beth ran through what she was going to say in her head. She would help him to understand why he should join them.

"Pass key...my pass key!" she mumbled to herself, while searching around her car glove compartment. She was nearing the gates now, and everything was always double checked there.

The engine revved as she came to a stop at the gates.

She pressed the buzzer...

"Hello!" There was no answer. "Damn those guards; they're hopeless. Why we employ thick arseholes like these I never know. It wouldn't happen anywhere else," she said.

She pressed the buzzer again. The gate opened without her using the pass key at all.

"What the Hell are these people doing? I could be anyone," she mumbled.

Beth drove her car through, parked it, and then began to walk up to the doors of the building. They'd been left open.

Beth felt uncomfortable. Something wasn't quite right.

As she entered the building all was silent.

Beth checked the first cell with an inmate. She was sat in her black prison overalls. Why was this poor woman there, you may ask? Well, it wasn't for being a thief or murderer; it was for using her powers without her master's permission.

Not a good idea if you live in Raithar. All powers were forbidden. Her Lord didn't like anyone challenging his power.

Beth entered the corridor. As she turned she felt fresh air hitting her face.

'Impossible.' The walls were thick, and there were no windows to the outside.

She sped up, heading towards the corridor, where her brother's cell was. When she got there, two guards lay unconscious on the floor by the cell. She noticed a big hole in the side of the wall.

"Damn! Those bloody useless guards," Beth shouted. "The only way they could have been knocked unconscious is by spell casting. That vile animal Lexis. I bet he taught Rellik how to do it; he must have," she said furious.

Bethadora pulled her sword out and swung hard, aiming down. Both the guards' heads rolled from their bodies onto the cold white floor. Blood poured.

Beth lit the prison fire (Belial had it there for the dead) and threw the two bodies and heads onto it, watching for a while as they began to burn.

"If you can't do your jobs properly, don't join the team," she said angrily.

Jumping through the hole in the prison wall, she began searching for tracks.

Rellik had left none. She would have to try a psychic scan, in the hope that she could trace him. But she would have to do this without being caught using her powers by Belial.

Beth cleared her mind and began to concentrate. She could only find fragments of his trail.

In other words, Rellik was long gone...

CHAPTER 20

The training began every day except for Stu. His human body couldn't take all the exercise. "Heart attack city," Orion said.

There were wrestling matches between the males and yoga for the females. The Voxians thought this was great exercise, loving the competition with one another.

Fighting styles were different. Voxians were faster than the Reptilians, everything becoming intense and precise.

Raidar believed that no human should ever stand in the middle of a Voxian fight. It would be like trying to stop a train moving at full speed.

Matches would last for hours, before either opponent showed any sign of fatigue. Amazing to other species, the Voxians fought without weapons; just sheer brute force and showed no mercy towards one another, except the usual no killing rule.

Vox had gone from reasonably populated, to full. It was like summer in Stratford-Upon-Avon on Earth, just as the tourists arrived.

Warriors who resided on different planets were returning, including the map makers and star gazers. They wished to be with Kathos, and fight by his side.

Ghost had decided to leave her cave in the mountains. When she arrived for training, she appeared concerned about something.

"Where is Shadow?" she said to herself, she teleported.

Ghost appeared at the Manor. Shadow wasn't anywhere on the Estate, so she decided to look in the woods close by. Surely he wouldn't be that far away from his family.

Shadow seemed to be off doing his own thing while the others trained, which wasn't like him at all.

Ghost remembered her psychic link with him when they were on Titan. Shadow was a comfort to her in that 'large dome shaped Hell,' and had saved her life many times. She had grown to love him. She felt relaxed when she stroked his beautiful black fur. She would breathe in her friend's calming spirit.

After searching the forests, Ghost headed back to Orion's house on the estate, he was at home. She went to the back of the house, walking through the garden area to Orion's home, where the music was coming from.

Orion was head banging. His hair waved through the air, long and slightly sweaty now, as he nodded his head backward and forwards, turning round as he played his 'air guitar.' He stopped when he noticed Ghost, so she signalled him to turn down the loud music. Orion sarcastically put his hand up to his ear and cupped it, mouthing: "WHAT!"

Ghost rolled her eyes, and then took a sharp intake of breath. She began to shout: "Orion! Turn off the music... "I SAID..!" And then she paused, as she heard herself loudly through the silence. "Idiot!" she said, just loud enough for Orion to hear. Orion smirked at her.

"What? What did I do?" he asked her, shrugging innocently.

"Where's Shadow?" she said, ignoring his attempt at humour.

"In the conservatory, behind the chair. He's usually there when he isn't out and about. I put his bed there, so he tends to hide there when he wants some peace and quiet. I think it's the moving from planet to planet that did it. But he's okay," Orion said.

Orion gave a whistle.

Shadow came padding through from the conservatory. Ghost watched as he entered the room. His body was more muscular. She was a little stunned at first. Standing on all fours, Shadow was around four feet in height. His coat shone beautifully, and he looked extremely healthy.

On Earth the humans would have been terrified of an animal this big.

Shadow wagged his tail and walked in. He sat down next to his master.

"Oh, My Goddess, he's gigantic!" Ghost said.

"I know, he's been growing since we got here. He's bigger than the other wolves," Orion said, patting Shadow's back lightly.

Ghost went to approach him, but Shadow's ears flicked to attention, and he growled.

Ghost was about to back off when Shadow jumped to his feet. Running past her, he began heading towards the gates of the Estate.

Ghost sighed; it wasn't her he was growling at. She watched as he threw himself at the gates, and they crashed open.

When Ghost and Orion arrived, Beth was already running. She was panicking so much she forgot she could teleport. You could see she was afraid of the massive animal. Well, she was the one who'd left him for dead years ago. Shadow hadn't forgotten her betrayal to his family.

"Run witch, run!" Orion shouted, laughing as Shadow gave chase.

She didn't turn back; she just kept running, with Shadow snapping at her heels.

The dog's mouth began to foam, full of saliva, his teeth bearing at her with his fangs out, gnashing and barely missing her. He caught her ankle a few times, making her leg bleed.

"I can't believe a Voxian would be scared of anything," Orion said.

He whistled, and Shadow stopped in his tracks, then the wolf returned to his master, leaving Beth almost tripping over her own clumsy feet.

Shadow sat at Orion's side.

Orion patted him. "Good boy, you got her a couple of times then? Shame those marks won't be permanent, mate. But well done anyway."

"Okay that's it...What have you done with the real Shadow?" Ghost said joking, also patting him on the head.

"Hmm... I don't know, but this one is kinda cool!" Orion said.

Stu stumbled around the corner, heading back to the Estate

gates from Limly, the nearest village. He was looking a little dazed, and was rubbing the top of his head, and holding the side of his right arm.

"Dude, did you see the chick?" Stu asked Orion. "She's the one from Titan, man."

The two friends ran to his aid. Beth had attacked him. She had entered the Estate, going for the weakest warrior. Her intention was to cause grief. She wanted to kill the Capalians new ally.

Orion sped to Stu grabbing his friend, checking him over.

"What did that bitch do to you?" Orion asked.

"She only had time to grab me. She knocked me hard with something on the head. Man, have I got a headache now," Stu said, as he held his head again?

Ghost began chanting, taking hold of Stu's arm. As her hands touched him he began healing immediately. She looked at him, "this won't hurt," Ghost said, with a cheeky grin, chanting once again.

Stu's headache faded; his head stopped hurting.

"That's awesome!" Stu said. He took his hand away from his head, which had been bleeding.

"We need to find Kathos and my mother, to tell them what happened," Orion said, patting Shadow's side.

Shadow followed.

Comet appeared, sword in hand, closely followed by Fantasia, Drakos and Kathos.

Comet became calm as he spotted Stu and the others, and they were okay.

"Beth got Stu, but Shadow heard her attack and gave chase," Ghost said, patting the dog proudly.

"Jesus, he's got big! What you been feeding him?" Halen said, stepping out from the gates of the Estate, sword in his hand.

The warriors laughed.

"He's been hunting. He doesn't eat tinned dog food anymore," Orion said, looking at the dog once more.

Halen went over to Shadow and began stroking his fur.

"You're getting a pretty awesome beast," he said to Shadow, rubbing him with his hand. Shadow rubbed into Halen with his head and face.

"Hey, why's Beth afraid of Shadow?" Orion asked, looking at his mother and father.

"Who knows?" Fantasia said.

The family and friends went into the Manor.

As they arrived, so did Sky, she appeared in the room.

"We are just talking about the new version of Shadow, trying to understand why he has grown to such a massive size." Said Orion.

"Shadow's the leader of wolves here," she said. "He got his powers when Orion, Stu and I did, when he was present at the ceremony," she smiled. Shadow went over to greet her.

"The more ceremonies, the more power he gains!" she said.

"Shadow's been twice to my knowledge," Orion said.

"Actually, he's probably attended more than that." Kathos said.

"Of course, that would do it, wouldn't it?" said Ghost.

Shadow's Voxian blood had rejuvenated, after lying dormant while he grew up on Earth.

"Can you describe what you noticed about Shadow?" Sky asked.

She pulled a small note pad from the pocket in her jeans.

Orion sighed.

"He has faster speed, bigger fangs, and his eyes change colour from deep gold when he's powered up to the usual dark brown when he isn't," Orion said.

He couldn't help thinking his sister was a pain in his arse.

"He originated from Raithar. On Earth he's identical to a breed called German shepherd dog. But the breed doesn't have abilities like Shadow."

Before Orion began getting sarcastic, Fantasia asked "So, how many wolves like him are there, I wonder?"

"I'm not sure; around six of them," Sky said, looking behind her mother.

As Fantasia turned, there in the gardens, by the patio window, stood five large wolves, gigantic white teeth smiling as they panted, with tongues hanging out.

They sat inside the doorway, while Fantasia took another look.

At the front of the pack was a cream and white bitch. She had got blue/silver eyes. She sat wagging her tail. Sky called her.

"This is Spirit; she's Shadow's mate!" Sky said.

Spirit went to run to Shadow, but then noticed Ghost. She began wagging her tail frantically, rolling onto her back. Spirit began whining like she knew her. Ghost looked on amazed that the wolf seemed to like her.

So, Orion started stroking Shadow. "You got yourself a girlfriend. Good for you, you dark horse!" He laughed.

Drakos started moaning.

"Not more bloody dogs, if they stay build them their own kennels, because I'm damned if they're all living in here."

"Of course, they can live with us," Fantasia said stubbornly.

"Great, that's bloody marvellous," Drakos said, storming out in a huff to the library, mumbling loudly all the way.

"We can breed them," Sky shouted in his general direction, just to rub it in a bit more.

"That's fine, but only if you keep the puppies at your house," Fantasia said loudly, playing along.

The others laughed, as they could still hear Drakos mumbling at every word said.

"They can stay with mc. I've no objections to that," Sky said.

Drakos was still mumbling.

"Spirit can live with me. After all, we already seem to have struck up a good friendship. She'll like the mountain terrain; plenty of fresh air, and close enough for her to still meet up with her other family," Ghost said. "I'll be happy to have her; my caves are big enough to accommodate our friends."

Sky nodded with approval, and Spirit didn't seem to be objecting either, so the attention changed from Spirit to the others, still sitting in the doorway.

"These two can come back with me," Halen said. "Dad would be pleased to have them." Halen stood stroking the two black and tan males.

"They're called Jake and Karn." Sky said.

Both sat firmly beside him, wagging their tails. Halen loved it; the wolves seemed to understand.

Sky looked at the two pure tan females who sat next to her. "Gem and Charm will come with me! It appears the wolves have picked where they want to go themselves, which is a good thing," Sky said.

The wolves disappeared to hunt, and on that the Voxian warriors decided that fresh blood would be good, so joined them.

"I believe we've found another ally against the armies of Belial," Halen said.

"Our warrior count is getting bigger by the day. We should inform Bellazard and the others about our new members," Kathos said.

"Don't tell me, Grandfather, we're having another meeting," Orion said.

"Well, that's one of your better ideas, Orion!" Kathos chuckled, hugging Orion.

"Meeting in one hour," Kathos said to the others with a smile. "Spread the word."

CHAPTER 21

Can a brother forgive his sister for imprisonment? For the separation from the family he loved. For the killing of his wife? Could Rellik forget his feelings of hate? The torture and the terror he had been put through at the hands of Beth. This, I doubt very much.

What about accusations of treason against his father the King? Even though Rellik was innocent of these crimes.

Rexus believed his brother was a traitor. Beth had already told him that.

Still Rellik put his faith in the Capalians. He believed that one day he would be allowed to defend his honour and be free once more to live amongst his fellow warriors.

~

Beth walked through the prison corridor, looking for clues of escape, but found nothing. She would have to really move herself if she wanted to find Rellik, one thing she did know, he hadn't reached Capalia yet, that was evident when she had her close encounter of the wolf kind, she bent down rubbing her ankle, it had nearly recovered.

Her feet were faster than the car she had left parked outside. Her hope was she could use her powers, without being found out. Death would be her penalty.

It was hard work running that distance, but she had no choice. All she could do was hope Rellik's captivity would have made him slow.

Replacement guards approached.

Beth shouted to them: "Fix this wall, and when you've done that, stay alert! We have an escaped criminal on the loose. He may double back. You need to be on the lookout...Oh and keep this information from Belial. You must close your minds," Beth said.

The two men nodded as Beth began to run, her speed blurring her shape. She vanished.

Beth could reach high speeds, but she never managed to outrun Rellik, not even when they were children.

Beth had to get to the border before he did, otherwise it would be too late. He would cross the water, and her life would not be worth living.

The Capalians would probably kill him anyway. They wouldn't recognise him. He looked nothing like he did before his captivity. The torturous treatment had changed him. He had gone from the beautiful young virile man that he was, to older than any Voxian she had ever seen; that is except for Mallick her father's strange friend.

"RELLIK!" Beth shouted.

Silence!

Only a small echo from her voice carried across the water. She waited and then moved to another part of the border quickly, she called again all the time aware that Belial could be watching, listening.

Beth sighed; she would have to stop! She realised she was too late.

~

Rellik didn't stop. He kept heading south, and just ran. He was unfit, finding every stride difficult, but he had to keep up his speed. He had a lucky escape.

The guards came into his cell. He pretended to be asleep. He was going to be questioned again, and he had been subjected to this every day.

They tried to talk him into becoming one of them, a traitor to his father. But he was stronger than they realised; he'd refused.

Radonna was murdered by his sister. He would never be the same without her; he had loved her so much.

He remembered her long silver/white hair, and those beautiful soulful eyes, he could stare into for hours. His love, the most beautiful woman he had ever laid eyes on, now wiped out.

Rellik kept running, even though he was exhausted.

Beth would soon catch up to him. After all, she had been able to feed properly, and was stronger than him now.

Suddenly he heard a noise. He slowed down, hiding as she

tore past him. Rellik adapted his camouflage; he held onto the bark of the tree and changed to blend into the woodland.

Beth STOPPED!

She began to look around.

"Rellik! Come on, I know you're here somewhere... I love you. Don't betray me," she said.

'Betray her?' Rellik thought, keeping still and silent. *'It was her who had betrayed him.'*

She looked over the water at the forests of Capalia, sighed and walked slowly away, turning now and heading back towards the prison building.

Rellik sighed. Beth looked around. All Rellik could do was hold his breath and hope she hadn't heard him.

She picked up speed again and was gone.

Rellik breathed out loudly. He had outsmarted Beth and the prison guards. She would have killed him. After all, she had already done a good job of torturing him. As far as he was concerned, she deserved everything she was about to get.

Rellik's wings opened. He struggled to take off; he had not flown for a while. He told himself it would be okay; this was his only option across the water. Too low on energy to walk across or run, it would be too much of a gamble. He still ran the chance of being seen, no matter what he did, so he opted for the fastest way off the mess he had escaped from.

He took off clumsily, hitting the surface of the water a few times, before gaining his flight pattern. His wings tired, but he got to the other side quickly, hitting the grass bank with a thud. He rolled behind some large rocks, and fell unconscious, dreaming of his own death...

Rellik woke up when a cold wet nose nudged at his face. He stirred, and then panicked, trying to struggle to his feet, looking at the black wolf with giant white fangs glistening as the animal snarled at him.

It must have been hours since he landed here. The sky had darkened.

He jumped to his feet, catching sight of a lizard-type creature, (Bellazard), who had been out walking with

Shadow.

"Hold on, now then, boy," Bellazard said to the wolf.

Rellik stumbled. Not only was he staring into the face of a giant lizard, but it talked.

It wore a large red cloak and a crown. Rellik shook his head...maybe he was still asleep and would wake up any second.

When this didn't happen, he thought of other reasons why the lizard would be here.

"Has there been an invasion?" Rellik asked.

Bellazard said nothing, and the wolf just snarled at him.

"Shadow! Good boy! Stay calm, I think we've found ourselves one of those Voxian spies," Bellazard said.

"Spy...I'm no spy. I'd like to know what you're doing here on my father's land," Rellik said.

"You know Kathos?" Bellazard said, surprised.

"Of course. I'm Rellik, his eldest Son!"

"Oh, I see, so you are a spy. So, did Beth send you here?" Bellazard asked him.

"I'm not answering any more of your questions. I don't know who you are, or why you're here, but I demand you take me back to the Manor Estate to see my father." Rellik looked panicked.

"Sorry, no can do!" Bellazard said. "He's away on business, but Fantasia's there. I can take you to see her."

Rellik agreed, and the three began to walk slowly home.

~

Every step taken, Shadow snarled and snapped at Rellik's legs.

"For Shylaya's sake, call off your hound!" Rellik said angrily.

"Shadow, come to heel," Bellazard ordered.

Shadow stayed with Bellazard but was keeping a close eye on Rellik. One thing was certain, Beth would not be following him because she hated this wolf and knew him all too well.

As they came to the village, people stared as the stranger

entered. They wondered if he was another ally, or if Bellazard and Shadow had found another Voxian traitor. Whichever it was, the news travelled fast.

Rellik hung his head in fear of being recognised. Without verification of innocence from the family he could be attacked, just for being there.

Bellazard sensed his nervousness, so picked up pace and took him straight to Fantasia, who was waiting outside.

"Fantasia...I'm not a traitor!" Rellik said.

"We need to talk. Grandfather has been informed that you're here. He will be on his way back soon. First he's to contact the United Nations of Earth. They need to negotiate with one another about the battle with Belial and Beth. I will listen to you and make my own judgement," Fantasia said very straight faced, very distant for her.

She could see by his condition; he had been through Hell. Or at least it appeared that way.

His gentle face had hardened; his long black hair had turned a ghostly white. Instead of looking in his thirties, he looked in his late fifties. His face had wrinkles, and his eyes dark circles under them. He looked tired.

"Perhaps you should have a lie down, Uncle. It'll be hard enough to tell of your time in captivity. Perhaps it would be better for you to wait for Kathos's return. You can tell us all your news then," Fantasia said.

Rellik nodded. She led him to a small room, with cream paint and a single bed, used usually for Voxians who had injuries, the bedding brightly coloured as if for a child. It was the old first aid room.

Rellik didn't bother looking around anymore and fell asleep almost immediately.

Fantasia touched his forehead, watching his escape through her telepathic powers. He had been through a lot. She believed him innocent. She connected with Comet, asking for him to make this clear before Raidar came home.

Raidar and Rellik were best friends, and to Raidar this had made his treachery worse. Fantasia realised the minute Raidar stepped foot back onto Vox, he would be out to kill his old friend.

As far as Raidar was concerned his friend was a traitor.

BLAZE & BELLAZARD

RAIDAR, STU, ORION & SHADOW

THE MOUNTAIN WARRIORS

THE CITY WARRIORS

KATHOS, BELIAL & THE LADY IN WHITE

THE GROUND BATTLE

CHAPTER 22

Beth stood in the forest for a while. She began to pace.

She knew she had to go back and face her master at some point. Better sooner than later, she thought. But what if Belial thought she had let her brother go on purpose?

"No...No, he wouldn't; he would know my loyalty was true to him," she mumbled quietly. Taking a deep breath, she headed through the forests, back to the prison and her waiting car.

"If Raidar is at home, Rellik will be dead by now anyway; headless and bloody, burning in the flames of Hell," she told herself.

Beth's mind raced. She knew the punishment for this would be bad. Belial didn't like being let down.

But how would he punish her?

So, jumping into her red convertible, she pressed the button, waiting for the roof to unfold. She watched as the roof slowly swung itself over the car and the sound of the click as it placed itself.

Driving was difficult when she was considering her own death. Her body filled with panic, palpitations hammering into her throat. She turned the key in the ignition. It was hard for her to concentrate on driving, she was shaking so much, but it would get her back slowly and she needed time to think.

"Perhaps I could find some protection; someone else to blame... but there's no protection from him. What a crock of shit!" Beth laughed nervously to herself.

Beth had nowhere to go but back to him. Her master would probably kill her for letting Rellik escape, even though she had killed the guards of the prison for letting him go. The blame would be hers, and she would be punished for their incompetence.

She could face eternity in the realms of Hell, when she told her master what had happened.

Within no time, Beth arrived back at the old woman's

house; she could see Belial already awaiting her arrival.

"So?" he asked.

Her mouth began to open, and a jittering sound was all that would come out.

His eyes looked deep and dark. He wasn't happy to see her at all.

Beth dropped to the floor outside the house, where he had come to greet her.

"You have failed me, haven't you?" Belial's face filled with anger; his arm raised. "Why did you let him escape? You are a stupid GIRL!"

His eyes darkened, then turned red. His black wings spread from his back, and he inhaled sharply. He began pacing up and down by the front door.

Beth stayed on her knees, just looking up at her master.

"I didn't let him escape. Those incompetent guards didn't do their duty. They were the ones who failed us," Beth said.

"But you hired them!" Belial's eye's shone red.

Then Belial stopped pacing.

He stared at her and smiled, but only the very corners of his mouth moved in an upward position.

"You are loyal to me?" Belial said.

He began stroking her face, as if she was his pet.

"Yes, My Lord. How can I show you?" she replied.

An evil smile came over Belial's face as he looked at her.

"Oh, you'll show me. I will tell you more when the time is right," he said.

Beth sighed with relief. At least she had escaped with her life. But what did he want from her in return?

Belial stood to one side, letting Beth through the door. He disappeared from the place, leaving Beth to wonder what proving herself would mean.

Little did she know that Belial was planning the greatest sacrifice she could give.

Beth had survived, but the cost she hadn't really thought about. Right now, she didn't care much about it either; she would face that problem when she had to.

For those who knew Belial well enough, realised how high a price Beth would have to pay.

CHAPTER 23

Orion stared at a fanged rabbit in amazement, as he walked around the gardens.

"Do all the animals here have the same defence mode as us?" Orion asked.

"Pretty much," Safire said. "The only creatures that don't are dreavils; they're a Voxian version of a cow."

The two carried on walking. As Orion looked around he caught sight of other animals all doing the same thing, with fangs showing in disapproval of being disturbed.

"You wouldn't want to put your fingers by them," Orion chuckled, putting his hands in his pockets. "How do you deal with these?"

"We just leave them; they aren't big enough to replenish our powers. We would have to hunt all year round to keep sustained! So, we just let them be that way no-one gets hurt," Safire said.

"They're really vicious looking. Is there anything here that don't have fangs?" Orion said.

"Yes...birds! They have beaks," Safire said, a little sarcastically.

Laughter came from the house. Fantasia and Drakos were talking to one another. Both Orion and Safire looked over at the kitchen window, which was open. Fantasia and Drakos were baking cookies.

"Tell me about mother, before Earth?" He asked, walking away from the smell of the baking, and further into the gardens.

"What would you like to know?" Safire said.

"I just wondered why she made the decision to leave Vox. Earth's good, but why would she give up all of this to be... on Earth?" he asked.

"When Kaos was killed, Fantasia was unable to deal with his loss. Saul had made the Capalian people look differently at her. She believed she had helped kill him," Safire said.

"But that's madness!"

"Your mother understands that now, but grief can make you do some funny things. She wanted to escape her own thoughts of Kaos's death and Saul's betrayal to Kathos. Earth was the closest to our life here and had a good atmosphere, that is before pollution started destroying it" Safire said.

They both sat on a garden bench.

"So, Hyedan's daughter: Is she Voxian, or has she got Earth ties like us?" Orion asked, going a little pink.

"Hmm. Azaya is Voxian. She's sixteen, almost seventeen now. Her ceremony will be next summer, so she's three years younger than you," Safire said smiling.

"So, she doesn't have all her powers yet then?" Orion said, trying to work it all out in his head.

"No.," Safire smiled.

Orion spotted Stu in the doorway of the house, large cookie in his hand, with a bite missing. He pointed in Stu's direction, and Safire suddenly realised the talk was over. With the mention of Azaya, he was feeling a little uncomfortable.

"Got to go, Stu's here," Orion said.

Orion got up and walked quickly away.

"See you later," Safire said, sitting back down on the bench, her nephew already meant so much to her.

The boys greeted one another. Stu looked over at Safire and smiled, waving as Orion ushered him into the house and out of sight.

CHAPTER 24

<u>UNITED NATIONS</u>

"A fast approach would look like an invasion," Kathos told his warriors, "so approach with caution."

"Father, can you clarify what the UN is?" Genesis asked.

"Yes, of course. In layman's terms, they're people brought together to represent all included countries. They don't have one main leader, but all countries involved have a spokesperson, and things get extremely complicated. They put together talks about global warming and war, making a lot of decisions. They debate peace, and intervene in times of crisis; like earthquakes, sending aid in. The war with Russia and Ukraine should be mentioned, as the Russian leader as forcefully attacked and killed many innocent people, this is against UN law, so the European countries and the Americans have got together and are providing the Ukrainians with weapons to help combat an illegal take over!" Kathos paused for a second. "They're people who negotiate and listen, so that they can prevent unnecessary fighting. Well respected by most, only now and again some countries go against them and don't listen, unfortunately."

"This sounds very complex," Genesis said.

"So, why are we here?" Halen asked, butting in.

"This time it is not another human they have to fight against, but one of the all-powerful. If the humans wish us to help, it would be polite to get the permission of those who are in charge." Kathos said.

The Voxians teleported down to the planet, they had precise location details and had put themselves an ocean away from the point of destination, on a private beach away from humans heading for Geneva, Switzerland.

"Remember, we all dance together." Raidar said with a smile.

He raised his arms from his side to above his head and his body left the floor, The Mountain warriors did the same, some with wings, some just floating above the water's edge. Then City warriors did a similar thing, but they added an extra buzz to their ability as the warriors placed their feet to the top of the water, they slid like ballet dancers across the top, it was amazing to see, like a small army of superpowers heading to save the planet.

All of them moved faster than the eye could comprehend, but if humans could see it, they would have been astounded.

All in sync with each other, it took only a few minutes to arrive on the other side.

Then they ran at Voxian high speed to the UN building.

Comet looked at the huge complex in front of him.

They noticed the humans who had been outside looked shocked as they suddenly appeared. They realised that the humans would be afraid as soon as they set eyes on the Voxians.

There were a few screams and the people at the front of the building began running.

There was no way to soften their abrupt appearance, without looking aggressive.

Also, a Mountain warrior's prowess and large stature, mohawk, leather coat, were not the usual suited and booted delegate that sat within these walls.

"The fastest way in will be to teleport in there. It's madness, but we have to," Kathos said.

"What if that doesn't work?" Genesis asked him.

"It will, but I may need my powers. We can teleport to the inside of the conference room. The humans are debating now. Our size will make them aggressive towards us. Also, the fact we're interrupting with no authority will really do the trick. They've armed guards, so try not to react - Halen. Please - try not to kill them before we've had chance to speak!" Ledawna said smiling.

"Me...React?" Halen said.

"Typical, you are just like your father." Ledawna laughed.

More humans on the outside of the building were causing a noise now, they knew they had to move.

"OK! NOW!" Halen ordered.

The Voxians teleported inside the building.

The ceilings were high, and there was row upon row of seats with desks, all full.

The men and women sat with the name of the country they represented on the front of their desks which were placed around the room.

The guards guns all pointed straight at the intruders.

The meeting fell silent, as the strangers walked down the stairs in silence, heading towards the Head Speaker.

Alarms began ringing.

The Guards were shouting orders at one another, and to the Voxians.

"STOP!" soldiers shouted. "GET DOWN!" someone shouted at the delegates.

"STOP YOURSELF!" Halen shouted back, watching with amusement as the delegates vanished under their desks.

The soldiers remained still, pointing guns, as they looked at the newcomers. The soldiers watched on as the Voxians paid no attention, and just continued down the staircase. They didn't take too kindly at being ignored by these huge invaders.

"STOP OR I'LL SHOOT!" one of the armed security men shouted.

Halen had his hand ready on his sword, which was lying in the lining of his long jacket. He was thinking to himself that, although a gun can't kill him, it may just hurt a little, like a bee sting.

"Hold your position," the officer said to his men.

"Yeah, hold your position," Halen laughed.

The Head delegate rose from his seat, trying to clear his throat to speak. The other delegates began popping up from behind the desks to see what was going on.

Halen stood in front of his King and Queen, offering himself as protection, if the shit hit the fan.

One trigger happy guard fired his gun.

The humans began screaming and ducked under tables

again. Screams could be heard outside the room as chaos reigned. More trigger-happy guards came running in, with guns firing in the air.

"STOP!" the Head delegate shouted.

Halen growled loudly. Kale grabbed him on Kathos's orders, the last thing needed was his hot-headed antics.

"Who are you people? Why have you come here?" The head delegate asked.

Kathos walked over in greeting, bowing at the brave man.

"Sir, I am Kathos, King of the Voxian people, and we are here to help you," he said.

The delegate looked a little confused.

"Why...? What would we need your help for?" the head delegate said, suspiciously.

"This world as you know it is coming to an end. We can help you prevent this," Kathos said.

"Why is it ending? Why would you help us?" the head delegate asked, still confused.

As far as these people were concerned nothing needed to be sorted out, all here were perfectly safe.

Kathos stepped forwards so he could stand alone, and then he glowed. He turned looking to his men.

Comet approached. The next step he saw in the human's mind wasn't good. The only words he picked up were ready, aim and fire!

"Sir, is that all you human people can think of for a solution, believe me you have already a bigger threat that is about to rear its ugly head than my people turning up on your doorstep. Our people have lived amongst you for many years, ever since Voxian technology became advanced enough to fly out of our own Galaxy," Comet said.

"Are you here to invade us?" the head delegate asked.

"NO! We're here to ask if you want our help. Your planet is in terrible danger!" Kathos said.

"Danger? We've not heard any such threats," the head delegate said.

"So, you haven't sent your academics away to Titan to

168

preserve human life?" Ledawna asked.

"W...well, yes..b..b..but..." the head delegate said nervously.

"Well, here is some good news. They're returning home as we speak. They wish to fight to save the planet you call home." Ledawna said.

"Who sent you?" the head delegate asked.

"No one sent us. We have human friends and allies already wanting to be a part of the battle. We can help you." Kathos sighed, feeling frustrated. "You'll need us, if you wish to beat Belial," he said.

Kathos opened his wings then, flew forward. Guns began firing again, only this time with no impact.

Halen jumped high, twisting, and turning in the air, catching bullets aimed at his monarch. He caught them in his hand. Landing back on his feet, he dropped them to the floor.

Nothing hit Kathos, but even if it had he could easily shield himself.

Orion and Kale had followed Halen, doing the same thing, so quite a few empty bullet cases hit the floor. The warriors were amazing; their swords out, moving with speed and elegance as they protected their leaders.

"You are just wasting your bullets!" Kathos said as he glowed silver white, his white feathered wings spread out from his back.

People watched stunned as they spanned ten feet each side of him.

Gasps were heard as the delegates came back out of hiding.

All went quiet..

"You're an Angel of God!" the head delegate said, putting his hands together ready to pray.

"No!" Kathos said, "I'm Galaxican. We do not follow your God!"

"Blasphemer!" was shouted from across the room.

"I'm a Galaxican; nothing more than that. I have not been sent; I am here to help protect your species. Loyalty to my family, keeping them safe on this planet for many years, has given you the right to my help, I have only one purpose, keeping as many of your people alive as possible." Kathos said.

The speaker got to his feet. "Who's Belial?" he asked.

"This..." Kathos said. "This is Belial!" Kathos showed the newspaper from Titan, with the British Prime Minister on it.

"NO!THIS IS A TRICK!" the head delegate yelled.

"No trick. Humans are all gullible fools. Who put together the evacuation of the rich and brainy?" Halen asked sarcastically.

In the background of the hall a hissing was heard...

The smell of rotting flesh began to sift through the massive room. The humans began heaving, and then vomiting, as the smell lingered in the air.

The Voxians turned around, looking for their familiar enemy. Orion brought out his sword, as the large, bloated ghost like spirit began appearing, turning solid.

"VARDU!" Halen shouted, taking a dive over some desks.

"You picked a bad time to try that, sucker!" Kale yelled, grabbing his sword.

Guns began firing, as the soldiers shot at the peculiar creature that had also got through their defences.

The soldier's bullets did nothing, just floated straight through the creature, who didn't even acknowledge them.

"You really need to do something about your security!" Halen said to one of the soldiers.

The Vardu began to disappear again as it realised its mistake.

The head delegate held up his hand, commanding the soldiers to wait and stand down.

With one swipe of his sword Orion beheaded the Vardu, before it turned back into spirit form.

People in the room pushed and panicked, heading for doors, but the Voxians remained calm, standing waiting as the exits became blocked. A third wave of guards arrived, alarms still ringing, as the UN went on lock down.

"Now do you understand. You have just witnessed just one threat to the human race. Belial has lied to you all. You've all gone along ignoring the signs. He's fooled you," Orion said angrily.

"The humans on Titan are returning as we speak. They will make it back very soon. Did you know they were coming home?" he asked.

The delegates all shook their heads.

Orion had an idea that would help.

"Listen, I can find a way to talk to the people returning on the shuttles. They could explain what was happening on Titan." Orion said.

Orion played around with a mobile phone.

He hooked the signal up to one of the satellites orbiting Earth.

"Unit one... this is Orion. Are you receiving me? We're on Earth, do you copy?" Orion said.

There were a few crackles and then waves of sound as the ships message crackled back.

"Yes, we hear you Orion," a voice said.

"Thanks unit one. Can you confirm your return to Earth?" Orion asked.

"Yes, we've tried communication with Salt Lake City, Utah, but nothing is getting through. We're just about to come into Earth's orbit, we are without permission to land, at Cape Canaveral." the voice said.

"Land!" the head delegate said. "We will contact Salt Lake. They may have a problem with their communication network."

The head delegate looked at Kathos. "I'm convinced sir, we'll fight with you. We need to tell the people of our planet."

"Perhaps our help with recruiting may be an advantage," Orion said. "When those academics have returned all will be revealed.

"Thank you, young man. We're happy for you to help," the head delegate said.

Orion knew his mother was a great negotiator, and she would be happy to return to Earth. If anyone could persuade them to stand with the Voxian people and fight, she could.

Orion thought; 'Stu could be of some help as well.'

"So, what next?" Orion asked.

"We must get organised, and fast...I'm going home now. Comet, come with me. Halen, your father has been doing a little hunting and a job for me. I would appreciate it if you could go and find him, but Halen...please, take a little time." Said Kathos.

CHAPTER 25

Rellik's mind wondered; nothing he thought of seemed to give him any comfort whilst he awaited the arrival of his father Kathos.

'The fact of a definite presence of evil in our lives. Look at Earth, and at the followers of Belial; we know evil exists,' he thought.

Rellik began pacing nervously. He was thinking of Raidar's return.

'But it's a scientific fact that we exist through evolution.'

Rellik was deep in thought and not making any sense. Raidar's arrival worried him most. He could convince most people that he was innocent, but Raidar would kill him anyway, just in case.

Firstly, Rellik needed to face his father and mother; let them make the decision whether he lived or died. That's if Raidar didn't do the deciding for them.

Kathos appeared, and Rellik's nerves got the better of him. He jumped, wondering whether to greet his father, or to just stand there, so he chose to stand.

"Your mother's gone home. She is hoping that all is well with you, and that you will see her later. Shall we walk?" Kathos said, gesturing to both Rellik and Fantasia.

They entered the gardens. It was summer and the topiary figures of knights on horseback towered high, with little animals hiding throughout the grounds, and bright coloured flowers of all kinds; ones that humans would not know.

There was a silence for a while, and then Kathos opened the gates of the Estate, and began walking out towards the village of Limly.

He turned to see Rellik hesitate!

"You have nothing to fear here, Rellik," Kathos said, as he looked at him with some seriousness.

They walked.

Rellik constantly looked around, surveying everything, until they entered Limly. The people looked on as they followed the footpaths of the village.

People began chatting to one another, some wondering if Rellik was their long-lost Prince.

Kathos smiled, gesturing hello kindly to them, nodding with politeness.

Nervously Rellik began to talk...

"When Radonna died, I found it hard to believe what had happened," he paused. Kathos could tell Rellik had no idea what to say in his own defence. "My mind was in despair; I need you to know that."

"I understand. Of course, I do," Kathos said.

Fantasia asked to take her leave. Kathos nodded his permission and the two continued together.

"As the battle ended, I went to the mountains, trying to get my faculties back - to grieve. In my head, I had a plan to move on when the battle had finished. I couldn't bear to think of losing any more people I loved, so I was going to find Flynn and go mapping the stars. It sounded like a great option. I hoped that we would be able to find Kayden out there, to tell him of his mother's death. I was sure that it would be best from me, his own father," Rellik explained.

"Continue." Said Kathos.

But Rellik remained silent.

"Flynn has been home now for over a month and has not mentioned Kayden in all the time he's been here. It may be wise to go and see him a little later; see if he has any news of him," Kathos said.

Kathos knew all had been chaotic. Death from all sides, and betrayal, had brought so much devastation.

It was one of the worst battles the Voxian people had been through. Raithar tried to take over Capalia, and they had to protect their own lands and people.

Kathos headed back to the Estate. Rellik was tired and weak, his energy was low. Kathos held back his emotion as he studied his son, he looked aged, ill and his fear stood out at every corner and every noise.

This man looked more like an eldar, the wise men of Vox

who preach as prophets and philosophers to the people.

His son was no eldar, he was a mountain warrior. So why had he aged like this? Tortured at the hands of his own sister! Kathos felt ashamed that his daughter had been persuaded by that devil to do his bidding.

As they entered the grounds of the Estate, Fantasia was waiting.

Kathos left, wanting to find Ledawna. He needed her to see her son; she had been waiting a long time for this, it was a pity she had to see him like this!

"It makes my decision to leave feel kinda selfish, but as your father has said, grief does silly things." Fantasia said to her uncle.

"The grieving process is a selfish thing, and you don't consider others, do you?" Rellik said, looking ashamed. "I should have stayed. It was such a shock; but grief overwhelmed me." Rellik wiped the tear from his face, it shone like a small jewel at the edge of his eye.

Rellik began to walk away.

"I've pissed a lot of people off here." Rellik said anxiously, as he watched a crowd gather at the gates of the estate.

Fantasia then asked the question he had been fearing.

"So, how did you find yourself in the company of the Raitharns?" she said.

"Stupidity! I was captured!" Rellik looked straight into Fantasia's eyes. "I'd gone to the mountains. I just hadn't any idea where I was, but something, a noise I heard, stopped me. I realised someone had been following me, probably from the moment I'd left the lakes. I had been fighting there when Radonna had been... lost." Rellik paused. "I'd come to the end of the border before they had caught my full attention. Something – shining straight into my eye. It caught me off guard, and then something hit me. I didn't have time to register what it was." Rellik started to cry, he held Fantasia's arm. "I was grieving, Fantasia. My life had just come to a standstill. The woman I loved was dead. I don't think I even attempted to fight back. My strength had been swept away..."

Rellik stepped away from Fantasia. Suddenly, like a fit, his eyes turned white. He began kicking and punching out blindly at the air as if hallucinating, with an uncontrollable anger.

Fantasia gave a telepathic call for help to Kathos.

When they teleported into her house, Fantasia was trying to hold him down, failing quite badly.

His mother and father ran to his side.

Rellik rolled on the ground, fanged out, and screamed in anger as he finally collapsed. Kathos had never seen this before; it was like he was possessed.

"It's alright, son. You've had enough for now. Let's get you some rest and food. Come home now, just for a while." Kathos picked him up, carrying him into the Manor. He had been through so much.

It was obvious to Kathos his recovery could take a long time. But truth was, they needed him; he would know some useful information.

"I'm not a traitor, Father; you must believe me. Bethadora took me...Belial spent years torturing me for information...I said nothing...NOTHING!" Rellik cried out.

Rellik fell unconscious as Kathos carried him through the house, lying him down on the sofa.

"You know, there's no way Rellik was a traitor. The emotion was pure animosity for Belial and his own Sister Bethadora!" Fantasia said as she followed them.

"I had already come to the same conclusion. Your uncle has been through enough mental anguish. He's aged more than I have ever seen a Voxian age before. Not even the eldars look as old as he does. What to do next; that is what I'm pondering," Kathos said.

Ledawna walked into the room, her long black shining hair swaying from side to side as she entered.

"I've hunted for fresh deer blood. Our son is very weak and has come a long way to find us. I will leave him to sleep for a while longer, and then he must eat. It will help him regain some strength. I believe this may be a long process," Ledawna said.

She sat down beside Rellik, stroking his long white hair, straggly and unkempt. His clothes were the same ones he'd disappeared in. She remembered the last time she had seen her son clearly.

The others left the room. They knew the news of Rellik's heroic return needed to be spread, before the other rumours took hold, and everyone believed him to be a traitor.

Fantasia knew he would win back the hearts of his people. But they would have to wait, firstly for him to regain strength enough to stand in front of them, and secondly to be able to fend off Raidar's need to kill him!

~

The next day Fantasia went into the meeting room at the Manor. The whole family, including Raidar and his sons, were sat around a feast of deer; rich red blood cupped in goblets of silver; the royal crest engraved into them.

She sat down, taking a cup. The taste of the deer blood hit her lips, warm and fresh. She felt it slide down easily, giving her a warm buzz as it emanated power through her body. She had missed this on Earth, and although the Voxians could do without it for a while, she loved it.

Kathos entered, then Ledawna walked in front of a less frail Rellik, he had been given his meal last night and it had at least given him some recovery.

"Can you walk by yourself, Uncle?" Fantasia asked him casually.

"Yes, Princess, it's been quite a while since I've been allowed to walk anywhere except up and down that retched cell. The escape from prison consisted of me running away like a fleeing animal, there were times I thought it would be my end." Rellik said.

An angry growl could be heard coming from the opposite side of the room. "Raidar!" Rellik said, cowering a little.

Rellik became nervous. Raidar's threatening attendance reminded him of his shattered spirit, and his broken body.

Like all Voxians, he was fast recovering from his ordeal. He had dark speckles of colour back in his hair, which had now been cut short. He knew that his people would accept him back. Well, they had already started to.

Rellik began smiling. "This is a long shot; does anyone know what happened to 'Spirit', my wolf?" he said.

"I believe Fantasia may be able to help you!" Kathos said, looking around at her.

"I know she has a long life. Do you think, after all this time, she'll be living in the forests with the pack?" Rellik asked.

A small animal cry was heard.

"Oh, My Goddess..." Rellik said.

Standing at the door was a large pack of six wolves; one he recognised almost immediately.

He dropped to his knees and opened his arms. Spirit, the white female, entered the room. The wolf went ecstatic; she jumped and rolled onto her back. Animal and owner were so pleased to see one another.

"Hello, girl. You remember who I am?" Rellik said.

Rellik rolled about while his wolf rubbed her head on him, crying and whining, pleased to meet and greet her master after all this time. Now he had something to keep him occupied that loved him unconditionally.

Shadow sat and watched for a short while, then nudging Spirit. He sat, wagging his tail, waiting for some attention.

Spirit nuzzled into her master with her head and began speaking to him telepathically.

"This is Shadow," Spirit said.

Rellik stared, a little surprised at first. His memories came back from his captivity. "Yes, hang on just a minute..." he said, then went back to his room. He had suddenly remembered something important. He searched his old, ripped clothes, and found a piece of paper.

"So, there we have it," he said, coming back out and to the table. Rellik observed the ripped paper, and then the two wolves. "You're the yin and the yang."

Kathos looked at his son, confused. When he looked around, everyone stood with the same vacant expression.

"What do you mean, Rellik?" Fantasia asked.

But Rellik was still fussing about with the paper, spreading out the crinkled page carefully and fully, laughing, shaking his head.

"These two animals have an important role to play in the banishment of Belial. We don't have a lot of time, but what I'm about to tell you is that everything you've worked for is important. Have you found the human yet?" Rellik asked.

"We have a human here. He lives amongst us. He is the first man ever to do so. A friend of Orion's from Earth, called Stuart... Stu," Kathos said, looking even more confused.

"That's Great! What's the date?" Rellik said.

"Earth time; 20th July 2512," Kathos replied.

Rellik's smile vanished.

"We've only five months left!" Rellik said.

"What do you mean? What for?" Kathos asked him.

"Earth's end!" Rellik said, now looking at Fantasia.

The house fell silent.

Kathos didn't seem surprised. Only Fantasia, Sky and Orion showed a small inkling of emotion at the news.

Raidar and Hyedan got up to look at the paper.

Kathos and Orion quickly jumped in front of Rellik, as Raidar growled in disapproval.

Halen stood by his father. They knew, when push comes to shove, there was no stopping Raidar. But he did respect his leader, so Raidar glared disapprovingly, sat back down, and said nothing.

The room began to fill with the others who had come to attend the meeting from the different warrior factions.

Rellik was given consent to speak.

"When I was imprisoned, the next cell held a man who was accused of being a traitor to Belial. He wasn't there long. His power was to prophesise the future. After being beaten and tortured, he was eventually taken and killed. When alone, we would talk about his premonitions. He told me of prophesies he had seen, including 21/12/2512. He was taken in the middle of the night. He struggled, risking more beatings, so he could throw this piece of paper into me before he was taken away. It fell at the cell door, before they slammed it shut."

Rellik held out the paper, A4 sized, with a drawing on it. The picture had been carefully drawn.

Kathos in his full Angel glory, wings flashing, pure white, glowing with power. On each side of him stood Fantasia and Orion. At the front of them, Spirit and Shadow - Rellik's yin and yang - then above the picture, the words: 'Belial's obliteration 21/12/2512'.

"So, this is why Bethadora was afraid of Shadow," Raidar said, standing.

"Oh yes. Spirit was found by the borders edge as well, abandoned. We took her in. She was so tiny, and had been left to starve," Rellik replied. "This is it! Beth must have seen the prophecy. She was there when we found Spirit and told Radonna to 'ring its neck'. We had found her just before we believed Beth had turned to the bad side."

"Belial was Beth's master two years before she finally disappeared to be by his side. Don't kid yourselves that she wasn't spying for that demon," Raidar said, looking with a hateful stare at Rellik.

Fantasia knew that Rellik had a lot to tell, but looking at Raidar's rage building, she thought that now would not be the time to say any more.

She called a close to the meeting, and everyone left. They knew of Beth's fear now when she had come face to face with Shadow. She knew both wolves had survived.

Rellik had time to get prepared and give details to all. It would be at Raidar's, home in the mountains of Capalia, the giant warrior would be there to greet all who arrived, this included Rellik.

The Reptilians had been invited, and Stu. All had been briefed and would be given the opportunity to speak if they wished.

Any ideas that would help had to be considered.
Time was getting rapidly short.

CHAPTER 26

The Morning was beautiful.

Kathos and some of the warriors had arrived back on Earth. They teleported to Fantasia's home in Worcestershire, UK.

The Voxian's looked around at the neighbourhood. It surprised them; the houses were terraced and were all strung together in rows. Vox didn't have terraced housing estates.

Humans seemed to live on top of one another here, the land was smaller than Capalia, but the population was much larger than Vox.

As they stepped inside the house, it was lived in and cosy. It seemed a little too small for Fantasia; yet there was something familiar, a bit like her house on Vox.

Kathos couldn't help staring at the inside of this small, yet neat house.

"So, you remembered nothing of your home on Vox?" he said laughing.

Fantasia smiled. She knew what he meant. It even had the same colours on the walls; similar, but miniature.

Red and gold decor in her front room, with cream and red furnishings and curtains. The place had been empty for a while. Dust and cobwebs on the ceilings, and in corners, showing that only insects and arachnids had intruded while she was away.

"I do apologise for not having time for housework!" She said sarcastically.

Fantasia sat down, dusting off a large cream cushion, smiling politely.

"Please, come and sit down,"

The others looked a little stunned at her.

"How on Earth did you cope in such a tiny place?" Halen asked.

"Tiny! No, this is a big house for Earth. It was often commented on when people visited it," Orion said to his friend. "Come on, we've a spare five seconds," he said mockingly, "I'll show you around."

Orion took them outside to look at the twenty-by-twenty-foot garden; all slabbed, with a small, brightly coloured Wendy house, that Emmina had played in when she was smaller. The rain and sun had discoloured the roof through time. The fencing was old, and the sides were splintering. It had the occasional hole where Shadow had been digging at it, he didn't like his neighbour, a miserable old man and his dumb son.. Orion smiled as he remembered his childhood here.

"Couldn't hold a meeting here with more than a few people, could we?" Stu said to the others.

The tour went on. It lasted for perhaps thirty seconds; not five. The men came back into the front room and sat with the others, as they made themselves comfortable, waiting out the time until they went back to the UN.

They Voxian's didn't want to give the wrong impression to their Earthly hosts, they needed to be seen as peaceful, especially as they didn't just have Halen with them now. Kale, Orion and Raidar had also taken on the recruitment drive.

So, Kathos spent some time trying to keep the men in a peaceful mood. He wasn't too worried about Raidar. He was the older and the wiser, but Halen, being like his father, may shoot his mouth off, if pushed.

"How do we show we've come to help?" Raidar asked, "After all, we can't just go in there, wave our swords, and expect them to all join in, can we?" Raidar looked over at Kathos, who was now sitting in Fantasia's chair, trying to get comfortable.

"These aren't built for Angels!" Kathos said standing again, he laughed, as he waited for Raidar to continue with his conversation, albeit sarcastic. Some of his points still made a lot of sense.

"If these men start attacking us, what are we supposed to do?" Raidar asked. "Bite their heads off?"

Kathos ignored his comment, looking at his friends and

family. "Ideas anyone? Not including Raidar's new head biting one." He looked at Raidar, who was looking up at the ceiling, with his booted feet on the coffee table, saying nothing. "No 'killing' ideas are welcome." Kathos swiped at Raidar's feet as they rested on the table, and they dropped heavily to the carpeted floor.

Orion's face lit up. He had an idea.

"Not all Earth's academics disappeared to Titan... You can't bribe everyone to leave a doomed planet, even if it is a matter of their life," Orion said, looking at his mother. "What about Samuel, our old college lecturer?"

Fantasia's face dropped. She didn't seem so pleased and cringed at the thought, but reluctantly said "OK."

"Samuel's a real studier... I've never met anyone like him. He knows everything possible about nearly any subject. I think if we can persuade him, he'll make a good human negotiator!" Orion said.

Kathos smiled. "How do we approach him?" he said.

"Mom?" Orion prompted her.

Fantasia wasn't sure about approaching Samuel after all this time.

"Okay, I'll give him a call, see if he's not got too many meetings today, see if he can take some time to save the Earth with us!" she said, a little sarcastically.

Orion crossed his two fingers together whispering the words "Good luck!"

Fantasia huffed at him then they both laughed. Samuel spent most of his life in meetings. It was as if he was born to be bored, walking, and riding a bicycle where hobbies (Obviously he never got any sex!).

Kathos looked on, confused. Stu smiled; he'd been taught by this man as well and knew exactly why it was so funny.

The others looked on a little confused.

"To know him is to love him, is all we can say. Isn't that right, Mom?" Orion chuckled.

Fantasia shook her head, mumbling to herself. "Bloody kids. Why is the crap always left to me?"

"Wow! What's up with her?" Raidar asked, giving Orion a nudge.

"Oh, he was Mom's friend. They slowly drifted apart. I think she feels a little alienated from him now," Orion said.

"Alienated! Dude..." Stu said laughing. "They haven't spoken in years. This should be interesting."

Kathos remained confused, but glad that all was coming together.

"We have to attend the meeting with the UN today. Will you be able to persuade your friend to come with us?" he asked Fantasia.

"Hmm, maybe... I will have to convince him that this isn't an elaborate joke!" she said.

"Do you need us to come with you?" Kathos asked.

"No, I should be able to persuade him. I just don't want to give the guy a heart attack. He's already highly stressed!" Fantasia said.

"Perhaps I should go with you," Comet said, volunteering.

"What? Be face to face?" Fantasia said, realising they were telling her to visit this guy in person.

Samuel had refused to do research with her for Titan, along with the other academics. He rejected any invitation to leave Earth, stubbornly. He was *'born on this planet. Nothing, not even its destruction, should be an excuse to abandon it.'* To be honest, she believed he would probably be dead by now, because his stress levels were so high.

"I'm sure Samuel's okay," Comet said, picking up Fantasia's thoughts.

"Oh... yes, he's lived through worse things than waiting for doom; I can assure you. I wonder if he still has his job at the old college?" she said.

"Do you know of a safe place to teleport? We don't want to frighten the students by just appearing in their classroom," Comet said, laughing.

"They keep rebuilding it, I should imagine I won't recognise it after all these years." Fantasia said.

Stu and Orion smirked. She really didn't enjoy her time

there at all, even with the great friends she had met.

Fantasia took Comet by the sleeve, and teleported.

"I need some help assembling a transporter, and Comet has gone with Mother?" Orion moaned.

Then standing at the back of his living room was Azaya. She had teleported to Earth along with the others. She was there to help Fantasia. Azaya was another negotiator.

"Could I be of some help?" she asked.

Orion went a little red faced and nodded. Stu, Kale, and Halen just sniggered at each other, as Azaya and Orion began to walk from the room.

"Oooh, want to be alone?" Halen said, making kissy faces at him.

"Get stuffed Halen..." Orion said, laughing at his friend's comment. Azaya and Orion left the room.

CHAPTER 27

SAMUEL

The two Voxians teleported to an old part of the college building that had been standing empty for a while, they appeared just outside it in a blind corner.

Fantasia didn't attempt the college reception; there was never any point. Instead, she went straight to the sixth form office block; but Samuel wasn't there. She stopped and thought, then looked at the time. It was 10.45 am, break time. She knew he would be drinking coffee in the dining hall.

She was tempted to teleport, but Comet shook his head. "No," he said. "We'll have to walk."

She sighed and walked to the stairs. No taking the lift now; she was fit and strong. But how was she going to explain her sudden burst of fitness to Sam? He was a stress freak... obsessive-compulsive disorder, phobias, paranoia, you name it, he suffered with it.

She had always been quite a lazy human.

"I don't understand why we need him," Fantasia said, wondering what his reaction to seeing her now would be.

"You said he was used to speaking to others. He's a teacher, and with a good reputation. The humans will listen to him."

"What am I going to say to him?" She asked feeling a little panicked.

"You, my friend, are about to come out, as an alien. He's gunna be really freaked out, now start walking" Comet said, as they looked at the three flights of stairs.

"If he says no, I may kill him!" Fantasia said, jokingly.

Fantasia stood, pretending to be breathless at the top of the stairs. Comet looked confused, and then realised she was acting the way she would have when she attended here. After all, if they saw that she had got a new lease of life, what would they think?

"Most humans look breathless and exhausted coming up

these stairs... that is, except for the sports kids!" Fantasia said, explaining her actions.

Grabbing Comet's arm, who was amused, he started to copy her. She walked into a large glass room. It was light, bright, and full of plastic tables and chairs. It had vending machines up against one of the walls, and a kitchen area, with serving hatches at the bottom.

She looked around at the people sat at the tables, and sure enough, in his usual spot, with a newspaper in one hand and coffee in a polystyrene cup in the other, was Samuel.

Samuel had the same full-faced beard and short hair that had been left to go a little wild. Only now he was a lot greyer than Fantasia remembered. Surely it hadn't been that long since she had seen him. A pang of guilt swept over her as she looked at him. She noticed he had the same look on his face as her. She was relieved about that, because that meant she had not been the only one who'd neglected their friendship. What she was about to tell this man would only be what you would tell a most trusted friend.

"Fantasia!" Samuel gasped, "long time, no see!" he looked down at his paper while he folded it, and he then threw it down on the table in front of himself.

"Oooh... awkward!" Comet whispered to Fantasia, she just threw him the, shut up look!

"Hi Sam, I know it's been ages, but I went to..."

Comet elbowed her. She went quiet. She couldn't say that. No one according to the news had come back from Titan.

"Mmm...I went abroad! Anyway, how have things been?" Fantasia asked him.

Samuel shrugged at her. "Rubbish, I guess," he said, sussing her lie out immediately, she was forgetting how well they had known one another, even if it was a while ago.

She could see a coldness in him she had never come across before; two old friends who'd fallen out and just met again by accident, well sort of!

'Now what?' She looked a little helpless at her brother-in-law, so Comet approached the table, hand out in greeting.

"Good morning. I'm Fantasia's brother-in-law, Comet," he said.

Samuel looked at his hand, hesitated, and then took it and shook it.

"I didn't realise you had a brother-in-law," he said.

Fantasia felt a little relief, and then realised this was the diplomat. He couldn't be rude, especially to a stranger on his own turf. Why would he be? After all, he was annoyed with her for not making any contact.

"I'm sorry, OK?" Fantasia said, sitting next to him.

Samuel looked down at the table, and began playing with the polystyrene cup, swishing the coffee left in the bottom. She knew what would come next.

"I've got to go. I have a class now," Samuel said.

Fantasia put her hand on his arm, and they both began to stand.

"Please, you don't understand... I'm no good at phone calls! This is important...I know you're angry because we lost contact, but you're to blame as well!"

He looked down. "I have got to go," he said, as he began walking away.

Fantasia had to stop him. She needed to find something to persuade him to stay.

"WAIT!" she shouted.

People looked around to see what the commotion was.

"Millions of lives are in danger!" she said as she sighed, sitting back down again.

Samuel looked stunned for a minute, then he walked back and sat back down.

"What? Who's in danger? Are you in danger? What has happened?" Samuel panicked as he spoke, and the people who sat in the surrounding area looked at him.

The dining hall fell silent.

"Fantasia, it's not wise talking here. We need to go somewhere out of the way," Comet said, looking at all the staring faces.

Comet went towards the door of the diner, but he was still

faster than he should have been, so people remained staring.

"I think it's time to make our exit," Fantasia said.

Samuel looked closely at Fantasia and Comet.

"Did you take that job in London? Are you on a mission? Your eyes... they're identical; not like any I have ever seen," Samuel said, his Middle English sounded quite tainted, just for a moment, with his northern accent.

Fantasia looked at him. "Not here, Samuel, please! We seriously need to get somewhere private," she said.

"I get it. I thought at first you had a new boyfriend, but it's obvious now, you're related... your eye colours identical. I mean, as unusual as it is, I'm sure..." Samuel began babbling, getting louder, which meant he knew something wasn't right, and was panicking.

Fantasia had to stop him because his next move would be to get hysterical.

"Come with me," Fantasia said as she pulled him up by the arm gently. She made it look friendly enough for people to glance, but then look away as they left the dining area.

Samuel stared at her.

"Stay calm, old friend," she said, also panicking now. Her eyes tinted blue, and her pupils enlarged, and Samuel panicked even more.

His arms resisted her, and he started to pull backwards, then he began turning back towards the dining area.

"Calm," Comet said, waving his hand in front of Samuel.

Samuel dropped into Comet's arms, just outside the lift, unconscious.

"You'll have to show me that trick!" Fantasia laughed.

Fantasia and Comet grabbed Sam's arms and waltzed him into the lift next to the dining room door.

Two students stepped into the hall as the lift began closing. They looked at the strange people holding up their drunken lecturer.

The lift door closed.

The two students glanced at one another, and then ran back down the stairs to catch one more glimpse of the inebriated teacher.

"Oh crap!" Fantasia said. "Now what?"

"Teleport quickly," Comet said. "Be out of the lift before it gets to the bottom. I have teleported before with Stu. Just be aware of the different chemical compounds in human DNA. It's heavier than ours." He yanked Samuel up in his arms, pulling his body in as Fantasia pressed the lift button.

"We've about fifteen seconds before it hits the ground floor, go!" she said.

Comet nodded at her.

"Nobody said to kidnap him, for Shylaya's' sake. He already hated me, so now what?" she said, panicking.

"Teleport now," Comet said.

Fantasia concentrated on Sam's human DNA, and then they vanished.

As the lift door opened on the ground floor, the two students stood breathless and amazed. It was empty; they had obviously been seeing things.

~

All three teleported into the house. It wasn't that far away from the college; a bus ride if Sam protested too much, she would walk him down and help him on the bus herself!. She really didn't mean to take him against his will. Let's face it; they didn't kidnap him because he had fainted before he could protest.

Kathos was standing in the lounge. He looked at the two of them as they appeared with Sam, he wasn't amused, so they looked a little sheepishly at him as they walked by with Sam still in their grasp.

"Diplomatic!" he said sarcastically, shaking his head. "Pray tell me, why we're now taking prisoners? Are we hoping to ask this man for help?"

Comet took away the temporary unconsciousness from Samuel, and he came round quickly.

For once Samuel didn't panic, and he didn't protest either, he just stared at Kathos.

"Good morning, my man, I'm Kathos. I have a lot to ask

of you and explain to you. Obviously, my granddaughter and her helper didn't do a very good job at persuading you to meet with me," he said.

Samuel said nothing, shook his head, and smiled as the glow from Kathos brightened the room around them.

"You're an Angel... did I die?" asked Sam.

Kathos smiled, shaking his head.

"So, how are you here?" Samuel asked.

Fantasia shrugged at Comet, and the two of them went to walk away.

"Not so fast, get back here... This man isn't even aware of what you are, is he? So, you didn't even get to tell him that!" Kathos said annoyed.

"No, Grandfather, it would have exposed us if we drew too much attention. We tried to explain, But Sam here started freaking out," Fantasia said.

She gave Samuel a look. He knew she had found his actions pathetic. He looked down, and his face turned red with embarrassment.

"I have known you for years. I can honestly say you have never shocked me to this extreme before. You call an Angel Grandfather! I don't know what to say to you...I'm sorry," Samuel said.

"For what? Being a complete chump, and not trusting me after all this time?" she said.

"That too! But mainly for not realising that you were not from here...Earth, I mean. Well, you're not are you?" Samuel smiled at her.

"No Sam, I'm not..." Fantasia turned 'battle-mode', white fangs glistening, face bulking out, showing her true alien form.

Samuel looked slightly startled but much to Fantasia's amazement, Samuel didn't flinch. He just studied her for a while, and then got out of his chair and walked over to her. She was his friend, and this was probably the biggest news she had ever trusted him with. He felt honoured.

"So, this is who you are?" he said, and gently touched her

face. His acceptance was amazing. They stood there just for a while reacquainting themselves, chatting about what had been going on whilst he was being a chump, while Kathos and Comet looked on.

"You think this is good, wait until you see the dinosaurs." Comet smiled at them.

Samuel looked on in shock.

"Now your friends again, can we please get on? Time's running short." Comet continued.

They all sat down around the small dining room table, and began to explain Earth's predicament, asking if he would negotiate for them representing human's to all species involved in the conflict. Samuel agreed immediately, without question, and sat listening to everything he needed to know.

"Yes, I'll help negotiate. I haven't missed a day at work in fourteen years, but for this I believe I can. We need a recruitment drive, Fantasia. You would be a good face to use; perhaps one of the dinosaurs too. Fear is one thought, but familiarity, as these creatures once roamed our planet, so humans should accept them quickly... after a scream or two!" Sam laughed.

Samuel looked excited. His son loved Dinosaurs when he was little. He wondered what he would think about them, being back here on Earth again.

Orion, Raidar, Kale and Halen suddenly appeared in the front room, as if by magic. They teleported in front of the sofa.

Samuel started panicking. Fear hit his face, and he tried to calm himself. He felt outnumbered by these huge aliens, seven to one. The odds were piling up, and he suddenly felt small and insignificant.

"Hello, my human neighbour," Raidar boomed, approaching with his hand out in greeting, it didn't help Samuel's palpitations, but he offered his hand in friendship.

Raidar towered over seven feet tall, he was wide with muscle. Samuel had never seen a man so big. To be honest, there wasn't another Voxian that big either. Halen did, however, come a close second. He had just entered the room too.

"Hello, I'm Sam, your human negotiator," he said nervously.

"Hello, I'm Raidar; warrior, killer and out 'n' out arsehole," Raidar said back.

Fantasia looked at Raidar, shaking her head. "No," she said to him, indicating for him to back off just a little, as she watched Sam's legs buckling with fear under him.

Orion smiled, always happy to be friends with everyone. Sam had taught him for a couple of years. Of course, his mother's friendship had been a big help. Orion had a lot of respect for Samuel.

Orion remembered that Sam was around when he was a small boy. He would meet his mother at college after school, with his friend at the time.

"Sam," he nodded respectfully at him, and sat on the floor by Comet.

"Orion my friend how are you?" Sam put out his hand and shook it. Familiarity made him relax just a little.

Orion had a sudden brain wave.

"Perhaps we could get scout groups and cadets to help with distributing any news." Orion said to Kathos.

"Great thinking," Kathos said. "What's your plan, Samuel? Do you wish to remain here, or go back to work? We can get you back in the lift in a second. Let's hope that no-one is using it. It may be a bit of a squeeze if they are," Kathos laughed.

Samuel nervously smiled. "No thank you, I'm happy to stay here. I am sure the UN can give me a decent excuse for not attending work today, but I will have to give them a phone call." he said.

They all laughed. Samuel was getting to grips with them already, and Fantasia realised that they had made the right choice. She just wished she could have handled the approach a little better.

"Hey, I just realised, I finally got you to visit my house,"

Fantasia said to Sam.

"Visit? You had to drag the poor man here with an accomplice," Kathos said. Smiling at her.

Her face turned a lovely shade of red.

"What? No come back. Now that has got to be a first," Samuel said, laughing at her.

"Bite me Samuel," Fantasia laughed, fangs protruding.

CHAPTER 28

Beth wanted to see Flynn, she was taking the risk of being caught, even though she chose to stay back and look at him from a distance; sneaking onto the mountains near his home, she watched as he came in and out of his house, so knew what she'd lost when she made an alliance with evil.

It was time for her to go. Contact with Belial was getting harder to face, especially now Flynn had returned home.

Beth wanted to be with Flynn more than anything. Even more than being with Belial and his warriors.

'Maybe Flynn loved her enough to join her and become a follower of Belial, recruit him, her master would love that!

"Here goes nothing," she said, as she ran back across the mountains and onto the Raitharn border.

~

Beth limped with one shoe on, the other lost in the Capalian mountains.

She stepped onto the pebble pathway leading to her lair. She was on her own side of the planet again, back on Raithar.

She stared up at the window from the large garden and began to limp, the pain in her foot shot through her shin. It was getting worse by the minute. Beth bent to take off her remaining shoe. She didn't get time to stand up again. A hand grabbed her, catching her by the throat and throwing her up the wall of the house.

Squeezing hard.

"You bitch... traitorous witch!" Belial growled.

"Master, please... let me explain," Beth said, her voice croaked as she began to choke.

Belial dropped her and turned away. He turned his body back, swinging his fist hard at her face, punching Beth. Her lip split open as her teeth gashed into the side of her mouth. Blood gushed just for a moment, and pain gripped her. She fell to her knees, foot forgotten.

As she pulled herself up again, all signs of the abuse had already gone.

Her anger almost began to show. She would have to control it, keeping herself from changing; otherwise, he would see it as a defiance.

Beth took a deep breath and followed Belial inside. He walked her into the front room of the dilapidated house. As she entered, he kicked her to the floor, and punched her again, this time harder. Her left eye socket rained blood, and she lost vision, but only for a second as her alien DNA fixed what had been broken.

"Master, please, I beg of you, listen to me," she said.

"This better be good. It would be better if you went onto the Capalian borders to kill your brother before he reached Kathos." Belial glared as he towered over her.

Beth crawled to Belial's feet. Tears began to fall as she begged for her life.

"I followed Rellik's trail as best I could... I came back to get more warriors to help search when you called me."

This was it. If he didn't like her version of events, he would kill her. She waited...

"Stand up! Come to me," Belial said, calmly now.

Beth wept a bit more and dropped to her knees in front of him again. He began stroking her hair and kissed her on the head.

"Beautiful Beth, I'm sure you didn't mean to be overpowered by your weak, traitor brother. But two good men lost their lives only hours ago because of him. He'll pay dearly for this, and you... you will need to show your love for me by proving your loyalty," he said to her.

Beth nodded. "Yes, My Lord, I will do anything."

Belial smiled his evil grin. "Yes, my darling girl, you will," he said.

~

Kathos needed to stay on Earth, while Rellik remained behind, regaining his strength, and recovering on Vox.

Ledawna his mother had taken on the job of carer for him, also his sister-in-law Genesis became counsellor to try and make his mind heal as well as his body.

Shadow stayed to watch over him, along with Spirit.

Bellazard, along with the other Reptilians, had stayed and continued training, but she would be visiting Earth to help with recruitments. She had been visiting and befriending Rellik, she felt a compassion for the man she and Shadow had saved..

Rellik had returned to training, avoiding Raidar as much as he could.

Ghost had disappeared in the forests of Capalia. She had made herself a home in one of the large caves and lived in peace amongst the animals there. Spirit would return to her occasionally. She was always happy to see her.

"Why don't you come with me Ghost, come to the city and meet my master."

"I am happy here at the moment, but I will come before the battle, I promise." Ghost replied.

As time was short, it was important to get training underway. Kathos had Samuel and Stu working with him. He was convinced that all would go smoothly before the battle.

"This is cutting it fine, I know, but we need Earths military on our side, and we should meet again and talk once more to the UN," Kathos said.

All the Voxians agreed, and the UN meeting on Earth was arranged.

Kathos discussed the situation with his warrior leaders, to be sure that he had everything worked out in his head.

The UN meeting would give the humans opportunity to join the battle, so he knew he would have to be persuasive.

CHAPTER 29

MEETING WITH THE UNITED NATIONS (NO.2)

"The military need to know that fighting the Raitharns, with the weapons you have, even the most advanced, are no match," Kathos explained to the people of the UN.

They listened as the Angel spoke. The room was silent.

"I'm the representative for mankind, and the Capalians," Sam said, getting to his feet calmly. "I'm here to help with recruiting our people to train with the new allies; the Capalians and Reptilians." He gazed at his audience.

They had their full attention on him, it was different than talking to his class of daydreamers at college.

"Why did the Voxians choose you?" the head delegator asked.

"Sir, I was chosen because I'm good with people, a teacher. I come across well with all ages. I believe I have gained Kathos's trust and respect," Samuel said, standing upright and proud.

"I see, and may I ask, what your name is, sir?" the delegator asked him.

"Samuel Kane. I'm the head of psychology at Brightnortan-on-the water College," he said proudly.

"Well, Mr Kane, I do hope you're as good as the Voxians believe you are," the delegator smiled.

Samuel looked over at Fantasia.

"Yes sir, so do I," he said, showing his nervousness just a little.

The delegator shook Sam's hand.

The delegator for the UK looked at Kathos. "So, now what?" he said.

"Now we recruit!" Kathos said. "Orion will stay here with Fantasia and Stu. Samuel will also be accompanying them in their short stay on Earth. All of them have a lot of experience on your planet."

"The plan is to broadcast to the planet in all languages,

which is where you all come in. If my people adapt, they can organize in the language needed." The Voxian's pentagram lit blue. "We need to make it clear; this is not a joke, it's a matter of survival. Our two negotiators will come in very handy. The people of Earth need to trust us, so Stu and Sam will demonstrate we are on mankind's side." Kathos said as he turned to Samuel, who nodded in agreement.

"Orion has contact with another shuttle that is almost home from Titan. They're just about to touch down," Fantasia said.

"The broadcast will go out at 1500 hours, Earth time, and will be broadcast at 1800 hours in Vox, due to time differences." Orion said.

"Good, we'll prepare for this. We can make a speech and find some good interpreters and subtitles in different languages. I'll personally announce the first alien contact. I must say, I feel extremely honoured," the delegate said, with a smile.

~

Beth lay sleeping. Her mind drifted as she kissed Flynn on the mouth, his naked body warm, close. She felt his breath close to her skin as the hairs on the back of her neck stood on end prickling, as she smiled. Her body rose in ecstasy at his touch. Her eyes opened slowly as he kissed her mouth again...

She was dreaming, surely?

Then reality struck.

She awoke suddenly. She began to struggle. Two strong hands grabbed her by the wrists, holding her there. Belial punched Beth hard in the face, and her nose exploded in a spray of her own blood.

She realised who it was and tried very hard to calm herself. After all, there was no point fighting. He stared at her, his red demon eyes glowing, and then he slapped her in the face again, then began licking the blood as it poured. He grabbed her thigh so hard it hurt. She stemmed her tears. Beth tried not to whimper. She wanted to cry. She felt dirty. Even if she had screamed, no one was there to help; everyone was

200

too afraid.

"Bitch!" Belial said, as he climbed off her, sitting at the edge of her bed.

He put a hand in his pocket, throwing money at her, coins from Earth. The money jingled as it hit the bed and floor.

Beth looked at the money on the bloodied sheets. She began to cry uncontrollably. She had left her family and her lover, for this.

"I'll pay you what you're worth, scum. Next time you betray me with your thoughts of Flynn, I'll kill you. Your ass is mine; don't you ever forget that!" Belial said.

Beth looked at her master. The red glow in his eyes stood out in the darkness. Beth turned away from him, hiding the tears.

Was this what she could expect from now on?

It would have been better if she had told him the truth, and he had killed her.

CHAPTER 30

Fantasia held Sam's arm and Orion took Stu's, they all teleported.

They appeared at the lake on Vox for some basic training in combat. Samuel felt extremely uncomfortable with this. He was a man of peace, after all, and the thought of fighting with weapons and fists didn't make him feel right.

Stu, on the other hand, loved it. He had come along to help show Samuel some of the first basic human combat moves, and to show off his sword.

"Dude. Anyone can do this; it's a piece of cake."

Samuel nodded nervously.

"It may be easy for you. But this isn't my style; fighting and killing...I don't like gore!" Sam said.

"Oh man! You're the Voxian negotiator. Look, Dude, not being funny, but you need to be able to escape if you're attacked, don't you?" Stu said.

Samuel looked down and nodded in agreement. Fantasia took his arm and led him away from the others.

"For Shylaya' sake...what's your problem, Sam?" she asked.

"I don't do fighting. You know that!" Sam said anxiously. "You left me. I was supposed to be your friend, and you didn't think for one second to persuade me to go as well. Left me for dead on Earth, to accept my fate! What am I supposed to say?" he said, suddenly turning angry.

He held back his emotions, and he began to walk away from her, shaking his head.

"I didn't leave you, Sam. What are you, my child? I had no choice. You didn't come with us. That was your choice, not mine. I asked you - no - I begged, and you were convinced that it would be okay on Earth, and it isn't, is it?" Fantasia barked back.

Samuel snarled. She was right and he was wrong. He turned his back on her and walked away again. This time Fantasia grabbed him, twisting him round, her face in 'battle-mode', her white fangs protruding, and her face filled with anger.

"DON'T! I know you, and this doesn't work on me. Even with the newfound fangs and face, I'm not afraid of you!" Sam said.

"Defend yourself from this, your stupid..." she said, lunging forward.

Fear hit his face.

"Fantasia! You would never hurt me would you?"

He had never considered, not even for a second, that she would attack him. She stopped, changing back to her soft human look, feeling quite ashamed of what she had just put her friend through.

"I'm so sorry Sam, but you need to fight. Tell me how you can defend yourself against someone like me?" Fantasia said, stepping back from her friend for a moment. She had not intended to make him feel vulnerable, but she did.

It was bad enough having to fight this battle at all. But now she had threatened someone she loved.

Samuel had been like her brother; he had helped her through some very tough times.

Sam watched as her vulnerability began to show itself. He caved in immediately, remembering their time on Earth, and walked over to her. He kissed her softly on her forehead, and then hugged her.

"It's okay. I just feel alone out here. I know that we've been there for each other for a long time. But although the thought of war is not a new concept for me, fighting a battle is," Sam said.

He shivered and turned, looking around. He had the feeling that someone else was there. He looked across at the trees and spotted Drakos watching, his face filled with hate as he stepped back.

Samuel said nothing. He just stood with Fantasia in his arms. He knew Drakos may be a problem but hoped he would realise that this was an old friendship, and nothing more.

EARTH'S TV BROADCAST.

Life on Earth had been good for Fantasia and her family, so when she was asked to recruit human warriors, she was only too happy to be involved.

Time was limited. The humans needed to protect themselves from the enemies.

The need to train them was urgent.

Belial had not been seen. It was believed he had gone back to Raithar, on the north side of the planet. Kathos felt his brother was close by, because no other people were being tortured, except for the ones who were his allies.

Samuel suggested a poster campaign like World War II.

The poster was of Orion and Kale, standing with Stu and Samuel; humans and Voxians together. Then towering above, teeth gleaming, stood Deathladon. All were pointing up to the words in bold yellow and red:

YOUR PLANET NEEDS YOU!
ANNOUCEMENT TO BE BROADCAST
3.00PM BRITISH SUMMER TIME ON PRIMETIME TV
AND RADIO.

The UN had made sure everyone knew about the broadcast. Posters and bulletins were everywhere.

Voxians volunteered to put up posters. Those with speed had the whole planet covered before 1.00PM. Orion hated doing this type of work but being one of the fastest (apart from Rellik), he didn't really have a choice.

The UN would talk first, explaining Earth's predicament, followed by Samuel's speech. *'Earth will be doomed if we do not stick together and fight evil.'* The title which he'd written in bold writing at the top of his page.

The Voxians and Reptilians would get their chance to talk, along with Stu. This was to show the humans they had no reason to be afraid of their new allies.

What they needed to avoid would be people who shot first

(not that it would harm the Voxians,) and ask questions later.

~

3PM. LONDON, UK

Looking as humanly welcoming as possible, Fantasia prepared herself to speak in public. She was nervous, so her 'battle-mode' kept trying to sneak in.

She paced for a while, trying to keep it together and stop her face changing. That would be all she needed: Telling the humans she was their friend, and growing a metallic tint, and giant fangs as she said it.

"It's okay," Sam said, stepping next to her. "Piece of cake, picture them all naked!" he smiled his face warm and friendly.

"Good grief!" Fantasia laughed.

Two men stood with cameras aimed towards the podium. Fantasia had been asked to give her speech immediately after the UN, and a woman with a clapper board shouted, "On air in 5...4...3...2...1!"

Fantasia gulped, and then stepped onto the platform, looking at the others, hoping they would follow. They stepped to the side, so she had people's full attention. Fantasia cringed.

She glared at Drakos and at Samuel, who both waved at her and mouthed "GO ON!!!!"

Fantasia cleared her throat. "Good afternoon." She paused "My name is Fantasia. I'm here to show you proof that life exists on other planets." She paused to no reaction, "I'm a Voxian, the daughter of Rexus, Son of Kathos, who is Galaxican. Our planet, like yours, is full of life and intelligence. We're here to help save your lives." Mumbles came from the crowd. "Our planet is called Vox, and is on the Mythus nebula, which I believe your scientists have wrongly named *'The Eye of God'."*

Chatting continued loudly now, this was all big news. Sam approached the stairs climbing them slowly until he reached the podium.

Samuel stepped forward, standing next to her, as the crowd began mumbling and chatting amongst one another. He waited for them to refocus again...

Samuel began.

"Many people of our planet have known Fantasia and her family for many years. She's lived amongst the human species. Like the rest of the Voxians here on Earth, she has not caused any harm to our people, and has lived here in harmony amongst us."

More mumbling, as those around the aliens looked on, both with excitement and fear. The press, however, began jotting everything down, and cameras flashed over and over.

"Okay...Please, can we have a little order? Perhaps some silence would be appropriate now. After all, it is our planet that needs their help, and not the other way round." Samuel said, putting on his serious face, as if he was talking to a class of students, and it worked as always, very well.

Fantasia began to speak again.

"Please, I'm asking you to listen to me. Your planet is under a great threat of destruction by the dark Angel Belial. For you to remain here, you'll need to hide the vulnerable, and stand up and fight beside us and our other allies. We're willing to stand beside you and defend those who cannot fight for themselves," she said.

A news reporter stood waving his hand in the air, like a small child in class asking for permission to speak to the teacher.

"Princess... how will we know that this is not an alien invasion?" the reporter asked.

"Sir...it is! But we're not your invaders. I can show you who is," Fantasia said.

She took out the familiar photograph and began holding it up. Samuel stepped to one side and pressed a button on the podium, placing the photograph flat on a scanner. The picture came up on a large screen behind them.

The photograph was of Belial, Beth, and Mia.

The people stopped chatting. This man was already known here.

"That's our Prime Minister!" one of the news reporters shouted.

"That is his deputy and the chancellor! This can't be true, can it?" A cameraman asked.

"My God, what a bunch of deceiving bastards these politicians are!" another reporter said, as they all looked alarmed.

The crowd went into a frenzy!

"We must keep our heads," Samuel said, interrupting the chaos.

"Be cool, Dudes. We're here to help...there is nothing to panic about," Stu said, forgetting the speech he had in his hand. There was already chaos, which needed his attention. He dropped his paper to the floor, and just tried to help calm his people.

One man turned to the person next to him. "This is why I hate politicians...they're all a bunch of lying hypocrites."

Fantasia was quite relieved to hear this.

"I knew I didn't like that guy; he has shifty eyes!" another reporter said.

Fantasia looked at the photograph. Belial's eyes were blue/grey, but as the crowd watched they turned black, Demonic.

"Evil magic." One of the reporters said as he pointed at the changed picture.

Evil had infected him so much that his eyes could not hide it, not even in a picture.

"Is that some kind of magic?" a reporter asked.

"No, it's evil!" Fantasia said "Now, we need to get on."

Still chaos, Orion thought to himself that he wished Raidar was here, he'd get this back under control!

Right in front of the podium the giant man teleported!

"SILENCE! Raidar shouted.

His voice boomed and the full yard fell silent.

"WE NEED YOU! DO YOU UNDERSTAND?" he

boomed; heads nodded silently.

"Thank you." Fantasia smiled.

Raidar vanished.

Everyone stood, prepared to listen.

Orion chuckled to himself.

"Now, you have a choice! Fight, or hide. Those who need protecting, we've found a good method of transport that's not disruptive to them, and even those who have medical conditions will be moved with no harm. The planet we will take them to has good air quality and is called Reptilia. Others, who wish to train with us, will come to Vox. Time for humans is running out," Fantasia said.

She looked across as a familiar snake-like figure appeared. First the people gasped in fear, and then fell into a strange silence, which said it all.

Bellazard's sleek and lizard-like form walked to the podium, and Fantasia knew that the humans would either accept her or run.

Fantasia introduced the new speaker.

"This is the Queen of Reptilia. She's strong, brave and descended from the dinosaurs that once made their home here on Earth. Try not to be alarmed. Like humans, Reptilians have evolved. She's not here to harm you, but to protect you. She's a trustworthy and loyal ally," Fantasia said, stepping to one side.

As Bellazard came into view, the camera began to shake as the camera man panicked, almost dropping it. He had been focusing on those he'd been filming, so a Reptilian stepping onto the podium gave him a bit of a shock.

Fantasia approached the man and helped him steady himself. She smiled at him. "It will be okay," she said.

The cameraman smiled at her and nodded as Bellazard stood tall and strong. Her speech was broadcast.

"Good afternoon people of Earth, our founding mother. My name is Bellazard De Reptil and I'm the Queen of Reptilia, a planet in the Mythus nebula, which is light years away from the Milky Way. My people would be honoured to give shelter to those who are in need. Our medical technology can be used to heal those who come with us. The Voxian King has allowed their technology to bring those sick or wounded to our planet and help them to recover. I can assure you Belial is not interested in our planet. We've enough people of our own species to defend it, should we need to," she said.

Bellazard paused as people from outside the studio gathered to look at the alien. Cameras again began to flash. Words like 'walking with Dinosaurs' were heard, which Bellazard found highly amusing. Well, after all, that is what she was, and yes they would be walking together; man, and reptile, for the first time in Earth's history.

The television broadcast took only twenty minutes, but to Bellazard and Fantasia it seemed like a lifetime.

Fantasia was an alien life form, and like Bellazard would either be accepted or rejected!

Bellazard could be teleported by Fantasia, so gun fire was not a problem if it happened.

The reaction from the humans was disbelief to begin with, and then what seemed to be a type of strange acceptance; probably because they were still taking it all in.

A good human negotiator helped. He wasn't afraid, so why should they be?

As Bellazard and Fantasia stepped outside, groups of people were heading towards churches and village halls. It looked like a scene from an old film that Fantasia had remembered loving so much from her days here.

"I like these humans; they're trusting. I understand that they were taken in by such evil. They are easy to persuade. You didn't even need to show them any power," Bellazard said to Fantasia.

"I know. Having a negotiator and a whopping great Dinosaur next to me must have been proof enough!" Fantasia said.

The two friends giggled with one another, as they watched with pride as the humans signed up for war.

"I'm happy they want to go into battle with us. It shows we're not doing this for ungrateful people who don't care. They'll need to make changes to keep Mother Earth alive for longer and cut a lot of their industrial methods out that cause pollution," Bellazard said.

The next training would be difficult. The super-beings fighting with those who have human strength to protect themselves with. This was no longer like protecting one human they'd taken into their hearts; this was taking and teaching others who were not quite as powerful as Stu. Also, there are more humans than Voxians, so learning to fight with them in a massive number could prove a hard task.

The task belonged to Raidar and Hyedan.

After the human's already meeting Raidar, He would have no problem holding their attention.

All admired the human species. They would face the enemy head-on with little knowledge, with hope in their hearts, and would never give up.

While the Voxians were on Earth, Fantasia had asked Orion to check on a few family friends.

CHAPTER 31

According to Raidar, the best way to protect the humans would be their own military forces. He explained how this would not do anything to help with the Vardu and Voxian rebels, but it would help with human enemies who had decided to join Beth's fight against them.

Beth could be very persuasive. The Raitharns knew this only too well.

Shadow was happy to go with Orion to the old neighbourhood.

Orion found one of his friends outside.

Jim stood five feet ten inches; tiny in comparison to his friend. His hair was the latest Goth fashion, so it looked like the wind had blown it hard from the back. It all came over the front of his face, which just about left room for his eyes, nose, and mouth to appear through the style.

Jim had known Orion forever, so he just ignored the height difference.

Orion walked with Jim to the pub.

"So, did you catch the broadcast?" he said as they approached the door.

"Mate, the whole world saw the broadcast with your mom. But look at it this way; you couldn't possibly be a normal human, could you? So being an alien would give a better explanation why you're just...gigantic!" Jim said, patting his friend's arm.

"So, we're slumming it then?" Orion said. "Mother wouldn't even come in here when we lived on the estate. She may have untold powers, but she still refused to come with me today."

"Now she's a Voxian, she's gone all snobby!" Jim laughed.

The men laughed as they walked into the bar. It was crowded with strangers who'd just left work. Some whose clothes were grubby and scented with oil and grease from the local factory estate, just across the road.

The people in the bar talked amongst themselves and seemed to ignore a young couple as they snogged in the corner. Two men played snooker, completely oblivious to all the people around them.

Orion and Jim could see that the carpets were worn, and the curtains had seen better days. So had the barmaid and her manager, who stood ignoring the punters, talking to one another on the other side of the bar.

All were ignoring the drunk, who was aggressively hanging over the bar, trying to get their attention so he could buy another drink.

"God! What a shit hole," Jim said, walking towards the bar. The manager gave him a glare, and then when Orion approached as well, he stepped back, now paying attention.

"Two pints of your finest brew mate, please," Orion said.

The barmaid stepped towards the pumps, poured the drinks into the glasses that she had picked up from under the bar.

"Cash or card?" she asked, snarling at them passing them their drinks.

"Mmm...Cash! Don't like strangers in here then?" Orion snarled back; the woman looked uncomfortable. Orion stepped away, as she held out her hand for the money.

Jim handed over the money as the barmaid gave no eye contact; she just looked at the ground and slowly walked off to the till.

Jim and Orion sat down at the table closest to the silent juke box. Orion put his drink down on the table and walked over to the player.

"What a pile of crap!" he said. Looking at the list of music on the jukebox.

Jim came over to look, sipping his pint.

"Bet the last time they changed the music in this, the Beatles were at number one with an original hit!" Jim laughed.

"Oh, I can't find Mozart's Requiem. Maybe it's not that outdated then," Orion said, and began to laugh. "Oh, here we go, what about this?"

Led Zeppelin began playing *'A Whole Lotta Love.'*

The two men sat down, while the other people went back to chatting and ignoring the newcomers.

"So, tell me, what's up?" Jim asked.

"We need allies to help fight," Orion said.

"Like who?"

"You, others, young, fit and even soldiers," Orion said, looking at Jim. "The military because they're already trained in combat, and they have more chance of survival against their enemies than humans who have no training at all."

"But surely this is a matter for the UN?"

"Our problem is that, although the UN can do a certain amount here, the armed forces still take their orders from the government," Orion said.

"That's a problem?" Jim said, a little confused.

"The British PM is your problem, Jim. He is your enemy. We need to save the people of this planet. A Demon for a PM means you will have no chance. He can find out our plans first-hand from the military under his control. He will just have you all put to death unless you fight on his side."

"HOLY CRAP! Now that's a problem," Jim said. "We need to get word out. The military are paid by the government to protect the people. But with a corrupt government, it doesn't work so well."

Jim got up out of his seat.

"How do you deal with terrorism in your world Orion? After all, you must have some crackpots there," he said.

"We've got Belial, who rarely has the nerve to come to Capalia. Bethadora is our 'terrorist,' and she spends most of her time getting it wrong and being punished by her master. Our King suffers no power hunger, and he doesn't get his thrills from being higher in the ranking order than anyone else on Vox. Oh yes, he is of course my great grandfather!" Orion said, as he smiled.

"So, I'm sat with royalty? My God," Jim chuckled. "Orion the prince of giants. That's well, justified."

"Let's not start bringing God into the conversation!" Orion laughed.

Jim thought about his family and the threat he had been asked to help his friend with.

"I will pass the good news on to Stu, if you are in?" Orion said.

"Stu's with you? You can count on me, but that's great news. Last I heard he had made it to Titan." Jim said. The two friends spoke a little more, "I'll speak to the rest of the guys, I'm pretty sure they will come as well."

The two men finished their drinks and got up. The drunk who'd been in the background suddenly approached.

"Fighting a Demon? COME ON," he shouted, putting up his fists. "I'm a blood sucking Demon..." he shouted and fell to the floor with one swing of his own fist.

The two men just shrugged, stepping over the drunk, who then began making a snoring noise.

"How do I get in touch," Jim asked as the two men stood in the pub car park.

"I'll give you my mobile number," Orion said.

Orion searched in his coat pockets for pen and paper.

From the corner of his eye, he spotted the silver glint of a sword.

It was speeding towards Jim.

Orion dashed forward, holding his arm up in defence. The sword slashed into Orion's arm, which poured with blood, but it immediately began healing.

Orion pulled his sword from his jacket, and Jim calmly stepped back.

The attacker wore a long white mac and had brown shoulder length hair; his teeth and fangs were on full display. Orion had also changed into 'battle-mode' as the Raitharn traitor panicked.

Orion grabbed the warrior by his hair, and with one slash of his sword Orion took his head off . He stood holding it as it screamed obscenities at him. Orion took out a small canister of something from his coat pocket and poured it over the head, which was still shouting.

"Son of a bitch!" the Raitharn tried biting Orion.

Orion smiled at him and pulled out his silver lighter and ignited the head, which then began screaming loudly. Orion dropped it to the floor, and it disintegrated into ash.

Jim looked on for a while.

"Anyway, where were we?" Jim said. "Oh yes, your number."

The two men stepped over the body, Orion pouring the stuff from the canister once again and then with a flick of his lighter the body was gone.

Putting the number into Jim's phone for him, Orion then took his leave.

It was like the old days. Jim walked into his house; Orion went across the road and back to the house in the next close.

Both knew it wouldn't be long before they'd meet again. They would fight side by side for the survival of Earth. Like the war games they played on their consoles as children... this time though, the battles were real.

CHAPTER 32

The TV was on the news as always, Fantasia didn't really watch it, but it always stayed on in the background.

"Here is a broadcast from the Prime Minister, Ted Watson..." Belial's face appeared on the large screen, calm as he was trying to control the situation. He was outside Downing Street stood at a podium.

"Good evening." Belial said, clearing his throat a little.

The smug look on his face made Orion's blood boil. Belial or 'Ted' as he was calling himself on Earth, stood dressed in a black pinstripe suit, and as ever, he looked charming. He had a small pile of papers in his hand, which he put down on the podium. They contained his statement.

"Good people of Great Britain, I'm appealing to you all. I'm not a monster. We are being invaded by aliens who are trying to take over our country. We must not let this happen. I appeal to you all to understand. I am no more an alien than you are. People of the UK, we are at war with these creatures," Belial said.

One of the reporters asked "So, you are saying that you are not an invader, sir?"

Belial didn't answer, he just glared at the woman.

"Sir, why would the King of Vox lie to the world, then offer to stand by us in our fight for freedom? You have to admit, this country is in a terrible economic situation at the moment. And sir, didn't you make a law that forbid our nations workers the right to strike over bad pay conditions?"

Kathos and the others watched in horror.

Kathos noticed Belial's eyes. They had become black, shining like onyx stones.

"Are you trying to get us transfixed?" A News reader asked.

"I have no idea what you mean!" Belial said.

Then the military arrived, Raidar had gone to meet the generals of all of the armed forces, giving an explanation about all of this 'Mad Man's' abilities.

Jim entered, "have you seen... Yes you obviously have!" He said hugging Fantasia.

As an old family friend Jim was always welcome to come and go as he pleased.

Fantasia turned to face him. "You're not safe here, but if you're happy to leave with us we would love you see our world. You'll like it there, it's warm all year, and you can get a tan without UV's," Fantasia said kindly.

Jim laughed at her.

Kathos and Orion continued watching as the news readers were asked to evacuate, as they turned to arrest the PM, he had vanished into thin air.

"Slippery guy isn't he?" Jim said. Paying attention to the TV.

"Oh yes. The sneakiest, evil son of a gun you will ever encounter!" Orion said.

"But what about Earth? We still need to train and recruit, surely?" Jim asked.

"Oh, I am sure they'll be coming with us, our problem will be working out who are fighting with us, or spying for our enemy?" Fantasia said.

News reporters and people alike stood watching as the armed forces stormed number ten.

Everyone inside, even the cleaning staff were taken by armed guard, put into vehicles and placed under arrest.

CHAPTER 33

Rellik was sat in the library, reading. He had become quite obsessed with books, not being able to read anything in captivity. Belial had banned all books, newspapers, and press releases in Raithar, plus he was a prisoner who got no privileges at all.

Fantasia's house on Vox had become Rellik's sanctuary. He spent a lot of time recovering from his ordeal there, just catching up with what had happened in Capalia after his long absence.

Drakos spent a lot of time in his company, they became good friends.

When Ledawna attempted to stroke his face, he still flinched, but less now. He was looking younger and more recovered. Although the white in his hair was still dominant, he had flicks of black through it, and all the facial abrasions had vanished, only emotional scarring had remained.

Ledawna put out her arms and gave her son a hug. He flinched again, so she backed off as she felt his discomfort.

"Sorry, my son, really," she said, looking a little rejected.

Sat in the chair just on the other side of the room Kathos looked on with sadness. This warrior had been broken by Beth and Belial. It made him angry. He would capture Belial and drive him back to Hell this time, he was determined to succeed.

"I...I'm sorry Mother," Rellik hesitated. "It's been a long time since anyone has stepped into my personal space without a weapon of torture...I apologise for my behaviour," Rellik said, bowing with respect.

Ledawna gave a small nervous smile. Her son approached her and hugged her. She relaxed into his arms, squeezing, and hugging him back.

"What have they done to you?" she whispered, hugging him closer. He cuddled into her, like a child with a favourite teddy bear. Her familiar warmth and smell brought relief.

~

Fantasia waited for the arrival of her family and friends, she too had returned to her home on Vox.

Her father Rexus teleported there a little earlier than the meeting was due to start. He wanted to talk with her.

His stance always reminded her of a vampire actor from Earth's films, a young Christopher Lee.

"Do you believe he's genuine?" Rexus asked Fantasia.

"Yes, Father, I'm sure he is," Fantasia said.

The two walked outside and into the gardens for a while, arm in arm, comfortable with each other's company. Rexus was seven feet tall; slim, with a slight limp. He had been in many battles, and this was one of the scars that never healed fully.

He wore black trousers with a white shirt and his red overcoat. Rexus was a proud looking man. Dark brown hair swept to one side in a parting, very handsome, and very athletic, you could see that he was the brother of Rellik. The usual blue Voxian eyes and a small moustache and goatee beard. The two of them sat down by the flower beds on a bench.

Fantasia glimpsed at her father's complexion. As Rellik had been recovering, she noticed how similar the two brothers looked, only Rexus looked noticeably young in comparison, with a much slimmer face, but his body was slight, not like a mountain warrior, he must have more angel genes than Voxian. She found herself smiling at him.

"I understand why you are suspicious. Kathos is convinced that Rellik was captured, and Father, so am I. You should have seen the wounds he had. We don't stay wounded for very long, but these, Father, were deeper than I've ever seen; even after a battle," Fantasia said.

Rexus acknowledged her. "Do you know what hurts the most? How could our sister be responsible for doing this to him? I am ashamed of her."

As Rexus spoke, he stood up, picking a rose from the gardens, placing it into his lapel.

219

Fantasia took his hand, then gave him a hug, and they headed back to the house.

"Comet will be here soon. The two of you combining your psychic powers can show everyone that Rellik is innocent, and they'll feel better with confirmation," Rexus said.

Fantasia agreed as they both went to sit in different parts of the room.

There were times before Belial and Beth when his word would have been enough. It's terrible how distrust creeps in when people are constantly under attack.

Fantasia didn't want this for Earth.

Talk was quickly over; battle plans and training were both discussed, Kathos believed by the picture that the fight would be on their own terrain, it looked like the edge of Raitharn.

The meeting was over quickly. 'They would meet Belial and his Raitharn followers in Vox on 21st December 2512', which was now only four months away.

Dinner was arranged the next evening, Kathos was happy to invite members of Earth's military.

The battle would be on the mountains of Raithar at 1200 hours precisely. Strategies were planned, although Belial and Beth would believe no plans had got out, Kathos knew they would try to ambush the Capalian warriors and allies.

The evening hunt put food on the tables for the Voxians who had blood in goblets to make it civilised for their guests, food from Earth had been cooked and prepared for the humans attending.

Raidar had got to like barbecued beef whilst on Earth, and salads, so he was tucking into that.

"Great for the digestion," he said, holding it out on display for those around the table. "Things come out faster with all this green salad. It makes you feel fitter not fatter," Raidar said laughing.

The human guests weren't sure whether they should be laughing at him, or just be disgusted at what he had just implied, so they gave a small laugh that was confused, with sheer disgust on their faces.

Of course, this made Raidar laugh even more. The boys just sat with their hands over their faces, as he indulged even more with both toilet humour, and blood and guts, while eating his food.

A lot of the human guests seem to quickly lose their appetites.

Halen pulled him to one side.

"Father, please, cut the shit jokes while we're eating. Humans are our guests, be polite instead of giving them images that are going to make them puke and want to run to help Belial!" Halen said.

Kathos tried not to smile at them both, at the end of the day, Raidar needed no encouragement. He tried to hide his laughter with a yawn, and then covering it with a hand, diplomatically.

"Halen, it's alright. I'm sure these people are aware that your father is only testing how far he can take them, before they are all disgusted enough to be sick," Kathos said sarcastically.

Everyone around the table settled, and Raidar stopped the toilet jokes. He just spoke about puke instead; the hint taken...well sort of.

"It's okay," Jim said to Halen. "If these guys had weak stomachs, they would not be in the jobs they are. Believe me, they've all heard a lot worse."

The human soldiers gave a smile and continued eating.

Orion had taken Shadow outside for a walk, and was just returning, having missed most of Raidar's bad humour.

"Look what I found!" he said, holding a letter in his hand. "This was pinned to the gate as Shadow and I came back in. It's from Belial," Orion said.

Rellik got up, taking the letter from Orion, then taking it over to his father and brother. He nervously handed it to Rexus, who began reading it aloud.

**"Rellik, you are a traitor.
I am your Lord and Master!**

I will allow you time to say goodbye to your friends and family before I come back to get you.
I will show no mercy. You will die for your crimes against me.

Belial

Rellik let out a shriek of laughter. "I believe I may have upset him," he said.

Kathos didn't see the joke and looked at Rexus.

"We must keep Rellik in our sight at all times," Kathos said.

"I'll be happy to look after my uncle. Raidar and his sons can also help to take care of him. We'll keep him safe," Fantasia said.

Rellik looked over at his old friend, who agreed with the decision. He wasn't happy; he still needed time to believe Rellik wasn't out to betray them all, and the letter on the gate got him thinking, what if he was just working for Belial?

Rellik was nervous. What would happen if Raidar decided he was lying?

Raidar looked Rellik in the eyes, growling as he walked past.

"He better watch his back." Raidar pushed into Rellik's side, and Rellik toppled to the ground.

"Stop!" Rellik said, picking himself up from the floor. He angrily sped over to Raidar, getting directly into his face.

Raidar ignored his friend's actions, pushing past him and heading to the door.

Rellik was back on the floor.

"You better watch your back. You may have more than just Belial to worry about," Raidar said.

Raidar growled as he lifted the side of his mouth up, showing his fangs.

Rexus put his hand out and helped his brother to his feet.

"Fantasia, I think I should look after Rellik when you're absent. I believe we have a long way to go before we can prove Rellik's innocence to our chief warrior, and Rellik would be in danger," Rexus said. "I'd rather Belial came after him than Raidar. He would let Belial kill Rellik, and we would lose another member of our family."

Rellik put his hand on Rexus's shoulder.

"If I spend time with him, he'll realise that I'm not his enemy. We should stick to the plan, and you should leave me with Raidar," Rellik said.

Rexus shook his head.

"Okay, but it's your funeral, Bud," he said.

"Yes, Brother, it is! I'm willing to take the chance on an old friend, rather than let him think he can't trust me. I can face the abuse. Let's face it, I have been through a lot worse," Rellik said.

"On your own head be it!" Rexus laughed.

CHAPTER 34

The thought of Raidar protecting Rellik was ludicrous.

Fantasia had to go back to Earth so that human recruits could be trained. The numbers were getting larger, more realising what Belial was.

Fantasia had no choice but to leave Raidar in charge of her uncle as he recovered from his injuries from captivity.

"How do we know, Fantasia?" Raidar said "He's been gone for years. How do we know for sure that he isn't still with our enemy? He could be giving them information as we speak. I have seen no evidence he's telling the truth."

Rellik stomped up to Raidar angrily, after overhearing their conversation.

"I'm not a traitor!" he said, heading towards Raidar with his fist clenched.

"What you gunna do there? Hit me?" Raidar asked.

Fantasia stood between the two of them.

"How can I leave you both alone together?" she asked.

"What do you want me to do Raidar? You know me; I was your best friend. This evil bastard has even threatened my life...Don't you get it? Do you really think I look like this because I was on holiday? I've aged like a human. I look older than any other Voxian, still after months in recovery. Do you really believe I would allow myself to be changed like this?" Rellik asked.

Raidar looked Rellik in the face.

"You can't prove anything; that's my point! You're just a weakling who got picked up by the opposing side. Did you believe you could just come back and spy for them? Live with your family, and kill your friends?" Raidar said angrily, walking around Rellik, watching him.

"Then why don't you just kill me and get it over with? I don't give a shit if I'm alive or dead. But if I am to live, I want it to be on the condition that I have your trust. I want to fight with you. Can't you understand that?" Rellik said, his fangs protruding in a rage.

The sound of someone approaching made the argument stop. Light footsteps drew closer.

"Who's there?" Rellik said, looking up.

Ghost was coming towards them. It was only seconds before she came into view.

"Hello, who's this hiding behind the mask? Why don't you give us a look at your pretty face," Rellik said? Smiling at her.

"Do I know you? Your voice sounds familiar," Ghost asked.

Rellik stopped smiling as Ghost peeled off the mask that had hidden her face. Fantasia and Raidar looked on in silence.

Rellik couldn't believe it.

"Radonna!" Rellik said, getting a little emotional.

He could hardly catch his breath. The figure of his dead wife stood there before him.

Rellik ran forward, arms open, and Fantasia found herself standing in his path.

"Stop!" she said.

Ghost stood back, looking confused. She didn't know what to say. The name she heard was familiar. The man seemed familiar as well, but she had no memory of him at all, just a slight memory of the name he had just called her.

"Is that my name?" she asked him inquisitively.

Fantasia looked at her closely, trying to put colour into the white figure. She realised why she had felt a familiar connection.

She wasn't only familiar; Radonna was always in the background. She had unfortunately been someone distant to Fantasia. Her masked face covered any familiar memory that Fantasia would have of her.

Ghost was a ghost! Not a shapeshifter!

No-one seemed to realise who she was, which was a bit sad. As far as the Voxian's knew ghosts did not exist, so this was a first.

Voxians kept memory books when people died, to honour the dead.

Radonna's book would have been the responsibility of Rellik, who was not there, so her memories were stored and logged onto a computer, waiting for him to retrieve them.

"Drakos, he must have known who you were," Fantasia said.

"Well, if he did, he said nothing," Radonna said, walking over to Rellik.

Explanations didn't matter. All Rellik could think of was the good news. His wife was returned to him, even if it was in spirit form, although there was no explanation why.

"What do you remember of your life before? Is there anything at all?" Rellik asked her gently.

"I'm sorry, I remember nothing. I get the odd flash, vague sounds and pictures. As soon as I came here I knew I belonged here. There were familiar images, all seemed to be swirling around in my mind. I believe I'm here for a reason, but I'm unsure what that is, I don't understand why if I died on Vox, why I became a spirit on Earth?" Radonna said.

Rellik softly raised his hand and tried to touch his wife. After years of torture at Belial's hands, there must be some good come from his capture, and he believed this was it; the balance for all his suffering.

His hand went straight through. He couldn't believe it. A new method to torture him. He could see her but not touch her. Rellik frantically tried again and again... but nothing.

"Why can't I touch you?" he said, panicking.

Fantasia took his hand. He was still frantically attempting to touch Radonna's ghost-like figure by trying to hold her hand.

Anger began taking over him.

"You have no memory of me at all? None?" he asked frantically again, reaching for her in disbelief.

"I'm sorry, nothing..." Radonna said, sensing his sadness; it distressed her.

Radonna's heart felt like it would break for him. Not only did she have Rellik's emotions and his memories, she also had to come to terms with her death.

"At least I can see you. I don't know, perhaps there will be something we can do to help make you corporeal," Rellik said, looking hopeful at Fantasia, who said nothing.

Radonna didn't know what to say. Her body had been sacrificed along with her head when she died, otherwise she would have regenerated. That's what Voxians did.

"I feel like I'm in a dream, Radonna," Rellik said, admiring his wife like she was living. Memory suddenly flashed before her. She smiled at him.

"Please call me Ghost, for now. I think I'm going to go out of my mind if you call me by my living name. I hope you're not offended."

Rellik realised she still had no idea who he was. Her feelings for him must have died when she did. The physical aspects of her mind leaving with her physical being.

He remembered the mask was placed on her by Belial as a joke when he tortured and killed her. Like a beheading from the days of the French revolution on Earth; one of Radonna's favourite parts of Earth's history.

He approached her...

"Are you sure you've no memories at all?" he asked, as he fought back the tears. "I just can't believe you have no memory of me."

Rellik composed himself. *'Well, what was the point in trying to explain, when Radonna may never be able to remember?'*

He needed to talk to his father. He may have some kind of cure.

Fantasia could feel Rellik's sadness. She couldn't decide what was worse; living with her memory forever because she had died, or looking at her while she couldn't remember him, or be able to touch her.

Rellik was already vulnerable. His recovery would be hampered by this. He was in such an emotional state.

Raidar watched with great fascination. Rellik was no traitor. He had been captured and tortured. Both had lost the women they loved; only Raidar hadn't been witness. His eldest son, Flynn, had seen his mother's death, Willamina had been Raidar's world. What would he have done if he'd seen her die?

"So, now what?" Raidar asked.

"I believe it's time to find Grandfather again," Fantasia said. She closed her eyes and called him through her telepathy.

Drakos appeared, he was about to enter his library when he heard the fuss.

"I understand your anger Rellick, but it is a delicate situation," Drakos began to say.

"You knew?" Fantasia said.

"Delicate, my arse..." Raidar said angrily. "I don't like deceit, so tell me why you said nothing, you arsehole?"

"Radonna coming back as a ghost! What would that sound like to a species that had never seen or believed that they existed. You would have locked me up. I don't think even you recognised her did you Raidar?" Drakos said.

Kathos appeared.

Raidar grumbled something, incoherent.

"Rellik, it would be only a matter of time before you met. But Radonna had gone to the mountains. I thought it better to deal with this when she returned from her caves, which is now," Kathos said.

Raidar stood fangs protruding.

"Who said you made the rules here?" he mumbled at Kathos.

"I DO, AS YOUR KING!" Kathos stood up to Raidar. He was the ruler.

Raidar sat immediately, showing respect for his King.

"I'm sorry when Radonna came back with no memory I didn't want to cause her trauma. Knowing who she was when I first saw her on Titan even with her mask, this had to be done delicately. Rellik was in no emotional state to receive such news when he had been found, not until he had made some recovery. Your mother did insist we tell you. But when I tried, you just seemed unable to cope. I had no idea how you would take this; you were so ill," Kathos said.

Kathos held Radonna's hand. With some concentration, she managed to make physical contact.

"How are you doing that?" Rellik asked with excitement.

"Radonna can become semi-corporeal, it must be part of her adaptive skills as a Voxian." he said to everyone in the room. "That's if you wish to," Kathos said to her. "The trauma of your death and the loss of memory have made you distrust. I'm an Angel, so you trust me. In time you'll get to know all these people better, and your trust for them will return... Do you understand?"

Kathos smiled as his hand suddenly drifted through hers, her concentration diminished.

"With some practise you'll regain the powers you once had. After all, you are back on your own territory. My advice, if you wish to take it, is for you to go home with your husband and try to build a new relationship together as friends for now. It'll be good for you both," Kathos said.

Radonna concentrated and held her hand out towards Rellik. They touched for the first time in many years. As this happened, some of her memories came back. He was with the woman he loved dearly, and that to her was all she needed to agree to go home, even if it wasn't as before, her search was over.

"Rellik, I apologise. I hope we can stand together and fight. If anything good can come out of this meeting, we can have our friendship back if you wish," Raidar said, looking towards Rellik.

"I don't mean to be a party pooper, but we're desperately running out of time," Drakos said.

"Still moaning, Father? Is there nothing that makes you happy?" Orion said, entering the room.

Drakos was right; they couldn't afford any more delays, not even a day.

Raidar picked up his sword. It gleamed as he walked into the daylight, and his three sons stood beside him.

"For Glory or Hell," they all said.

"Cheesy!" Halen said sarcastically as all four of them fist bumped.

"Now this is going to be fun! Let's go and do a bit of clobbering," said Raidar.

"Yeah! Bring it on, puppy dogs!" Rellik said, joining them. He put his hand on his friend's shoulder and turned to his wife "I will see you at home later."

Radonna smiled at him and nodded.

Orion joined them, taking out his sword. All had their fangs on display.

The six men stepped outside pentagrams lighting blue, and picked up speed, going swiftly to the training facilities in the mountains.

Kathos, Radonna and Fantasia watched as they disappeared into the distance.

"I believe Belial may have one hell of a fight on his hands, Grandfather," Fantasia said.

"He doesn't stand a chance!" Radonna added.

Kathos smiled at them both because they were right.

CHAPTER 35

Stu looked out at the green fields and hills that led to the mountains of Capalia. Cal was sleeping amongst the fields, in the grass, under an orchard of apple trees, his tail tapping as he dreamt of a happy place.

Stu chuckled to himself as he watched this giant creature's body move up and down in rhythm.

The Manor Estate was his home now. He had been given a house by the Voxians. He couldn't believe he'd ever settle down, especially in a different world. This planet was almost identical to Earth, fanged animals and no money or greed. All the creatures here had one hell of a bite, so he didn't try to give them a cuddle, even if they were cute. But it added to his love of the place.

Stu walked towards the conservatory, attached to Fantasia's house. It was made of glass, rectangular frames which built a giant structure, with a telescope just poking outside one of the high windows to get a glimpse of the night sky. This was the home of his college friend and mentor on this planet, Orion.

"Jeez, that must get hot!" he said quietly to himself.

Stu was grateful to be away from Titan. He thought he would be stuck on that metal Hell for the rest of his life.

He wondered. *'Would he have been returning to Earth with the others now? Who knows?*

Stu felt at home here. It wasn't like he couldn't visit Earth any time he wanted to. No expensive flights or only the richer could go, now anyone could come and go on the condition they would do no harm.

Deathladon approached Stu. He had been given a place to stay amongst the Voxians. Deathladon (unlike Stu) was going back to Reptilia at the end of the battle so for now was staying with Stu in his home.

"We need to talk," Deathladon said in a gruff voice, which echoed through the Estate grounds. Cal stirred a little, making him aware of how loud he was being. He brought the volume down, which to him was a whisper.

"Okay, old friend, tell me is it a chick?" Stu asked, whispering as well.

Deathladon laughed. "No...NO! No chick involved."

"Oh, Dude sorry, I didn't mean to pry," Stu said.

"We have both trained hard and done all we can here. I need to go back to my planet. Will you come with me?" Deathladon asked.

Stu looked at the Reptilian with some curiosity.

"Dude, why are we leaving here? It's my home," he said.

"I understand this, Stu. But there is an ancient tribe on our planet that I believe will help us. Come with me to see Raidar. I believe he will agree to us leaving to persuade this species to join our fight, I think Sky may appreciate this as well." Deathladon said.

"Sure, man, whatever you think will help," Stu said.

"Please climb on board, little friend," Deathladon laughed quietly.

Stu climbed onto Deathladon's shoulders, and they both headed towards the mountains. Raidar and Bellazard were waiting. Bella had been staying in the mountains as Raidar's guest. She loved it there.

Raidar, Deathladon and Bellazard walked away and spoke for a while, out of Stu's earshot, and they agreed that the three friends should go.

They decided Markus should take them and wait on the borders in the caves; taking supplies to last them while they negotiated talks with what they hoped would soon be allies.

Markus was Raidar's head warrior, he was a kindly and reliable man, so Raidar would trust him with his friends.

Sky didn't get what the silence was over or what they were going for, but she went anyway.

The group teleported, appearing near the Reptilian Mountains. Markus began to set up a small base camp for them, lighting a fire, so that they could be comfortable and sleep for the night before they began their journey.

"I want my own tent!" Sky demanded, "I am not sleeping

with three burping, farting men!"

This was agreed.

The next morning, the human and dinosaur had had plenty of sleep and Sky was rested enough to start their journey.

Stu, Sky and Deathladon found themselves in a remote part of the Reptilian Mountains. Hard terrain for humans, but of course Stu relied on Deathladon to pick him up and carry him on his back.

Sky looked on, she had to keep waiting for them. She didn't mind because this was a bit of an adventure.

The three came to a large set of caves that were so remote even Deathladon had problems remembering how to climb them.

Sky took hold and teleported them to the edge at the top.

"Dude what's this? It's like a story that I had read to me as a young boy about dwarves and stuff. Hey, we aren't going to persuade a load of little people with pointy hats to fight with us, are we?" Stu asked curiously.

Sky let out a laugh.

"No, I've heard of that story. These are not dwarves, but I think you may be surprised when you see what they are," Deathladon assured his friends.

They approached the dark entrance to the caves. There was something sparkling in the distance. It was pitch black, but as Sky looked around, it had the occasional torch planted on the side of the walls, which Deathladon lit as they climbed down a large, tunnelled pathway.

Stu and Sky began hearing a loud snoring sound, and then growling. They held on a little tighter to Deathladon as the sounds drew nearer.

"Dude, you don't have yourself a resident giant or something, do you?" Stu whispered to him nervously.

Deathladon made no response, just a very quiet. "Shh."

As they entered a clearing in the cave, a massive curled up figure lay sleeping soundly in the corner. Stu couldn't quite work out what it was. Although Sky had caught on and was trying not to dance with excitement. As they turned to observe their surroundings they noticed more of these figures, all snoozing around this massive cave area.

"WHAT THE HELL ARE THEY?" Stu shouted.

Deathladon looked with surprise at his friend. "They are our ancestors," Deathladon said.

Deathladon was talking louder now. The creatures began to stir from their rest.

One of them, an extremely large creature, stretched out. As it did, its face hit the light from one of the torches. The creatures body also came into view. Wings spread out, and a serpent like tongue whipped out of its mouth.

"NO way, Dude! Is that... Is that a...a," Stu began panicking. If he could have run at that precise moment, he would have, but he was on Deathladon's back, holding on with all his might.

Sky of course was on the floor, walking next to them both, no fear at all.

"A Dragon?" the creature said, as its golden scales hit the light. The bed of gold and brightly coloured jewels the dragon had been sleeping on were revealed. The giant creature got up, yawned and stretched some more, walking over calmly to Deathladon.

"Greetings, my friends," Deathladon said, signalling for Stu to climb down.

Stu sat tightly gripping on for dear life.

Sky stepped forward, not sure how to greet this magnificent animal.

"Dude, that's a Dragon!!! I'm not going anywhere...Dragon... Dude!" Stu said as he remained grabbing on to Deathladon tightly.

"He's not going to harm you Stu, he's beautiful." Sky said, extremely impressed.

"Yes, young Voxian, well observed. Don't worry, young man, I'm not going to eat you. Well, I don't think I am. Human meat is a little tough you know. A cow or a sheep is more of a delicacy...Now, are you going to get down so we can talk?" the Dragon asked.

Stu nervously slipped gently down onto the ground, and the Dragon watched with curiosity. "Deathladon, you have brought a human here. This, I'm sure you know, is forbidden. So, this is either very brave of you, or very stupid. I'm not sure which," the Dragon said.

"Be calm, Blaze, he is a friend. A human from Earth willing to fight for his own kind, and ours..." Deathladon began saying.

The Dragon beat its tail on the cave floor and began to laugh loudly. The sound echoed through the whole place.

"Fight...? Deathladon, how can this small creature fight?" Blaze asked, looking very amused.

Sky just stood observing.

Stu stepped over to argue, but Deathladon caught him by the arm and pulled him back beside him.

The other Dragons awoke and were now beginning to approach. That would mean Stu either stayed beside Deathladon or died at the first opportunity. Blaze was their negotiator, and the others may not prefer cow or sheep; they might prefer to eat human and ask questions later.

"You must stay close. Dragons are sometimes very unfriendly," Deathladon whispered.

Blaze began to laugh. "Unfriendly? Now that I believe, is a little unkind." Blaze's eyes glowed red.

Sky readied her sword.

Deathladon thought the Dragons would ignore Stu. He began to realise at this point that perhaps he should have given some warning that would have prepared his human ally. Deathladon was worried that he may have put his friends in mortal danger.

As the Dragons approached, Stu stepped from his friend's side and stood in front of Deathladon, who was still trying to keep Stu behind him. The Dragons were confused by his actions, so they all stood still, and looked at one another. The Dragons wanted to see the next move the human would make. They had not expected him to make such a bold move, no one seemed to pay any attention to Sky at all.

"Do you know the legend of the Dragon slayer?" Stu asked Blaze.

"Yes, we've heard of this. What about it?" Blaze smiled at Stu.

"I was appalled that one of my own ancestors would ever be a part of killing such magnificent creatures," Stu said.

Blaze looked at the other Dragons, who had now sat waiting for the human man to feed them more compliments. Stu had realised that Dragons were very vain creatures, so he had thought that feeding their egos would persuade them to be allies of the Voxians, and hopefully not eat him.

"Go on, young man!" An older blue Dragon moved closer and sat beside him.

"The one thing humans regret is the loss of your species from our planet. We've been told stories of bravery, magic, and power, which have been passed down from the generations of our families. No one believes you ever existed, that your species are just stories. It's a privilege even if you kill me right now, to have met the most beautiful creatures in this Multiverse."

"Keep going...you're doing great," Sky whispered to Stu.

The old Dragon turned and began to speak to the others. He asked them to go with him to decide what would happen to this 'exceptionally fine young man,' as Deathladon held back the laughter.

"What do they mean?" Stu asked, a little panicked again.

Sky could still not quite take it all in, being brought up on Earth, she too believed Dragons to be fairy-tale.

"That was amazing, my friend. You may have got yourself killed, but bravery beyond the call of duty," Deathladon said, patting Stu on the shoulder.

They watched and paced as the Dragons talked loudly about 'this magnificent young fellow,' and his love for them. How could they kill him?

"Great, the Voxian doesn't even get a mention." Sky whispered.

What about his species, who loved the Dragons? Surely

they would like to meet them.

He began to realise that his speech had worked.

There were six Dragons in all. Not so many, when you consider they were once a thriving species. They'd fled with the dinosaurs and could remember how their older ancestors evolved into Reptilians, good people. Deathladon would not let any harm come to them. He was, after all, still one of them.

Blaze was the leader of the Dragons. The blue Dragon was Grail; he was the oldest of the group of Dragons. Then there were two green coloured called Hotshot and Firly, and lastly two black with red horns, Daster and Bail. All had dark red eyes and long, snake like tongues that kept slipping in and out, like a lizard. The black Dragons also had a red outline on the skeleton of their gigantic wings. They really were magnificent to behold.

Grail approached Deathladon. "Why have you come here?" he asked.

"To ask that you help in our fight against a Demon. He's going to destroy all planets if we cannot defeat him and his army," Deathladon said, bowing.

"Why does this concern us?" Grail asked.

"Because when the evil one has destroyed Earth, we may be next. And then, my friend, where will we live, supposing any of us survive?" Deathladon said.

"What kind of evil is this?" Grail asked him.

"A fallen Angel; he has escaped captivity from Hell!" Sky butted in.

Grail looked down at the Voxian, it was like they had finally noticed her.

"We all know Hell, so what species are you? I can smell your blood, it isn't human." the old Dragon said, standing beside his leader.

"I am Voxian, we live in the same solar system." Sky said showing no fear.

Grail stepped back into the group of Dragons, and they spoke loudly for a while longer. Stu was amused as they seemed to ignore that everyone could hear them.

"Okay, if things go wrong here, I will stand in the way while you run for it. Have you got that?" Deathladon whispered to Stu and Sky.

Stu nodded, preparing to run, Sky again put her hand to her sword..

The Dragons went back, and Blaze looked at Deathladon, then at Stu and Sky, who were awaiting their fate.

"What will we need to do?" Blaze asked Deathladon.

"The one thing that Dragons are fantastic at; you must fight with fire," Deathladon said.

"BLOOD, FIRE, WAR, HATE!" both Sky and Stu chanted.

The Dragons had agreed to fight.

It suddenly dawned on them why he was here. Deathladon wanted a way that the enemies could be destroyed quickly. If the Dragons stood with the humans they could incinerate all that came their way, no beheading necessary.

Stu thought for a moment. The Dragons would protect their human allies against Belial, Beth and the Raitharns. But surely the Voxians must realise that they could be killed by them as well if they got in the way of the Dragon's fire.

Orion would be the one to sort this problem out, maybe with some kind of fireproof armour?

CHAPTER 36

Kathos assembled the leaders together. He had news and needed their advice.

All the warriors had been training; mountain and city warriors alike in their own environments.

Hyedan arrived with Azaya. They had appeared ahead of the others who were securing the city borders.

Raidar and his sons were sat next to Fantasia and Orion on the grass by the lakeside.

Kathos was at the water's edge. The place was beautiful, the water so clear you could see the fish that swam in it.

Kathos watched while warriors set out seats in small rows, all placed carefully so the leaders would be able to sit with him.

"I need everyone not to react when our allies arrive," Kathos said into a microphone. Kathos moved away from it uneasily as the sound of his voice echoed across the lake.

"What new allies?" Hyedan asked.

"The Reptilians have a flying species on their planet. They have kindly offered to fight against Belial. Now, I must warn you, they're vain, so we've been advised by Bellazard to praise their beauty. They will not harm our people; of that I'm sure," Kathos said.

Hyedan and the other warriors looked confused. All, that is, except for Raidar, who knew of the Dragons already.

Suddenly the sound of wings flapping echoed through the air in the distance.

The warriors all stood and looked up towards the sky.

The other warriors teleported back with Markus by the side of the lake. Sky looked really excited as she began waving frantically.

"Dude, look what I brought yah home!" Stu said.

Orion's mouth fell open.

Stu looked around to see the rest of the warriors all staring in amazement, as Blaze came into sight; his golden scales glistened as the daylight hit them. Grail followed, his scales looked almost like petrol, as the spectrum of colours on his body all began changing as he flew. He gave out a high-pitched roar, and fire from his mouth was blasted into the sky.

An entrance that even Kathos had to admit was impressive.

The Voxians all watched, taking a sharp intake of breath. Kathos began cheering and clapping as the Dragons made their entrance, so the Voxians copied. The Dragons loved every minute of it, lapping up the attention.

Raidar walked over to the Dragons to greet them with Kathos.

"Thank you for coming," Kathos said, holding out a hand of friendship to Blaze.

"We are happy to help, Kathos. It was your kind who saved us from extinction and gave us our new home, and therefore we can't refuse the Angel's descendants."

"Descendants?" Kathos said a little confused.

"Yes, it was an angel from your galaxy that brought us here to this nebula," Blaze said.

"Ah! Not descendants, you mean Galileo, my brother!" Kathos smiled as he said this.

The Dragon looked impressed at the Angel.

"You are like us? Your lifespan is long?" Blaze asked.

"Yes, you could say even eternal," Kathos chuckled.

Raidar stepped up next to them. He admired these creatures, they were at least forty feet tall, and their wingspan must have been the same again on each side; all of which were out on display like a peacock.

"A magnificent sight," Hyedan whispered to Azaya.

She nodded, saying nothing.

"Now you are awesome!" Raidar said excitedly.

"Mmm thanks! I think!" Blaze said, looking at the warrior.

The Voxians looked a lot like big humans to the Dragons, but the technology around as he flew in seemed far more advanced. Blaze had never seen such a place before. But there again, since the move from Earth, he had not seen any type of place with corporeal occupants.

Orion looked over as the city folk were slowly arriving in abundance, and the lake area started getting full.

The excitement becoming subdued as the creatures displayed themselves to their new allies.

Elen arrived. She was Hyedan's wife and one of the most beautiful women Orion had ever seen. She had long silver/white hair that looked almost diamond encrusted in the Voxian daylight. She stood six feet tall, with a slim figure, wearing a long blue gown and a hooded cape in silver.

The Dragons watched Elen eagerly, like a piece of jewellery that walked and talked.

Grail walked over to her, and she smiled at him, stroking his long, blue/green coloured face.

"You are indeed the oldest creature that has ever lived," she said, still stroking him.

"Thank you," Grail said, gently nuzzling his face near to her shoulder.

"Grail, is it?" Elen asked him.

"Yes, I'm honoured to meet you. Can I ask your name? I'm not blessed with second sight," Grail said.

"I am Elen. This is my daughter Azaya, and husband Hyedan," she said.

"Honoured, I am sure." The Dragon's tongue flicked out as he stood staring for a while.

Blaze looked around. He could see mountains, higher than in Reptilia, snow-capped. He would love to live there, because despite the Dragons heated bodies they loved cold.

Hyedan gestured Orion to come and meet his family. He was happy that the fire breathers were on their side. It could have been quite disastrous if Belial had persuaded these creatures to fight with him.

Luckily he didn't know they existed either.

"Orion, have you met my wife? She's the woman stroking the Dragon." Hyedan pointed Elen's way.

Orion nodded at her in greeting, "Yes sir, I have," he said.

"As I'm sure you remember, this is Azaya," he said a little sarcastically.

Azaya put out her hand, and instead of Orion shaking it, Orion held onto it, swinging it to and fro. Raidar and Hyedan immediately began to smirk as Azaya pulled her hand away and looked at Orion confused.

"Have you quite finished?" she asked him a little abruptly.

"Mmm... yes! Oh yes, sorry, oh sorry!" Orion went red, letting go of Azaya's hand.

"What's this? 'Love at first sight,' my boy? Is that what you were thinking?" Hyedan said, smiling, Orion looked at the floor and anywhere else that didn't involve Hyedan, Raidar or Azaya.

"Please excuse me," Orion said, walking past them, stepping towards his mother.

Hyedan elbowed Raidar in the ribs, and they both began to laugh with one another.

"Think he may be a little embarrassed, he must have a bit of a crush," Hyedan said.

"Oh, grow up, for the Goddess sake!" Azaya said, annoyed. "Parents are such a bloody humiliation." She walked away in the opposite direction.

"Oh, that's intense," Raidar said, making one last comment before she left.

A sudden cry came from the side of the lake. A withered woman appeared on the horizon.

Everyone fell silent.

The Voxians and their allies watched as the woman slowly approached, collapsing only feet away from them.

Orion ran to assist her, but Kathos held out his hand, signalling for him to wait.

Kathos walked over. She was covered from head to foot in scars, bloody and wounded. He listened as she wheezed loudly, her body battered and bruised, her clothes torn. She made one last wheezing sound as her throat crackled, and she gargled, choking on her own blood.

Then there was silence…

As the women lay dead, Kathos walked over to her. Her hand fell open, and inside it was a piece of parchment. Kathos opened it and read it out loud.

'Dogs,
We are to meet at the destination of my choosing. I choose the northern mountains of Raithar, where you and your idiot allies are unfamiliar. These have remained barren and unused for many years now, and like you, Kathos and your people, they are surplus to my requirements.
Brother, I will kill you myself, and your pet Rellik will die at my hand too.
You can trust me when I tell you that I will take every opportunity to make your armies less in number.'

Belial

Kathos looked on in disbelief.

"Why would anyone do such a thing? The sooner we have him captured, the better," Kathos said, looking down at the woman's body again.

"This is what he's good at; threats and mind games," Raidar said to his King.

"Orion," Raidar said, "we need a shield, and good walking boots for the humans, if they're to take on the task of fighting. I have knowledge of the Raitharn Mountains and the terrain there is extremely rough."

Raidar looked at the people who'd been there and witnessed the death of this poor woman.

"You see, this animal has no mercy for anyone or anything, he did this to her just so he could pass on a message." He said.

Orion knew what he was fighting for. As he looked on at the human's body, she had been abused; like something, not someone.

"We need our Reptilian friends to be equipped with boots for their feet, to keep them from slipping off the mountain edges. Also, they all need grappling hooks if they find

243

themselves falling," Raidar ordered.

"On it!" Orion said, leaving quickly, heading back to his science labs at the Voxian University in Capalia.

Kathos knew that Orion could move faster than any of the others. It would be quicker for him to do as Raidar requested.

Hyedan and Raidar began talking battle strategies.

Rellik and Radonna volunteered themselves for battle. Hyedan and Raidar accepted their help.

"I've been through this area recently when I escaped. I will be of some help, hopefully. But I must warn you, Raidar's right in presuming that the terrain is rough. It's derelict and hot, with no water for miles. Our devil enemies have chosen well. We can investigate," Rellik said to Raidar, Hyedan and Kathos.

"I'm going too!" Fantasia volunteered.

"I'll come with you. Fantasia," Rexus turned to his wife Genesis "Will you stay here and get everyone prepared? We'll be back to report our findings as soon as we know exactly what's out there."

Kathos and Ledawna led the way, teleporting to the mountain side, knowing full well that they would be heading straight for a trap.

Rexus and Flynn took another route, along with some of the warriors who insisted on protecting their King and Queen.

Their swords hidden well inside their jackets, and long white gleaming fangs ready to shred whatever they met.

They began to climb, and soon enough they could see a sea of colour in the distance, as the Raitharns approached, red hair waving in the breeze and fangs already on display. They were ready to attack and had come in their thousands.

"This is not an ambush, my friend," Rexus said to Flynn. "This is the war!"

"We must warn the others, before it's too late," Flynn said as his wings spanned out, flying high into the air.

Kathos looked at his enemies, his brother, and his followers, humans, Vardu and some of the winged men of Isis the third and smallest planet in the Mythus system. His people had never interacted with them so, would have no idea how to face them in battle. He was grateful therefore to have the dragons.

"Are you joining us?" Belial asked.

It suddenly occurred to Kathos that the winged men may not have decided whose side they were on.

"If you wish to fight for the good, then we are your neighbours, perhaps becoming our ally would be an advantage." Raidar said.

"So, Belial could not deceive you so easily with his lies?" Kathos asked.

Kathos brought what little men he had together, standing almost face to face with Belial and his army of men.

They all stood swords out, ready to fight and hissing loudly as Belial's followers stood inches away from them.

Belial smiled, face to face with his brother.

"You have followers, Kathos," Belial smiled. "Are they so few because you believe them invincible and strong? Or did you really believe we would not be here waiting for you, so we could destroy you all quickly and little by little?" Belial laughed loudly, looking over at Beth, who just smiled at her master.

Raidar turned to look straight into Belial's face and laughed back. To Belial's surprise, regiments of human soldiers suddenly teleported to the side of Kathos; Jim leading them. Four of Kathos's warriors using their powers in unison so that the soldiers could be at the battle zone quickly.

"I thought you may need a little help," Jim said.

A massive bolt of light appeared in front of them as Reptilians teleported in next to the humans. And then the thing that Beth had dreaded; Flynn appeared with thousands of warriors at his back.

"Did you really believe I would be taken in by your lies? You believe everyone is as selfish as you are Brother! I think perhaps you see now that we guessed your plans, you really are that predictable!" Kathos said.

The men from Isis laughed, flying high into the skies

above. When they landed, to Belial's anger, they had joined the warriors of Capalia. It was apparent now who would be defeated, and the Capalian's knew it wasn't going to be them.

Stu appeared riding on the back of Deathladon, with a sword in his hand. He had brought with him the Dragons, all fire breathers.

Deathladon roared, teeth gnashing as he aimed with a snap, biting at Beth. He purposely missed and laughed out loud as she jumped to safety.

Belial attacked Jim whilst he was focused on Stu's arrival. Belial going for what he believed to be the weakest link in the chain of defence. As he did, Rellik pushed the soldier backwards, and Belial's sword flew, missing Jim's head.

It caught Rellik's instead.

"NO!" Raidar roared, running towards his friend; but it was too late. Rellik's head was met with a flamethrower held by a Vardu and incinerated. The ashes fell to the floor, like a sprinkle of icing sugar on top of a cake.

Rexus grabbed Raidar, who began to run to Rellik's body as it convulsed on the floor, bleeding. "Wait, Rellik needs transition!" he said.

Raidar looked puzzled.

Radonna sat on the ground beside her husband's headless body. A whirlwind circled them both as she began to chant something in another language; four words, over and over. Her eyes turning white.

"In morte vivimus, in morte vivimus." Radonna repeated.

"What is that?" Asked Stu.

"In death, we live." Raidar answered.

As this was happening, Orion suddenly took his eyes from Radonna and looked at his best friend. "Blood, fire, war hate!" Stu mumbled, turning a deathly white; he then began chanting her words in English, "In death, we live!"

Stu had complete control of the Dragons. They had placed themselves around Rellik's body and began to fly in a circle around it.

Belial and Beth stepped backwards in fear. These giant

creatures had amazing power.

"What kind of magic is this?" Belial yelled at his brother, who was also entranced by what had been happening.

Rellik's body lifted from the floor. Vardu with the flamethrower tried to burn Rellik's body with fire, but a shield had appeared around it. He was untouchable as the Dragons drew their breath.

A rainbow of colour spread over him and disappeared as if by magic, then Rellik reappeared, head intact only now like Radonna he was a ghost!

Kathos smiled, greeting them both, as the others remained stood on a knives edge.

The battle had been momentarily stalled.

Raidar laughed, and shook his head at Rexus. "You arsehole, you knew didn't you?" he said.

Rexus just smiled back.

"Well not quite knew but had a feeling. He's back with her now, and with us as well. What better reward could we give him?" Rexus said.

"Go, be free from this world, if you wish," Kathos said.

"No, Father, we'll stay. We can still be of help to you, especially with Orion's power," Rellik said.

The conversation abruptly stopped because they still had Belial and his soldiers in front of them. Now really wasn't the right time to start asking questions.

"So, Brother! The day has finally come were I take you from your people. Are you ready to ask for my forgiveness?" Belial said.

"I am never going to be your brother. This is the day you're banished from this planet. You have taken too many liberties. Belial; you're not the lord and master of all. Are you ready to kiss the doomed caverns of Hell?" Kathos asked him.

Belial laughed loudly as the two Angels began to glow with power.

Kathos shone a beautiful yellow, a golden light illuminating him. It was overpowering to those who stood close by. Belial, in all his darkness, shone red, as blood.

Kathos's army stood solid and together, next to their leader.

Raidar roared: "BLOOD, FIRE, WAR, HATE!"

The Capalians raised their fists and began to chant with him, while Dragons and Reptilians roared along with them.

"We must all remain strong in our beliefs, and fight against this evil!" Raidar shouted to his men.

"We need to stay focused at all times. Never let our enemies defeat us," Hyedan commanded.

The warriors stood together, leaving no gaps between them.

The humans, Reptilians and Voxians stood side by side, ready to fight for what they believed was right.

The noise was loud, so loud that Beth covered her ears. She was afraid of Belial, something inside her head knew she was on the wrong side, but she had made her choice.

Belial's whispers began to ring in her mind, taking over every thought, leaving no room for her lover anymore. Only anger and revenge filled her heart as her face turned to 'battle-mode'. She pulled her sword from her jacket and struck with one mighty blow.

Flynn's head left his body.

Beth looked on with tears flowing. She had chosen.

Belial laughed loudly, kicking hard. Flynn's head flew into the air, and the Vardu hit it with a flamethrower, perfect aim.

Flynn was gone, his body left bleeding on the floor.

Beth screamed in rage, tears flowing as she dropped to her knees.

Belial grabbed her arm, pulling her away.

Kale's eyes filled with anguish, as Comet went to comfort him.

"We must continue the fight my friend, otherwise Flynn would have given his life for nothing." Comet said.

Anguish disappeared from the young warriors face, replaced with determination, he nodded and continued.

Rexus lunged forward with his sword, but Belial struck

him down. It was like being hit with a lightning bolt.

Kathos grabbed Rexus and pulled him away from the line of fire.

Raidar was in full 'battle-mode,' anger and sadness tearing through him as Halen grabbed him. But Raidar was too strong, even for him. He knelt at the side of his son's headless body, stroking and holding it. "My son, my boy." Rage filling his heart, he turned and looked at his enemies.

Raidar's screams were heard as Belial grabbed Beth, and the two vanished from the mountain side, with just an echo of laughter left behind.

"This isn't over. Princess or not, she's dead meat," Raidar said, as he walked away from his son's body still bleeding on the mountain floor. "You're dead, you evil bitch. I will tear your throat out myself."

Belial's laughter echoed through the atmosphere.

Grail approached his friend. "I'm sorry; there was nothing we could do. It's a pity he didn't have angel blood, like Rellik we could have brought him back in ghost form." Grail hung his head.

Raidar picked up and placed Flynn's body on the ground at the Dragon's feet.

"To his maker!" Grail said, taking a breath and igniting the body with his fire, which disappeared in a golden coloured vapour as the body burnt.

Stu brushed the ashes into a small box, carried by another warrior then handed them to Kale.

"I'm sorry, man," Stu said.

As fast as the confrontation began, it was over. The Raitharns and Vardu had vanished.

The rest of the Capalians and their allies teleported back to Capalia, except for the Isisians, they flew back to their own lands.

~

The mountainside became a place of mourning.

Raidar walked around holding his son's ashes, days passed.

"*Ave, princeps mi, qui nunquam inter nos ut homo iterum ambulabit. Sedeat loco suo inter iustos. Astra sequar in aeternum, vestigia post se linquens astra, ut in nostris inveniamus mortibus illum." Raidar said, in prayer to his Goddess.

"*Hail, My Prince, who may never walk amongst us as a man again. May he sit in his rightful place amongst the righteous. May he follow the stars forever, leaving a trail of stars behind him, so that we may find him again in our own deaths!" (translation according to google).

Raidar was ready to allow his son to move on from this life.

Kathos stood in front of his people.

"Those of us who walk amongst the stars, we ask you to take our brother. Protect those who have lost him, give him peace on his journey," Kathos said.

Raidar and his two sons stood together, Flynn's ashes were spread on the highest peak of the Capalian mountains.

~

Rellik's ashes had also been taken to the mountains, where they were scattered alongside Flynn's.

He and Radonna were together now, with nothing able to part them again.

Kathos smiled at the thought. What would become of the two Voxian ghosts? Would they remain with their family? Did it also mean that Radonna had some angel blood?

Kathos had a feeling that this would not be the last they saw of them. He could at least find some comfort in that.

Raidar was sent with Stu and Jim to engage with the humans of Earth, in the hope he could teach them how to use the Voxian's powers to their advantage.

The other Voxians could do no more than to plan the battle they knew they would have to fight against Belial.

CHAPTER 37

Jim stood in military uniform, khaki jacket, and combats. He took names and gave out suitable equipment as the humans waited in a newly made airbase, recruits joining the men to protect their planet.

For Fantasia, she was there to greet the people of Earth, along with Orion and Safire after training on Earth, to get them familiar with Voxian terrain as well.

All humans were assigned places to stay.

The houses at the border of the Capalian Mountains were filled quickly as Voxians took in their human allies.

There were rows of tents, camp showers, toilets, and field areas for those wanting to play games like football. Food was laid on for everyone. All were supplied with uniform, black trousers, and red coloured t-shirts. Distinguishing them from the enemy would be difficult, armoured jackets and other hardware would be provided as well.

The Voxians did everything possible to make the humans feel at home.

The evacuation of the sick and injured from Earth began. Medicine was far more advanced, and the human infirmed stayed in medical huts on Reptilia.

Humans were fascinated as the Reptilians moved their belongings. Gigantic beasts that had a kindness never believed of their ancestors. They may have only been huts, but they were massive and full of luxuries.

Bellazard greeted the human warriors, giving instructions for their new living quarters.

"Hey! You're the Reptile woman aren't you? You know, from the telly?" a young man said.

"That's correct, young man, and who may I ask are you?" Bellazard said.

"Just a volunteer," the man replied.

"Not JUST a volunteer; a warrior in the making. You are very welcome..." Bellazard hesitated, looking down at the piece of paper he was filling in, waiting for him to put in his name. "Nick...pleased to meet you," she said, holding out her lizard-like hand. Nick held out his hand and smiled at her politely, and Bellazard shook it.

All seemed to go smoothly. The humans settled into their temporary homes, with a list of training schedules handed out and placed on a large notice board.

~

"Well," Raidar said., now back on Vox. "These humans do tend to be a little more forgetful than we are. Stu was saying that he was always forgetting to do his 'homework'. Which must mean they need all the help we can give them."

The people who were listening from Earth found this amusing, although Raidar didn't see the joke. They believed students did no homework, and this was not a condition, but laziness.

Orion didn't complicate matters by trying to explain.

Deathladon gave out a roar as he passed through the rows of people. The humans scattered.

Bellazard laughed, explaining that this was just his battle cry.

The training began with all species in attendance.

As they began to learn more battle strategies, something occurred to Raidar. The Dragons were the last of their kind, and all males. To put them into a fight may cost them their lives, which to the Voxians would be reckless and stupid.

He decided to talk to Kathos.

"You're right. We can't let the Dragons risk their lives. If they become extinct we've lost a most powerful and beautiful animal, especially as the fight isn't theirs," Kathos said.

"I'll speak to him. But I'm not sure if this will offend him," Raidar said, as he watched the Dragon playfully training his allies.

Raidar went to see Blaze, who'd been training with the humans, teaching them to dodge his fire.

"Perhaps I can help," Samuel said, going towards Raidar. "I believe I may have a good idea. You say that Voxians can adapt to anything?"

"Yes," Raidar said.

"You have two ghost types: Radonna and Rellik. So why don't we see what happens if Blaze or Grail gave them a blast of their fire," Samuel asked.

"Too risky, I can't allow that!" Kathos began. "It may destroy our ghosts."

Samuel signalled for Rellik and Radonna. The two ghosts approached him. He explained to them what he believed they would have to undertake to gain a new power. That is, if his calculations were correct.

Radonna and Rellik spoke for a while and agreed with going ahead with Sam's idea.

"But we may lose you both forever," Kathos said, looking concerned.

"Radonna and Rellik, as they are now, should be able to withstand the fire and release it again when they need to, can you imagine the advantages this would bring them?" Samuel said.

Samuel waited for Kathos's response.

"I can of course try to negotiate, but we know they will refuse to leave, so, do we let them risk the death of their species?" Samuel said.

"We're willing to risk it, Father. Remember, we're already dead, so I can't see how a bit of fire could kill us more," Rellik said with a smile.

Kathos wasn't sure if it was worth the risk.

"Okay, negotiate!" he said.

Samuel smiled.

"I'm coming with you," Raidar said.

Samuel fiddled with his tie for a second and looked at Raidar. "Ready?" he asked.

Raidar didn't reply. He flipped Samuel over onto his shoulder. Samuel looked tiny in comparison as he sped through the crowds of training men and women, like a whirlwind.

Samuel felt motion sickness due to the movement and speed, as they slowed down and then came to a stop next to

Blaze, who was flicking his wings and tail at the human allies, who were dodging him.

Blaze chuckled loudly, as if it was all a game. He had really begun to enjoy the humans' company, and to be honest they had become attached to the Dragons.

"We need to speak," Samuel said, as he was put down on the ground.

He retched. "Sorry, air sickness!" he said.

"Put your head between your legs lad!" Blaze bellowed.

"Will it help?" Sam asked, bending down a little.

"No!" Blaze said with a bellow of laughter.

Blaze looked at Raidar. They both smirked at one another.

"Humans!" Raidar said, his eyes rolling.

Samuel retched again and put his hand up to steady himself on the side of Blaze's large, golden stomach.

Samuel realised what he was doing and took his hand away quickly. "Sorry!" he said.

Blaze and Raidar began laughing.

"Oh Sam, just get on with this. We haven't got all day," Blaze said snorting, smoke billowed from his nostrils.

"Okay.... it's about the risk to your species," Samuel began.

"No!" Blaze said. "We will fight amongst you. All species are risking their lives, not just ours."

Samuel explained his idea. Blaze nodded in agreement at the suggestion, explaining his contempt at the sheer thought of standing to one side.

"While I appreciate your concern for us, Sam and thank you you're very kind, but it's our choice. The idea of flame throwing the ghost species is fantastic, and we're happy to help. It will give our warriors a head start that Belial will not expect. But understand, we are resilient. How do you think our species survived all these years?" Blaze said.

Raidar and Sam took their leave.

Blaze turned away and began to train again.

Raidar grabbed Sam, putting him back up on his shoulders, and then sped off.

Raidar picked up speed and off they both went, back on the other side of camp in just seconds.

Retching again as he reached base camp, "I'm just a small ant living amongst big giant red ants" he moaned. Raidar put Samuel down. He patted Samuel on the back.

"My friend, look at all this. Do you believe this would have been possible without your intervention?" Raidar pointed at the fields of training men. "You humans really do suck at praising yourselves for the good you've done. Stand here, just look, you made this possible, and we're all profoundly grateful," Raidar said to him.

Samuel stood and watched. "Thanks," he said.

Raidar took off at speed again, leaving Samuel to kit up and join in the fight. Jim handed him a shield, and then he handed him a weapon that Sam really hated.

A gun!

Fantasia caught up with Sam.

"Wow! That really isn't you, is it?" Fantasia said, looking unhappy.

"This is how it has to be, Fantasia. What am I supposed to do? I can't call my species to arms, and then watch on the side-line," Samuel said.

"Well, yes." She hugged him. "On the side-lines, at least I could be sure you were safe."

"But I negotiated with the humans to fight and save our planet. What would I be if I didn't want to fight with them? Fantasia, I'm not a coward." Samuel took her hand and kissed the back of it.

"I can make it that you remain in Capalia. Negotiation is important for us all," she begged him.

"No! The time for talking's over. Now is the time to show Belial what we have. Humans and all species threatened by this devil must stand up and be ready to protect the weak and susceptible. And Fantasia, I'm not one of the vulnerable or defenceless," he said.

Samuel turned his back to her, and headed into the crowd of warriors, disappearing.

CHAPTER 38

Beth's evil laughter rang out across the Raitharn forest. She described to her soldiers how they had 'taken two of the key warriors from the pack of dogs', and how they called on 'weaker species' to help in the attack.

"You see, we're the stronger," Beth said. "We have enough power to make this an easy battle." The followers were pleased. So was their master.

The Raitharn warriors began stamping and chanting with excitement. Belial looked pleased. Grabbing Beth at her waist, he pulled her close to him, whirling her around in a waltz, dancing to the sounds.

"Now I know you're on my side, my beauty, my lover," he said. He glared at her eyes, pure evil poured from them, dark, almost black. He kissed her, long and hard. She didn't struggle because this was her place now. Flynn was gone.

The dancing stopped, and Beth called for the attention of her soldiers.

"There is no time for play, my warriors!" she shouted, holding up her hand to quieten them all.

She turned to Belial.

"We must take arms against them. Build them to be stronger, to destroy and annihilate them. We may not need power, but we need to show them that this world is not going to be theirs much longer. We don't want to overpower them, but eliminate them," Beth said.

She had a glow about her, red and orange, like fire. She had become as her master had wished.

Evil...

Belial was pleased with her words. He stroked her hair, like she was his favourite pet, and kissed her forehead.

"What are you planning, my darling?" he asked.

Beth smiled at Belial, and took his hand, her fear of him gone.

"I have an idea. We'll be able to massacre the Capalians. But why should we make effort when we can just kill them?

Outnumber them, we can leave the dogs with nothing, by choosing to battle on unfamiliar territory." Beth said eagerly.

Belial laughed.

"Oh, my little Angel, you really aren't your father's daughter, are you?" he said.

"No, My Lord, I'm not!" Beth said, dancing around him like a child going to a party.

Belial hugged her. She knew that the only emotion the Capalians would have for her now would be 'pure hate!'

Beth had seen Raidar's face when she killed his son. Frankly she no longer cared.

So, Beth set to work.

Before long, machinery noises were coming loudly from her iron foundries. The sound of humans screaming, begging for their lives could also be heard.

"Oh, shut your mouths! You wanted to work for Belial, didn't you? Work, you greedy fools!" Beth shouted.

Belial was intrigued, but thought it better to stay away, rather than spoil his surprise; whatever it was.

The advantages were, it got rid of the human surplus by killing those too old or disabled. So, he was sure he would be happy with her hard work.

Beth walked out of her foundry, wiping blood from her hands, smiling, and throwing the cloth to one of her other frightened human workers.

"BOO!" she said, laughing as the human dropped to his knees in fear.

"How's it going, my lover?" Belial asked on her approach.

"Wonderfully, My Lord." Beth gave a smile. "But tell me, the humans...they're of no real use to us, are they?"

"None. They make up numbers; nothing more. This means the Capalian dogs have to face more useless people and have to kill them before getting to anything worth fighting, like my glorious warriors, and Vardu allies," Belial said.

"So, would it be alright if I took another hundred?" Beth asked.

"Take as many as you need. Just remember that their sole

purpose is to tire out the enemies, while I fight with my brother. You can do your magic by killing off the others, so don't be too greedy," Belial said, and laughed.

"How many are left?" Beth asked.

"Four or five thousand, which is quite enough to occupy those who have sided with the Capalians," he said.

Beth pointed at the human male who'd accompanied her out of the foundry.

"You! Old human! Fetch me one hundred volunteers. And hurry. If you don't get here fast enough, I'll be happy to use you as a subject," she said.

"Y-y-y-y.....e-e-e-e....s." the human said, stammering nervously, and ran.

"Oh, stop snivelling, your pathetic, an old meat bag, get on with your job!" Beth shouted, snapping her fingers at him.

The old man tripped over his own feet, continuing to run to pick up more 'volunteers.' He knew his life would soon end. Beth was wicked and, to be honest, the old man would rather be dead. At least the punishment would be over, and he could be at peace.

"Ooh, dead man walking!" Belial said sarcastically.

Beth laughed. "Now let's not be cruel. He serves his purpose. Greedy little human, thought being here would bring him more wealth. Snivelling little coward."

"So, how long now?" Belial asked, a little impatiently.

"Oh, nearly completed. I believe you will love this. Let me just say, try sticking your sword into these and see what happens!" Beth laughed loudly.

Belial was intrigued as she stepped back into the iron foundry, waving at him as she disappeared through the large industrial gates.

She left him pacing on the outside, waiting for his chance to see what glorious invention she had created for his war.

CHAPTER 39

The humans stood side by side with the other allies.

The Isisians returned, flying high, watching, waiting to give the news of the Raitharns' advance, their weapons were bows and arrows, Kathos still had no communication with their leader, but he did notice the absence of women.

"They'll try to surprise us," Raidar shouted across to his allies. "Do not fear...we're all strong!"

"BLOOD, FIRE, WAR, HATE!" the warriors cried back to their leader.

The king of Vox stood tall and proud, Shadow and Spirit were by his side. Fantasia and Orion and all the others stood around Kathos, with a golden Dragon stood next to Deathladon, who had Stu on his back.

Standing with Fantasia was Samuel, the teacher, peaceful and law abiding. Kathos looked on with pride. He had come a long way since their first meeting. Together, these people were a powerful army of warriors; the Dragons, Humans, Isisians, Reptilians and Voxians.

Lord of the city, Hyedan stood to the left of Kathos, along with the warriors from the city, with Jim and the elite warriors of Earth. Bellazard and Cal were both standing with them.

As the soldiers passed the Reptilians, they bowed in respect. Turning towards Kathos they all saluted him, taking their places behind the Voxian warriors.

"Remember." Lord of the mountains, Raidar shouted "At every corner we have Voxians who can teleport large numbers, if the battle twists and ends up somewhere that Belial believes will give him an advantage, we will go."

There was a sound of metal spinning, clanking sounds.

The earth beneath the warriors feet shook!

Large footsteps in the distance echoed through the mountains as the hour struck.

Belial stood on the mountain top in front of his allies, Beth and the Raitharn warriors standing behind him, as they began their advance.

Kathos saw his lost daughter, hair blowing out of place as she walked in the breeze. He felt sad that she was now lost to her family forever.

Beth looked up and, spotting the opposition, she looked terrified, and stopped.

Belial let out a roar: "WHY DID YOU STOP!" he yelled, swinging his fist into Beth's face.

She fell to the ground as her poor mother and father looked on.

"You said they were few! You'll pay for this deceit!" Belial screamed at her with anger.

Belial watched his enemies standing alongside his brother. More arriving in their thousands, rows of warriors, far more than his own men.

He turned back to Beth, striking her hard. She fell to the ground again.

Kathos felt his own anger surge. He wanted to kill Belial there and then.

Belial's army stood, humans in the front, followed by the Vardu there in their thousands, bloated, cracked faces all in solid form. All there for one reason, to make sure nothing and no one could reach their master.

Beth moved in the front of them all, and the Raitharn warriors stood much further back, all a mingled mess. They had broken weapons, dirty and unkempt. All their powers were forbidden.

Fantasia looked sad. "What has that vile creature done to these people?" she asked.

"He doesn't allow anyone to be more powerful than him. He distrusts those who fight with him," Kathos whispered to her.

"That, my dear friend is what we're going to use against him," Hyedan said.

"He'll be banished in this battle. We will make sure that your grandfather has every opportunity to get his hands on that freak and pull the feathers out of that arsehole's wings.

Put him back where he belongs," Raidar said, as he smiled at Fantasia. He had powered up into 'battle-mode', his sword ready, ready to fight for his King.

Belial placed Beth at the front in full view of her family, making the Capalians angry.

Fantasia looked down at her hand. She had forgotten her mark. Her pentagram star shone brightly, displaying itself in a beautiful blue colour. She noticed Orion and Sky were also staring at their hands. They looked down as their faces all changed to 'battle mode', and their fangs protruded.

"This is awesome! Everybody's mark is glowing!" Orion shouted.

"Your 'power of speed' comes with a gift! It's possible for you to turn tornado!" Radonna said, appearing next to him with Rellik.

"How the Hell do I do that?" Orion asked.

"Give the boy space please," Rellik said, clearing a large area. "Keep him covered out of the enemy's sight. Okay, think of your speed, and run in a circle."

Orion nodded. He began to run, getting faster and faster. He had gained so much speed he was practically unseen.

"Okay, SPIN! It's okay, you won't get dizzy!" Rellik shouted.

Orion did. The sound of a gale force wind started to fill the air. Turning faster, his movement became a massive tunnel, howling and screeching, picking up objects as he went along. As he got faster and faster, his feet left the ground. It was strange; he picked up and began flying in the circle, and the tunnel followed him.

"Now, that's what I call a tornado," Sky laughed, making sure she was well out of his way.

Orion focused himself and stopped.

"What about Sky? What can she do?" Orion asked, coming to a standstill in front of Raidar.

"As well as an absolute wiz with a sword you mean? She calls on the animals, any animal, remembering that all our animals are fanged up and ready to bite. Sky can make them do anything!" Raidar said, as he put his arm around Sky, hugging her. "You, my friend, are pretty awesome!"

"What can calling animals do?" Orion asked.

"Wait and see, you'll be surprised!" Sky smiled.

"Fanged up creatures biting you; not sure I could concentrate on fighting with that going on,' Raidar said.

"I can call the wolves and other bigger animals?" Sky said.

"Now, that's a creature with bite!" Raidar laughed.

"Orion, how did you solve the problem for the humans and the Reptilians walking and fighting on the mountains?" Kathos asked.

"Simple really Grandpa," Orion said, pulling up Deathladon's foot. "Err, sorry, excuse me, sorry big fella, just showing off the merchandise."

Kathos looked down at Deathladon's foot. Attached to it were spikes that could retract and shape to pick into ice as he walked. They gave enough grip to help steady the Reptilians on the rocky surfaces, giving the Reptilians the sensation that they were always walking on a flat exterior.

The human foot-grips were similar but had been adapted into steel toe-capped rock-climbing boots, so they had protection for their feet.

"It was easy. Sometimes the simple things are effective," he said.

The king of Vox was very impressed.

Deathladon put his foot down. As he did, the metal spikes contoured into the ground, so that his foot remained equally balanced. Stu smiled.

"I had to use a strong metal, these Reptilians are pretty heavy footed!" Orion said.

"It's as smooth a ride as I have ever had. Well, on a Dinosaur anyway, Dude!" Stu said.

Kathos looked at the humans. They wore armour; it was silver and looked heavy.

"It's lighter than clothes. The material moves into every crevice of their body. It's like the humans had been coated in a strong aluminium paint; the suits are close to their skin,"

Orion explained.

"This stuff is fantastic. Watch this," Raidar said.

He decided to swing his sword at a human, who'd stopped to pull on one of his leg guards.

The sword bounced off the armour, and the human fell, sprawling.

"What a fuckin' idiot!" he yelled at Raidar, going red-faced as he saw who he had just sworn at.

"Oh sorry, sorry my friend...I was just showing off your armour. Hey, at least you know it works!" Raidar said, with a little embarrassed laugh.

"Prat!" the human said, under his breath as he walked into the gathering.

Raidar shrugged. The others laughed at him, including Halen. As Raidar spotted him, he knew he would never live this down.

"Oh fuck!" Raidar said.

"Father, did you know the ones with the silver coating like you're baking a turkey belong with us? On our side. Even if they do look ready for the oven. You know; FRIENDS!" Halen said, as he pulled an exaggerated thick face.

Raidar walked away and approached his human allies.

"My friends remember you must only attack your own kind. We'd love to have as little loss as possible," Raidar said to the troops.

"Says the armour tester!" Halen laughed.

The human warriors cried back at their fearless leader. "BLOOD, FIRE, WAR, HATE!"

"My Goddess, we have been with them for five minutes and they already sound like us," Raidar said.

The humans' swords and guns waved in the air.

"Acting like us too!" he added.

Kathos liked the silver armour.

"You did a great job, Orion. I'm proud of you," Kathos said.

"Great job," Raidar said, sarcastically patting Orion, mimicking Kathos.

Orion laughed as they both took their place and waited for the approaching enemy. They seemed miles away but were getting closer by the second.

"This battle is for those we have lost; our kindred spirits, our family and our friends," Orion said, as he stood with Kale and Halen, swords at the ready.

"May he be with us in spirit; hey boys?" Raidar said, sword ready, gleaming in the daylight.

"TO FLYNN!" All four men shouted.

Raidar stood with his sons, waiting for Kathos to call the battle cry.

Halen turned and looked at Kale, their anger still strong for the loss of their big brother, both men well trained, so there would be no chance of them losing their heads.

The enemy was upon them. They could see the whites of their eyes.

Capalian fists flew in the air. Cheers rang out. The Raitharns stopped dead in their tracks for one moment, poised ready to attack.

Beth picked up a blazing torch, lighting a line of fire between them, leaving only a few small gaps for the Capalians to get through.

"Well, it's not the fire the Voxians need to avoid, Brother. We just have to keep our heads!" Kathos said with a smile.

All Capalian's began chanting: "BLOOD, FIRE, WAR, HATE..."

Kathos looked at Raidar and nodded once.

"Come to Papa! You blood sucking animals. It's time to die. Who's going to squeeze you like a lemon? I'm not! I'm just gunna bite off your heads," Halen began shouting, fangs in full view.

"Remember these blood suckers don't play fair. You need to watch one another's backs," Kathos reminded his soldiers.

Swords held high.

"CHARGE!" Raidar yelled.

The battle began…

CHAPTER 40

The warrior's chants got louder, with the humans and Reptilians chanting along. The Isisians flew above with crossbows and shields ready to come down on the ground to strike the enemy, the crossbows were useful from the air.

Raidar looked at them.

"Those fuckers are fast," he said.

Kathos watched his brother, who'd began shouting at the Isisians first.

"You'll die by my sword," Belial yelled. "You traitors will be incinerated. They will double cross you, Kathos. Believe me, these winged monkeys will start to diminish, and come running back to me!"

"You'll join me in Hell!" Beth Hissed.

She fired a blaster gun, hitting one of the Isisians flying overhead. He exploded, fire and blood plummeting down on those below.

The Isisians began firing at her from above, and the humans fired their guns from below. Bodies began to fall.

Beth and Belial laughed. Beth headed in Safire's direction with her sword held high.

The Voxian enemies clashed with one another. Capalians and Raitharns hit head-on, making the sound of a thunderbolt. Power hit power as enemies came together, fighting, slashing, and dying. Streaks of lightning span across the battleground and through the air. The Dragons and Reptilians swerved to avoid death.

The humans spread out as much as possible. Jim made sure his men didn't walk straight into the Raitharns.

The Reptilians pushed themselves forward.

Pentagram stars glowed on the hands of Voxians, and the armoured skin appeared as they touched the skin of the Reptilians.

Orion and Fantasia stood by Blaze, touching him on the side of his stomach. Scales appeared and turned a golden colour.

In rows next to each other, points of contact came together, and all those who wished linked, turning gold and scaled, some green ,others blue or black and red which ever dragon had been closest.

"Impressive!" Blaze laughed, as they walked towards their enemies together.

As the armour developed, they discovered a surprising side effect. Those who'd touched the triceratops' descendants gained hoods with spiked horns.

Deathladon called upon his dino-warriors to charge!

Kathos watched on as Belial began ranting with anger.

"Don't think he expected that!" Shadow growled to Spirit.

"We didn't expect it, so why would he?" Kathos said as he patted his wolf friends and moved swiftly into battle, getting closer to Belial. The wolves saw 'the devil' was trying to move as far away from Kathos as possible.

"Time for some battle tactics," Shadow said to Spirit.

The two wolves crawled on their stomachs. When they stood up again they were standing one on each side of Belial.

Shadow and Spirit growled fiercely, baring fangs.

"Don't mess with me you mangy hounds," Belial said, kicking hard into Spirit.

Spirit flew, yelping in pain.

Shadow growled harder this time, leaping for the Demon.

"Get off, I hate you bloody animals!" Belial shouted, shaking the wolf, who had hold of his arm with his teeth. Black blood poured from the wound, and Shadow began to choke on it.

"You see? Poison, you stupid mutt!" Belial laughed.

Shadow dropped to the floor, choking and spitting.

Belial turned and ran in the opposite direction to Kathos. Spirit gained on him again, this time she'd brought the other wolves.

"Shadow are you ok?" she barked.

"Yes, go! Spirit, stop him," Shadow barked at her.

She helped Shadow back on his feet. He was okay.

All the Voxian wolves turned 'battle-mode,' as Belial ran.

The numbers were unequal. To one Raitharn there were eight Capalians.

The Raitharns were outnumbered.

Kathos believed Belial had sent spies, but surely he wouldn't allow so few to fight so many? He had no way of winning. He must have something up his sleeve.

"Belial will not face us with so few men," Raidar called. "He must have known that we were bigger in number."

Raidar was fighting a Raitharn soldier. He made it look like a game.

"Come on then, use your powers. What the Hell is wrong with you?" Raidar shouted at his opponent.

The soldier looked scared, and then with one massive scream, fanged out, thrashing at Raidar. As Raidar was about to retaliate, a sword flew through the neck of the soldier, and Beth stood on the other side of the soldier's body as it hit the ground.

"My Goddess, you bloody witch, you killed someone fighting on your side." Raidar said in anger.

Beth looked at him afraid, then she ran in the opposite direction.

"Not staying to fight. Keep doing that and we'll all be able to sit down and rest while you finish off your own," Raidar shouted after her.

Kathos looked over at his warrior. With a small gesture he turned to face the front and walked calmly into battle.

Hyedan was tiring but stayed by his King's side.

"I'll keep you covered until you've reached your destination," he called. Kathos nodded, it was important for him to face Belial.

Beth came into sight. She began chanting a spell in Latin, and the humans who followed her dropped small silver pods on the ground in front of them. After a few seconds, the pods grew larger, developing into metal, human shaped, robotic warriors. They grew large and stood there, they were still for only a few seconds, their hands turning into swords that could extend and retract.

"Now the fight is even!" Beth said with a smile.

"Crap, now what?" Raidar asked.

He swung out his sword, slashing into the robot's body. As it sliced through the layers of robot's skin, the metal was like mercury, and the sword sped straight through, leaving no damage.

Raidar looked at Fantasia. She ran into the battle so she could pull Orion out of the fight.

"Looks like we've another problem," she said, pointing at the robots.

"I'll be seconds," Orion said teleporting.

Raidar looked in surprise at Fantasia, and the two of them got quickly back into battle.

Now people were dying as the robots on Belials side seemed unstoppable.

Raidar spotted Deathladon.

Raidar's pentagram star began to shine He tapped the side of the Reptilian and gained dark, almost black, body armour; it looked snake-like. Raidar ran his hand down his arm; it felt like silk.

He gave out a laugh "How awesomely cool is that?" he said, admiring his arm.

"Awesome," Halen said, running through and pressing his hand on Deathladon as well. "Thanks mate!" Halen said as he jumped high, landing smack in the middle of the fight. "Let me take you to Hell! Die, you fucker!"

The sound of his sword thrashing with speed sent a shiver down Fantasia's spine, Halen was the same age as Orion, and her children were fighting with her in a war against the biggest enemies of her time.

Sky had called upon her animal friends, they had attacked Belials weaker human allies, swarming together some biting, some stinging, as Sky battled alongside them with her sword.

Fantasia heard a cry in front of her, as Stu and Deathladon pointed. "The VARDU! They're forming! Come quickly, the humans are at risk!" Stu shouted.

The smell began to billow over the battlefield. The strange

hissing sounds came from all around. The humans were surrounded, by the deadliest of enemies.

Fantasia and Raidar looked on as a grey mist began to appear right in front of their human soldiers.

Grail swooped down from the sky and watched as Orion teleported back in front of the humans, grey smoke beginning to engulf him.

Two new figures materialised, becoming solid.

It was Rellik and Radonna.

Grail took in a deep breath and blew fire at the ghost Voxians as they began to power up. The flames hit them, and their figures turned into an inferno of fire.

Rellik called to Orion.

"TORNADO!!!! Orion...NOW!" Rellik shouted.

Orion gave one of the humans a canister, "Hold it, don't let it get into our enemies hands!" He began swiftly turning, Rellik grabbing his hand, Radonna grabbing the other. Fantasia watched the tornado turn into a ball of flames just as the Vardu turned solid. The trio swirled through them, burning them to ash.

Before their flames burnt out, the trio flew in a giant fireball to where the other half of the Vardu had appeared; and in Raidar's word 'they got barbequed.'

"There's one enemy gone for now." Fantasia said.

Kale watched. "Awesome!" he said. "I don't think we'll see too many others; their queen won't want them to become extinct."

Two Vardu appeared behind him. Before anyone could warn him, the Vardu pounced. Kale took his sword without even turning and swung quickly. The heads came clean off both, and the Vardu turned to dust.

"Now, that was a bit sneaky, wasn't it?" he said, as the dust hit the atmosphere. "She seems to have enough of her ugly species left, she doesn't mind a few more dying."

"Be careful not to breath that in son, you don't know what contaminants are in these soul suckers!" Raidar said.

Belial stood smiling, admiring his new robotic army, as

they slammed into the Capalian warriors, tearing shreds of skin from them.

"Is this slowing you down a little?" he said, taunting them.

Kathos looked at Belial as he continued after him. "Well, my Brother, when have you ever been able to fight fair?" he asked him.

Kathos was close, so Belial vanished quickly into his people.

Rexus appeared, giving Kathos a small, orange, liquid bomb. "Be sure this hits only the metal men. It's full of a corrosive acid. Orion has sent word to the humans, and others with skin, it will burn if they get hit. He tried hard to find a better solution, but it was impossible in the midst of the battle," Rexus said.

The mountains of the north had become a giant battleground, with good men losing their lives for what they believed in.

All that could be seen was violence, and those who were unprotected died first. Humans who fought on Belial's side diminished quickly.

Jim ordered people to guard the captives they had managed to save. This battle was at its beginning, and it was clear to all, it was nowhere near ending soon.

With the strike of swords heads flew, ash mingled in the air, and the ground turn into a mass of dark red mud and ash.

CHAPTER 41

Orion watched the new robot soldiers as they erupted from their pods. "We need to find a way to weaken these things, perhaps as they are dropped and are evolving?" he said to Raidar, the two continued fighting whilst looking for the soldier with the acid spray.

Blaze roared at the men as he stood beside the human soldiers, their silver armour shining in the daylight. He opened his largemouth... At first the human soldiers thought he was going to attack them, so crouched, but instead he sprayed out a golden mist. Masses of it covered the allies.

"The enemy are silver. Pass the word, our side are in gold. We must get all of the armour changed," Orion said.

Humans moved quickly to have their upgrade now before hitting the main battle and for speed all the dragons had joined in.

"You're awesome. I'm amazed by our new Dragon family," Raidar said with some pride.

Blaze took the compliment, watching as more lined up next to him. He continued spraying golden dust, yet he was ready to blast his fire if any enemy came too close.

Jim gave orders to fill flame throwers with the acid liquid now found by Orion.

"You only need a drop in water, and it will still kick ass hopefully." He said.

This would dispose of the enemy quickly. The gold armour was tougher, so there was no need to protect it from the liquid acid anymore.

Blaze watched as a small spray came their way, but it didn't damage anything.

"Our human's are almost indestructible!" he said with a smile.

As the robots approached, large hoses had been placed in a line, all fed with the acid-based liquid.

Jim shouted an order.

"NOW SPRAY THOSE BASTARDS!" he said.

The humans attacked the robots with the acid. They began to erode, melting quickly onto the floor, leaving large metallic puddles.

Beth gasped, looking afraid at Belial. She got angry.

"NO!" she screamed. "I hate you all."

Rellik appeared at her side.

"Oh dear, Beth is having a hissy fit! What's the matter? Did you really believe we wouldn't outwit you?" he laughed.

Beth couldn't believe she was seeing him.

"But you're dead! You arsehole, you are dead! I saw you!" Beth shouted.

She began thrashing her sword through him, but of course as we know, Rellik was a ghost!

Rellik laughed at her, saying nothing. He didn't need to.

Beth swung her sword, and it went through him as he turned to flames.

He began to step nearer and nearer to her, tormenting, jumping, swiping his flaming hot arms at her as if to hug her.

She fled quickly into the battle. He didn't give chase, he just stood laughing, which made her so angry she began swinging and hitting her own men.

"What's the matter, Sis? Don't you want to hug me now?" Rellik shouted.

Across from him was Orion, fighting everyone that stepped in his path that wasn't on his side. It had been good spending all those months adding new allies and training with them all, their may be many but the Voxians knew them all.

Orion shouted to her.

"Hey Beth, your robots had been spotted before you had even taken them from their little warehouses! The little man you killed had already sent news to us."

"I killed that rodent with the last batch of human tests. Traitor or not, he was of no use." Beth smiled as she spoke.

"Ah, that's why he isn't creeping around here. Treat them mean and they'll give out information to anyone!" Orion said.

He jumped into the air with speed, swinging his sword and beheaded a Raitharn, who thought he wasn't paying attention, so had gone to attack him.

Beth screamed with rage, swinging her sword again at anyone, killing another two Raitharns.

"Wow, at this rate Belial will wonder what side you're actually on!" Orion said.

The Raitharns were fighting with swords in their hands, slashing, biting, blood all mingling in with the Capalians, and the humans were fighting their own kind.

Some had begun to surrender.

Beth began heading back towards her enemies, with more of the robots and human allies of Belial.

Beth marched in formation, moving towards her family. She had no regrets, and no emotion that would save her from attacking.

Raidar saw a glint of emotion in his King's face, so he approached him.

"Sir, you must focus. We've tried to save Beth, and look what happened; we lost our sons," Raidar said.

Kathos knew they had to fight her, but it was a terrible thought.

Rellik, Orion and Radonna decided to kill the Vardu. 'Tornado power' and 'firepower' together would get rid of them quickly and efficiently, leaving only the humans and Voxians in the battleground, while the Reptilians fought with the Dragons who had remained in the air, biting, and destroying the enemies as they came close enough, Isisians firing arrows down from the sky, killing those who tried to run the other way.

Kathos was fighting for his planet, and for all planets that Belial had decided to destroy in his fight for the Multiverse.

Capalians teleported into the fight on the side of the King. Masses of melted silver covered the ground where the Dragons had set the robots on fire and the humans had sprayed the acid residue. There was hardly anything left of them, but Beth would still produce more.

Belial looked at his army. It was only a few hours into the fight, and already he had suffered great losses.

The humans from Raithar were facing huge numbers of enemies from all over the Multiverse.

Belial hissed loudly at them. They had no choice but to fight. Fleeing meant death sooner rather than later. Their master would kill them for deserting.

The soldiers from Earth marched forward, those on the front line dying immediately.

The humans were standing alone against giants.

Raitharns had fangs and swords, blood dripping as they bit into flesh, tearing off arms and legs, biting into faces, tearing away their victim's heads, even if they were on Belial's side, killing their own. To them it was just a massacre.

A lot of their victims came from their own side, killed just because they were in the way.

Jim stood in front of his men, spurring them forward.

Raidar happily found himself occupied, fighting the witch herself. He felt anger against her as he lifted his sword to fight, but he was a warrior, so held his anger in. He needed to concentrate; losing his head with her now could cost him his life. He began to think about his son, and Rellik, trying to put it to one side. Thoughts like this could lead to mistakes.

Raidar's rage was contained, yet there was something different in his powers. Raidar could smell Beth's fear. She watched as his face and hands turned blacker than she had ever seen. His knuckles and forehead broke out in sharp spikes. Metal, like tiny needles, piercing through his skin. Raidar's eyes turned red, and he gave out a loud laugh.

Raidar had gone 'Demon mode'...

Beth screamed. How could she fight against this?

Belial became enraged. He saw Raidar, had even more powers.

All would be used to kick his Demon arse.

x

CHAPTER 42

Stu and Deathladon (or Big D as Stu now called him) joined Bellazard as they moved slowly through the mass of the battle. They headed towards the Raitharns. Fighting through with a shield for Stu, the fight intensified.

Deathladon bent down, biting hard. Blood flew, speckles hit the air, and Stu automatically put his shield up. Big D then spat out the Raitharns head, which was still shouting.

Grail flew behind them and incinerated the head before it hit the ground.

"Nasty taste. I don't like traitor!" Deathladon said.

Grail laughed as they continued the pattern; bite, spit, throw and burn.

Bellazard watched as the warriors from Raithar got smaller in number, and the ash mounds got bigger.

Raidar energised himself in Demon mode. His fangs stood out now a blazon white, shining and hanging full length over his bottom lip, sharp and ready. "COOL!" he shouted, looking at his hands as the razor-sharp points stuck out of his knuckles.

"Look boys, your Daddy's a Demon!" Raidar shouted.

"Stop showing off, you mad son of a gun. Fight or you'll get yourself killed: Demon or not," Orion shouted to him, whilst swinging his sword.

Raidar let out a howl, and jumped over heads, bouncing through the cascade of people, striking with his sword, slashing with his sharp, needled spikes.

"This is brilliant!" Raidar said.

A human soldier in gold armour passed, touching the side of the Reptilian, just as Raidar jumped past and patted him. His pentagram shone an electric blue on his hand. The Reptilian turned, as his scales became metallic. Now, not only was he lethal, but nothing could penetrate through the Dino armour. Raidar grabbed the soldier by the arm.

"What? I'm sorry, what have I done?" The human female went into panic.

"Nothing girl." Raidar tried to sound as friendly as he could, but under the circumstances even that was enough to frighten her out of her wits!

"Thanks to you we have an even stronger ally. Come with me," Raidar said.

"Sir, where to?" the girl said.

"We're about to make Belial's day even worse than it is already," Raidar smiled.

As the two went by, patting every Reptilian and Dragon on the way, they all began to change and became metal. Kathos laughed as he watched.

He knew he had to get to his brother. And that if he didn't this would all have been for nothing, and so would the loss of those who had given their lives for freedom.

Belial kept his distance from Kathos, an essential part of his battle strategy.

Belial hissed with anger as he watched Raidar adapt the Reptilians. They too had impenetrable armour, powerless to do anything, especially as there were only around 2,000 Reptilians in this battle, some had been lost, others had remained on Reptilia to protect the vulnerable there.

"Feeling outnumbered?" Raidar called, laughing at him.

Beth watched the Raitharns become less in numbers. She decided that even Belial was not worth this.

She ran from the battle.

Safire watched. She knew Beth would survive this time; not because she was brave, and would kill everyone to win the battle, but only through cowardice.

Safire was determined that Bethadora would die one day by her hand and her sword.

~

Raidar looked around, surveying all. He watched the Isisians call to the warriors, pointing at areas where there were weak points. They were firing arrows of fire into the paths of the enemies as they fought alongside Kathos.

Suddenly Raidar was attacked from behind. As he turned his face toward his enemy a sword sliced, ripping into the side of his neck. Raidar back flipped over his assailant, keeping his head, but only just. He swooped lower than expected on the second attack. The sword sliced down Raidar's face. Blood particles flew into the air in a cascade of red, but Voxians heal quickly, so in a matter of only seconds Raidar was ready to retaliate.

The Raitharn watched as Raidar's face quickly knitted itself back together, leaving nothing, not even a scar on his black Demon skin.

"Mmm," Raidar said, tilting his head to the side. "I seem to be all better!"

The Raitharn panicked, realising he had picked on the wrong man. Raidar made his move with precision, swiping hard and fast at his enemy. The Raitharn's head flew into the air as Blaze's roar was heard, and fire exploded, turning the Raitharn to ashes.

The Lord warrior of the mountains took another blow across his back. His metal armoured skin felt nothing. Sparks flew out as his enemy's sword slid on metal spikes in huge lightning bolts.

Raidar struck, flipping himself over again as fire filled the air above him once more. The Raitharns began to run in another direction, afraid to fight him.

"Well, this is easy," he laughed, as Daster, one of the red/black Dragons took to the air, circling around, looking for enemies to burn.

Raidar stood in the middle of the battle, watching the chaos just for a moment.

One thing that had not happened was Kathos had not got to Belial, but Belial was still running in the opposite direction.

"To Victory! Come on, you fuck..." Raidar said, running sword in hand in the direction of Belial.

Kale and Halen stood back-to-back with their swords swinging into their enemies. They spotted their father fighting. He was surrounded by ten Raitharn warriors, so through the mass the two men ran, joining him, fighting together.

Raidar stepped in front of Belial, and they began to fight, Demon on Demon. Raidar didn't want to kill him, just distract him until Kathos had got to them.

Fighting the dark angel was hard, even for a big Voxian warrior like Raidar.

"Now boys, this is what we were born to do!" Raidar said, turning to Halen.

Raidar looked towards Kathos, who was almost face to face with Belial, much to the Demon's surprise. Kathos pulled out *'The sword of Justice.'*

"Thank Goddess!" Raidar said. "Now you're gunna get what's coming to you!" He smiled at his enemy, walking away with his sons.

Belial smiled attempting one last swipe at the huge Voxian, but Raidar had gone before it could hit him.

Raidar spotted Beth watching in the distance. Halen and Raidar looked at one another. As Beth let out a laugh, he headed towards her.

Raidar had to fight her. She had killed his son, and he wanted payback, and as he had brought Kathos and Belial together, he wanted revenge now.

As he sped towards her, she seemed to panic, and teleported out of sight.

Raidar stamped his foot hard on the ground in frustration, looking around for her, but she was nowhere to be seen.

Safire approached him and held onto his arm, trying to calm his anger.

"You will pay for what you have done to my family, blood sucking bitch!" Raidar shouted.

Safire held on to him, working her magic.

"Calm, my warrior friend, Calm..." she said. "She will live to fight another day Raidar, and when she does there are plenty of us that feel as you do," Safire said, gently stroking his hair.

Raidar calmed, Safire was right, Beth would be caught one day, as today was the last day on Vox for Belial.

Kathos had waited centuries to finally get his hands on Belial. Surely he could wait to find Beth, but when he did she would pay for everything. Raidar believed it was better to take it out on some of the Raitharns close by for now.

CHAPTER 43

Two brothers stood, Angel and Demon, for what seemed like an eternity. Everything came to a standstill.

All the warriors and their allies lowered their weapons.

Silence fell on the mountain side.

"You cannot defeat me brother." Belial said.

Kathos swung *'The sword of Justice.'* "Go to Hell!" he said.

The battle snapped back into action and the angel and demon were left to fight.

As Kale stood on the hillside, his head filled with the sense of danger.

He sniffed at the air.

"Vardu!" he said, looking around.

Halen and Raidar jumped to Kale's side as his pentagram star shone. A bright ray of golden light gave Kale's powers a boost.

Blaze flew above them.

Two Vardu turned solid, mouths open, full of fangs, ready to bite into Kale's throat. His hand pushed against the Vardu's chest. Light power emanated as it burned through, disintegrating his enemy into ash. The second Vardu attacked as more began to appear, spirit first on the battleground.

Suddenly Kale and his family were facing ten or more.

Orion jumped to his friend's assistance. Fantasia and Comet also picked up speed. Heading over to the forest edge to help Kale.

"Kale, that's awesome. Show me that again," Halen laughed.

Kale stood holding out his hand, making another ray of light that beamed in the shape of his protective star. He blasted it and it brightened, hitting all of the Vardu who were coming towards him. They fell in a pile of ash.

"Son, I think you have just found another power. There seems to be a lot of that on this battlefield. You rock, kid!" Raidar said. Turning back to fight, he showed off his Demon powers, and got on with the fight, which had burst back into action.

Belial smiled. He looked at Kathos just for a while, then like a werewolf changing at the sight of the full moon, Belial's skin began to rip apart, his clothes falling to the floor. Black fur began to grow everywhere on his naked body.

Beth reappeared, she stood in the background, it would seem her need to see what was going on outweighed her need to live. Looking on in disgust as Belial changed from man to beast.

Belial's eyes glowed red as his giant wings fanned out from his back, and a long, black, furry tail rolled from the back of his spine. Suddenly beauty had shown his true identity; he had become the beast.

The fighting accelerated between Belial and Kathos, the battle raged on, this time it got intense.

No one could distinguish who was who anymore, as both Capalians and Raitharns became awash with blood, in their hair and on their clothes. It was swirling in large pools on the ground, and sinking into the dirt, making a strange red/brown coloured mud.

Belial, after only a short fight, realised his mistake and tried to flee, but Kathos followed him.

The fight would be hard, but Kathos knew that to save Earth and his own people, he would have to be victorious.

Beth stayed and pulled her sword from her jacket. Halen moved close.

"This time, bitch, you really have turned up at the wrong place and at the wrong time!" Halen said. His eyes glowed red, his strength heightened, and he bulked out, bigger than normal. He too had found a new power, but he did not have time to show it off to the others.

He flipped in the air, still as agile as ever. Four Vardu landed in front of Beth, she laughed, but they turned around facing Beth and clawing straight across her face.

"Traitor!" A Vardu screamed in Belial's voice, the Demon

taking over the creature for just a second.

Halen swung out with his sword, and the Vardu was no more.

Beth clung to her face and attempted to teleport. She appeared again a little further down the mountain.

Three more Vardu appeared, replacing the ones that Halen had just killed. Kale zapped them to ash before they could attack Halen. The air filled with ash, which made Beth choke and grab her throat for just a second. Halen moved towards her, and swiped again, but Beth saw it coming and stepped back, bending as she did. His sword caught the front of her throat. As blood trickled down, she vanished once again.

"Coward!" Halen said, frustrated. He had her in his reach and she had escaped.

"Come on, keep fighting, Halen," Kale said to him. "There are a lot of us who are baying for that witch's blood. One day we will get it."

Belial and Kathos flew high, grasping one another as they fought hard. Belial began an incantation, which was in a language that only Kathos understood.

Like a giant explosion of fire, Belial's wings began to shake and turn into a mass of bright colour, igniting with bright orange and red flames.

Kathos showed no fear. His wings fanned out in white. He began an incantation, the very same words as Belial's. Kathos's wings illuminated gold, and an aquamarine blue ultraviolet light. An overpowering light shone from him. Seen by those fighting in the battle below, the power was so strong that humans held their hands over their eyes, scattering for shelter.

As the two higher powers fought, it sounded like an earthquake erupting; no swords needed, only sheer brute power.

The forces of good and evil clashed together and proceeded to lock in battle.

No one from the surface would intervene, and Kathos's warriors stood in silence, watching as their King, their Lord, battled head-to-head with an evil monster.

The surface fight was over, there was nothing left on the Raitharns fighting side, they had either been killed, captured, or had run alongside Beth.

"You are weak, Kathos. You are too busy grieving for those of no importance," Belial said cruelly.

Belial struck at Kathos. As the beast's claws extended, ripping a deep wound into Kathos's chest, his body tore open and blood poured, hitting the air and the atmosphere. Droplets began to rain down onto the watching crowd.

"Brother, before you die, let me tell you how your little daughter begged and cried when I took her. She wallowed as I tortured her soul, letting all my Demon minions have her, one by one. Even together if they wanted. Again, and again. It took weeks before she would agree to be on my side, to join my cause. But like your weak, Voxian people, she gave in to me," Belial laughed.

He wanted Kathos to be angry, to try and bring him down by making him lose control.

But Kathos would have his revenge when he captured and summoned this coward back to Galaxican Hell, so he held on to hope instead.

Beth had meant nothing to Belial, but she wasn't an innocent party either, she had done some unforgivable things.

Kathos showed no sign of anger. He drew a breath, and as he did his power and speed took a sudden boost. He rushed head-on into the fight with Belial, drawing out a smaller dagger. The hilt was gold in colour, and the blade began to glint in the daylight. It had a diamond edging, and the hilt fit exactly into the hand of its user. It was made only for him.

Hyedan had been commissioned by the Goddess herself.

Belial looked shocked when swiftly Kathos swiped at Belial's throat. This knocked Belial off his feet for a while, and he plummeted to the ground from the air. The body of Belial hit with force and left a giant dent in the ground where he landed.

Then Belial flew back up to his enemy and held Kathos

hard by his throat. Kathos twisted around to his side, swiping again, and with one motion the dagger slid into Belial's side, and the Demon became motionless.

The two brothers vanished.

CHAPTER 44

The two angel brothers appeared in another dimension. Belial looked in panic. He began to struggle and fight hard now for his freedom...

The two Brothers had appeared in their childhood home, Galaxia.

Belial began throwing powerful lightning bolts, and they lit the Galaxican skies with red shining lights.

"Well, if you didn't want to get our mother's attention, I think you have just failed," Kathos said.

The sky began to burn with dark purple and blue flames.

Belial threw another bolt, this time at Kathos with rage. Kathos was hit, the pain was excruciating. Blackness swirled around him, and the pain seemed to spread down his arm as his veins throbbed. He could feel and hear his immortal heart beating. The bolt knocked him onto his back, and he began to lose consciousness.

"You can do this. You were made to do this. Get up and fight!" Fantasia's voice echoed through.

"Fantasia!" Kathos came round quickly. He jumped back to his feet, pulling all his power together in a last attempt to rid the world of evil.

The fight raged on.

Kathos had to focus all his energy now. The immortals were never made to battle one another.

A soft breeze surrounded Kathos, and he saw his Galaxican mother appear, dressed in white.

"Lily." He said.

Belial cowered as the light from Kathos became even brighter, almost blinding him. Now he began to struggle, trying to slip away again out of this dimension, firing bolts of lightning, hitting anything and everything in a blind panic. But Kathos held on to him, keeping him in the Galaxican dimension, and not allowing him to leave.

Kathos and Belial raised swords in one last face off. Swords clashed; punches flew as they got close enough to one another.

Kathos knew that the lives of those he loved would be lost if he didn't succeed and beat his brother.

Suddenly, the grip on the Galaxican dimension was lost and both Belial and Kathos teleported back to the battlegrounds on Vox. All Kathos's men were still there waiting for him. They stood together and began chanting for their King: 'BLOOD, FIRE, WAR, HATE!'

Belial caught Kathos's arm, and blood poured from it. Kathos still stood his ground and began to glow golden light from his body. This healed him and produced a massive lightning bolt which smashed into Belial. The Demon shone red.

Kathos's sword hit Belial hard across his wing, and with a second blow hit his beastly face. His face bled, his blood black as tar, as all the evil of the Multiverse began to pour from him...

~

Samuel wondered through a small forest alone, nothing but a gun in his hand, looking for the enemy. As he drew nearer to the mountains the atmosphere felt strange. He saw mist appearing all around him. As he aimed his gun up he was surrounded by six Vardu. He had no idea how to kill these creatures.

"I'm coming old friend, hang on!" Raidar shouted over.

Raidar turned 'Demon mode,' looking over at the forests edge. He could hear and see movement. At first he believed it could be Beth hiding, then he saw Sam was in trouble, so he approached.

Raidar spotted the Vardu and jumped to Samuel's aid. Halen followed with his new super strength. The three men with swords and one gun took on the Vardu and Raidar beheaded them quickly before they could sink back into the soil.

Comet appeared on the scene, ready to fight, but all was well now.

"I must ask you a favour, Comet," Fantasia said. Who had

also come to Sam's aid. She looked slightly bewildered. "I need you to take care of Samuel. He will probably wish to go back to Earth after this battle."

"Of course." Comet said. "I will take care of him,"

Sam looked a little puzzled, then a small hint of dread ran through his body, a feeling that something may go wrong.

"I will see you very soon," Fantasia said, nodding at Samuel as she left.

CHAPTER 45

The battle raged on. The sky turned black as the volcanic moon erupted, black ash raining down on everyone.

"You even bleed evil!" Kathos said, aiming his dagger again.

Belial hissed, swinging his sword in the air, attempting to slice Kathos in two. Kathos moved before it touched him.

Kathos took a step back, catching Belial's sword between his hands. He pulled the sword closer to him and twisted it. He swung over Belial's head and landed, standing behind him. He jabbed Belial sharply with the dagger in the opposite side. This time Belial dropped to his knees, letting out a garbled scream as black blood spewed from his mouth. Belial grabbed Kathos and pulled him close.

"I will return!" he said.

Fantasia appeared with 'The Book of Demons.' Belial was horrified, watching as she tore the book in two, throwing the one half of the book towards a raging fire. Belial tried snatching it before it hit the ground.

The woman in white appeared and caught the vandalised book before it landed. Her eyes emitted a cold blue ray which covered the book, and it disintegrated.

"Mother!" Kathos said.

The Galaxican Goddess smiled at her son, saying nothing. The humans believed these alien life forms to be heavenly and seeing Lily on the battlefield and by her appearance you could see why.

"You can't travel so far when you only have half the ride, Belial!" Kathos said.

"You can't travel at all!" Fantasia said.

She began chanting, throwing the second half of the book in the air. Belial screamed as Orion and Rellik blazed through in a tornado of fire.

The other half of the book was gone.

The ashes sprinkled in the air, landing gently on the ground, in amongst the volcanic ash.

"Kathos, are you alright?" Ledawna shouted.

Belial swung angrily at him with his claws. The book was gone, but Belial was still free at that moment.

Kathos began chanting once more. A power bolt of blue left him, and then a golden rope of light lassoed Belial, going around his torso.

The battle was at an end.

Lily was at last at peace knowing this fallen angel could never be called to Earth or anywhere in the Multiverse again.

Belial was forever in captivity.

A cheer raged out, dancing and chanting: BLOOD, FIRE, WAR, HATE! In victory.

Fantasia headed towards her family. They were all tired from the days of fighting. She smiled at her children. She was so proud of how they had adapted to this life, after years of not knowing who they were.

Suddenly Beth appeared, swinging her sword,

Fantasia's head left her body, heading to the fire beneath...

Her family screamed, running towards Beth.

Orion, thinking quickly, sprang into the air over the blazing fire before his mother's head dropped.

"Oh, please no." There was silence. "It's too late!" Rexus screamed.

Orion sped into the distance.

Fantasia's body incinerated as it dropped into a blazing circle of fire. Beth turned towards her family and laughed loudly as she looked over at her master. One last gesture of her loyalty to him.

"I will come for you," she called to him as she disappeared again.

Belial, still in the chains, growled in disapproval.

Drakos stood horror-struck.

Samuel fell to his knees. His friend was gone, there was so many things that had gone unsaid, things he knew he would regret for the rest of his life.

Kathos couldn't believe it. His whole family came to a standstill, bitter grief pouring from them.

The Goddess approached and held Kathos's hand.

"I'm sorry for your loss," she said. Walking over to Belial, the two vanished in a white light.

All Kathos could think of was the cost. He knew there would be losses, but why her? Vox had only just got her back.

Raidar called to his warriors: "VICTORY IS OURS!"

Tears began falling from the warriors faces. Fantasia was their warrior sister.

The Voxians roared, covered in the blood of their lost friends and of their enemies.

All warriors teleported back to Capalia.

The Raitharns who were left disbanded. They were free now their leader had been taken to the Hell dimensions.

So, what of Fantasia?

Orion vanished, and no one had seen him. Even Kathos had not got enough speed to follow him. He headed towards the Capalian mountains, but no one knew if Fantasia's head had survived.

If a Voxian loses their head, there is still a chance for them to regenerate their body. It was the family's one and only hope, but no one had been able to see if it had burnt in the fire.

The Raitharns needed to know what their future would be now that their leaders Bethadora and Belial had disappeared.

"This is not a takeover," Kathos said. "This is bringing together all that remains. I ask that you care for the lands, and tend to those who have sickness, and rebuild your lives for the better."

"Who shall lead us? We've no one to follow," one of the Raitharns called out.

"I will!" Hyedan said, stepping forward. "I am happy to move onto your barren lands and show you how to work them. To build and teach you our policies."

"We will be in touch at all times, my friend," Kathos said proudly to Hyedan.

"I am sorry, my friend, to add more to your burdens. As

warrior leader you will need to appoint a new city leader." Hyedan said to Raidar. He nodded with pride.

"You are the one I do not envy, Hyedan. There is a lot of work to be done now, and perhaps you should consider calling Raithar something new." The two shook hands.

Hyedan turned to his new people. "What say you?" he asked loudly.

The Raitharns cheered. "I believe this to be a positive response," the two friends laughed.

They turned and faced their King.

"I believe we shall call it Valour, in respect of our battle and for those we've lost. These people need to begin again with a clean and fresh start," Kathos said.

"Be warned, my fellows, we have much to do, and there will be no time to sit about anymore. We have grass to grow, building foundations to put together new homes, shops, schools and any other building you wish. I will take no slacking. I will allow no traitors," Hyedan said.

One of the humans asked. "What about Beth, sir? What if she returns?"

"She knows better. We'll keep a scout on the lookout at the borders. Nothing will be able to get through. I have arranged for supplies, so that you can begin to build lookout posts on higher ground, while we are rebuilding. Believe me, you are all safe now and hopefully with practise you can hunt deer again and regain what was taken, your Voxian powers. We will not let her dictate to you anymore," Kathos said.

The people left on Valour were so few, they gave out a cheer to their king.

Kathos smiled "Good luck my friends, this is a second chance at a new life, go live it to the full and be happy."

"About the new leader for the Capalian city?" Kathos asked, turning to Hyedan.

"Halen!" Hyedan said. "He is so like his father. He would make a powerful force against any enemy."

Raidar agreed. "This is true, but will he leave the mountains to become a leader of the city?" Raidar asked.

Both Hyedan and Raidar looked towards him.
"Me? I'm already packing!" Halen laughed.

CHAPTER 46

There had been no sign of Orion. Weeks had gone by with no word or trace of him. The family believed he had gone away to grieve.

"This is bad, isn't it?" Bellazard asked.

"I'm not sure. Comet still feels as though Fantasia's spirit is with Orion. We'll just have to wait it out," Safire said.

Time passed, while the Voxians waited for news.

Valour had begun its rebuild, and the land was beginning to look more like it should. Replanting the forests would take the longest time and growing crops and farming animals (deer mainly). But they had a good leader to organise it. They all worked hard.

The humans boarded spaceships home, and the Dragons flew off, returning to their caves in Reptilia; all except for Grail.

Stu had remained with Deathladon, and they had stayed on the Manor Estate.

Samuel left his teaching post as soon as he returned to Earth. The UN had taken him on as the Alien Negotiations Head of Department. He laughed and thought how silly Fantasia would have found such a long-winded title.

Earth's ozone layer began to repair now that Belial could no longer draw his power from it. And the Mythus nebula had been added to the Earth's map of the Multiverse.

Vox, Isis and Reptilia had become members of the UN, through talks arranged by Samuel. He was proud of his work.

Peace had been restored, and everyone had the job now of rebuilding the damage and the future for all species looked wonderful.

Kathos and Sky had taken to cleaning and dusting Fantasia's house, in the hope she would return.

Drakos vanished, and took up residency on Earth, helping Samuel build good relationships with the allies. Samuel was his boss. Fantasia had been his friend for a long time, Drakos felt he owed her enough to at least take care of the old guy, well he looked pretty old. But it could have been that Voxians didn't really age much.

~

Sky was dusting some months later, when Orion walked in through the front door alone, slamming it behind him.

Sky jumped. Her mother didn't follow.

So, Fantasia was gone forever.

Ledawna saw him come home and had grabbed Kathos. They had both followed closely. Ledawna held out her arms to her grandson. Orion shook his head. He looked angry and bitter at his loss.

Orion said nothing as he walked out of the main house and into his own domain, shutting the door and locking it.

Hope was lost.

Silence fell upon those who had been waiting for so long for news. Vox was now in mourning for their Princess.

~

Bellazard had stayed with the Voxians on Valour. She had found the rough terrain there had suited her. Others had joined her; they had all become attached to their Voxian friends. She appointed Callouradon as leader of Reptilia, which was pleasing to all who had returned. He was strong and had a great head with negotiation.

Cal had realised that the Dragons would need to find mates. They needed females to lay eggs and make their species survive, and this was a negotiation he had made with the UN. They had agreed on a Multiversal search, to see if the species had survived anywhere else, this was a priority.

Leading the mission was Sky of course.

~

A memorial service had been held on Earth to remember the dead of all planets, and names had been read out to pay respect to the dead.

A Wall had been erected that held the list which read: 'The fallen of 21.12.2512.' There were thousands of names on it. A duplicate had been put on the battlegrounds of Valour, which had been flattened and made into a ceremonial circle

294

as part of the rebuild. There were ploughed fields, and poppies growing from a whole section planted by the humans, as a symbol of loss and respect.

All the Voxians had stood in front of the wall on Earth. Orion looked on at his mother's name. The Valourians had come to pay their respects because they had taken the biggest amount of loss during this war.

Hyedan made a speech:

"It is appropriate to mourn our enemy at this time, remembering that many had no wish to fight us. Belial was unable to live amongst man. He would not allow any to use their powers." He paused, looking into the crowd; never had he seen so many at a memorial. "Beth misunderstood everything we stood for, and therefore acted in a way that would cause harm to all in her vicinity. We must be grateful to our allies who fought at our side and helped to fix what she had broken. Let us give thanks to our leaders who understood the dangers," he said.

Comet held Safire tightly as she saw Fantasia's name amongst the fallen.

The people of Earth had mourned her with the Voxians, as they too had lost a member of their world. She had lived amongst them for many years, and had saved their world from destruction, and they all honoured her.

Next to the wall was a small plaque which read: Dedicated to Fantasia of Vox. A poem was written underneath her name.

I have gone to a far distant country
And you cannot follow me.
It is not where I thought I was going.
But it's here that I want to be.

You will see me once more in spirit.
And then you will understand
How my soul was transformed into glory
As I enter this waiting land.
Anon

Comet knew deep inside that Beth would be back, he spent his time sat at the borders of both Capalia and Valour, just watching and waiting.

Sky had continued her work so spent time with her Reptilian friends, including the Dragons which she had grown to love very much.

Emmina was at school. She was studying the Multiverse and different solar systems. She would become a great map reader in the future.

The family had begun to accept their lives without Fantasia.

Orion had never spoken of his disappearance, and no one hurried him into doing so, or asked where he had gone that day. They had assumed Fantasia's head had been ash in the fire, and he hadn't been able to get to it on time. He remained silent about the whole matter, never speaking of his mother at all.

Orion became owner of his mother's house. Sky and Emmina had moved in with him, wolves in tow. He'd turned part of the house into a laboratory to experiment, to try out new inventions for the good of all, using his intelligence to keep all Voxian science working and advancing.

Medical advances were passed on, including a cure for cancer.

Earth thrived, and everyone on it became more occupied with working for the good of man and not for money, as they had done before the battle in 2512.

They had found a new way to power the Earth, not draining its natural resources for their own good. A lot of solar powered inventions came into being, also wind power was used to light up and power buildings.

Everything used for the good of the planet, and all this was made possible by the people who occupied it. No one took things for granted anymore.

Not that the species from the Mythus nebula ever did.

ONE YEAR AFTER THE BATTLE...

All gathered on the first anniversary of the battle's end, in a memorial service which had taken place in the Royal Square. A minute's silence, as in human tradition, had begun the ceremony.

Orion stood up on the platform "I believe I owe my family and friends an explanation." He said, "My mother's head was safe in my arms when I left Valour and my plan was to take her away to recover in the high mountains of Capalia. I was rushing as she didn't seem conscious hoping if I hurried all would be well. I met Mallick, a great friend of our King, he asked me to trust in him and took my mother's head to the gates of the Multiverse, seeking the help of the great white dragon Queen Layottae. There he would ask permission..." Orion squinted his eyes looking out into the distance. He went silent.

Comet looked like he was squinting as well, and he began rubbing his eye. He nudged at Safire as the silence continued to take place.

In the distance a hooded figure came slowly towards them. As Safire looked at Comet he began to smile.

Orion looked over as the figure began to get closer. They could see it moved quickly, like a Voxian.

Raidar and Halen pulled out their swords, getting themselves geared up.

"It's Beth. The bitch is back!" Raidar said, turning 'Demon,' getting ready to fight.

"No!" Orion shouted, as it moved a little closer. "It isn't, put down your weapons!"

The figure began to slow as it came closer. The men held their hands still on their swords, ready to fight.

Emmina squeaked in excitement. "Grandma?" She shouted.

Fantasia was revealed as the hood blew away from her head.

The family were overjoyed as they hugged, while the

Voxian people stood in amazement.

She had survived.

Orion was amazed, Mallik had found the place he had been looking for, a place of peace he called it Crystilia.

Raidar stood looking on. 'This is just so wild!" he laughed.

Reunited, the family had been rewarded for their bravery, and their loyalty to the Galaxican higher powers, their beloved one had been returned to them.

"Listen," Fantasia said. "I am here for a reason. You must all be on your guard and listen to me...............We have a problem!"

Orion looked at Raidar, and the two began shaking their heads. Laughter reigned, filling the whole of the square.

"Will this never end?" Drakos said, hugging his partner. "You have only just got back here," he said with some amusement.

"I'll never stop the fight. We need to move quickly," Fantasia said, looking at her father Rexus, who stood proud and strong.

Orion and the others stopped as Fantasia began her tale.

But that my friends is another story...

EPILOGUE

Kathos's eyes opened. His vision blurred as he tried hard to get his surroundings into focus. He came across a familiar face stood chanting in Latin in the corner of the cavern.
Bethadora stood with a large book in her hands. This one was black with red/gold trim and on it. He could just make out the words 'The Book of Demons.'

As Kathos began to focus a little more now, he tried to stand up. He found that he had been restrained by golden coloured chains. These must have been immensely strong to hold him. As he pulled, a light force appeared on them; the chains were enchanted.

As Kathos began to come round properly, there in front of him appeared a beautiful young child with long black hair, eyes placid and brown, warm enough to make any mother love him. He looked around five years old.

The boy stared at Kathos for a while as he smiled.

"Kathos," The small boy said, grinning.
"Brother?" Kathos enquired.

The chanting stopped…

ABOUT THE AUTHOR

Ruth Watson-Morris is a graduate of Psychology and comes from the UK.

At N.E.W College UK she started her education from scratch working her way up to Worcester University in 2000 with the help of some fabulous friends, she majored in Psychology BSc hons with Education studies minor.

After graduating in 2008 she decided to pursue her dream of writing her first book. The Voxian series along with others is a dark fantasy series based on a vampire, alien lifeform, with many adaptable superpowers.

The aliens are led by an angel called Kathos who has changed the planet for the good of the people who live on it.

So here it began…

VOXIAN 101

Kathos – King of Vox (Angel)
Ledawna – Queen of Vox (Voxian)

Children
Rellik – Eldest son   - Radonna (Ghost) wife
Bethadora – Daughter (Enemy)
Rexus – Son   - Genesis wife

Next Generation
Kayden - son of Rellik and Radonna
Fantasia - daughter of Rexus and Genesis   -Drakos husband
Kaos - son of Rexus and Genesis
Safire - daughter of Rexus and Genesis

Next Generation
Sky daughter of Fantasia and Drakos
Orion son of Fantasia and Drakos

Next Generation
Emmina - daughter of Sky

Mountain Warriors

Raidar – Lord High leader of the Mountains
Willamina (RIP) Lady and wife of Raidar

Children
Flynn – son of Raidar and Willemina
Kale – son of Raidar and Willemina
Halen – son of Raidar and Willemina

City Warriors

Hyedan – Lord High of the City
Elen – Lady and wife of Hyedan

Children
Azaya – Daughter of Hyedan and Elen

Reptilians and Dragons

Bellazard – High Queen of Reptilia
Deathladon – Leader of Reptilia
Callouradon – (Cal) Leader of Reptilia

Blaze – Leader of the Dragons on Reptilia
Grail – Blue dragon and wise old dragon
Hotshot – Green dragon
Firly – Green dragon
Daster – Black and red dragon
Bail – Black and red dragon

Some of the human superheroes

Sam – Chief human negotiator
Stu – Dude with an attitude
Jim – Orion's friend joining the military to lead the fight.

Enemy

Belial - a fallen angel, brother of Kathos bringer of war!

NEXT STORY...

ORION

COMING 2023...

Printed in Great Britain
by Amazon